He noisily let  been seeing a counselor, and he had one of his patients, Ashton." HB paused his thoughts. "I talked to Ashton, who told me he had tried to kill himself but failed."

"Oh, no!" Alison cried. "Please don't tell me you want to kill yourself!" She leaned forward and tried to grasp his hand.

"No, I want to live again!" He let her touch his fingers before pulling back. Although contemplating suicide might be easier than telling Alison he was her dead husband—Robert.

"Anyway," HB swallowed, "Ashton told me about soul walk-ins."

"What did you say?" Alison asked, alarm creasing her brow. "Wait!" She jumped up and hurried down the hallway while he waited. He moved his forefinger over his thumb, wondering what would make her leave like that.

She returned with a small book, sat, and clutched it to her chest as if protecting it. Then, slowly, she eased the book onto her lap and opened it.

He murmured the title. "*Communicating with the Dead*...So you believe in that?"

"I don't know what I believe. But this book mentions walk-in souls and—"

"I think I have Robert's soul in my body," he exclaimed before he could change his mind.

HB didn't mean to interrupt her, but it just happened. He couldn't help it. He watched as Alison's eyes rolled back, and she slumped over.

"Alison?" He patted her hand and then her cheeks until her eyes fluttered open.

Walk-ins Welcome

by

Sue C. Dugan

Walk-ins Welcome

Cover Art by *Kim Mendoza*

The Wild Rose Press, Inc.
PO Box 708
Adams Basin, NY 14410-0708
Visit us at www.thewildrosepress.com

Publishing History
First Edition, 2023
Trade Paperback ISBN 978-1-5092-4908-4
Digital ISBN 978-1-5092-4909-1

Published in the United States of America

Dedication

As always, my books are dedicated to my wonderful and loving family and especially to my parents who had 70+ years together. 4EAEA—For ever and ever always—Jane and Dave.

And I need to thank Amy Tipton (Feral Girl Books) for her editing magic, Marti Tote—my idea generating and movie-making partner, my Tuesday critique group, and to everyone who has offered suggestions and encouragement.

And a big thank you to Dianne Rich and the talented staff at The Wild Rose Press for their belief in me and "behind the scenes" hard work.

Prologue

Ali and Rob were kissing by a tree. K I S S I N G.
First comes love, then comes marriage, and
then comes death in a twisted carriage.

The soul transfer occurred right after the accident beside the crumpled, twisted cars—three of them. One had caught on fire, and the other two had smashed front ends looking like demolition junkers. And the car in the middle, driven by the older man, was bent cruelly both front and back. The accident stopped the 6:30 p.m. rush hour traffic.

The older man, Robert, aged thirty-five, a doctor and volunteer high school baseball coach, was on his way home to his wife after buying her ice cream for her pregnancy cravings. Henry, the eighteen-year-old man, was driving behind Robert when Leo, confused by the fog, hit Robert head-on, causing Henry to ram the back of Robert's car.

Robert and Henry decided to change places— Robert's soul would take over Henry's body, and Henry's soul would leave with the dead boy in the burning car. The process, known to those who wanted to leave this world, was called a soul transfer. Those mortals who, if they remembered, called it walking in and walking out. Robert still had more love to give, a baby to nurture and raise, and needed a body.

"Hey! Can I have your body? I need it. Your body

1

gives me a shot at living. You're going to die if you don't," Robert said to Henry's soul. Henry was banged up pretty good but would survive with help from the EMTs. He was fed up with this life and ready to let go anyway. He was still alive—just barely.

Henry didn't know who spoke to him. Not a voice for all to hear but one in his head, but he was willing to let the body go and walk away.

"We can change that," Robert's soul said. His best chance at living again was trying to leave. They needed to make the soul switch quickly because the low whine of sirens was coming closer.

"How?" Henry asked, his voice tinged with skepticism.

"We switch places. My soul in your body and your soul can go on its merry way to its just rewards."

When the boy didn't respond, Robert continued his sales pitch, "I'll take over for you, and you won't have to have a sucky life anymore. Find another body that doesn't have it as bad as you."

"Can you do that?" Like bar hopping in a way?

"Yup! Just say the word," Robert's soul said.

And just like that, Henry's soul walked away without a backward glance, leaving the broken body—complete with scars from other attempts at killing himself. And just as he succumbed to the emptiness, Robert's soul took over.

First things first, to mend the body. A siren was almost to the scene of the accident. Oh, good, help was here. Robert's soul slid into the body and nudged the heart to start beating again. Not too vigorously. He didn't want it to be easy for the paramedics to revive him. Then a screech of tires, pounding feet, and hands on him, *opening his eyes, shining lights.*

"He's alive!" Robert heard someone shout. "Irregular heartbeat."

Then with a jolt, Henry's heart and Robert's soul combined. Once he had healed—he figured he should be good for a few years.

Robert felt himself lifted onto a stretcher. And what of his old body? He knew it was covered by a sheet. They couldn't save the body or the departing soul. They were on their way out of this world.

Chapter 1

Henry

The boy awoke slowly, not exactly sure where he was. He knew he was a boy by the square, blunt fingers, and muscular forearm. He guessed he could be a girl, but deep down, he knew he wasn't. His head hurt, one arm was in a plaster cast, and one leg felt numb.

"You're awake!" the nurse, wearing green scrubs, said.

"What…What happened to me?" His fingers climbed up his chest to his bandaged face and skull.

"You were in a coma after a car accident."

"Hmmm. How long?" he asked her.

"Almost two months."

"Wow!"

"You're lucky to be alive," she confirmed, staring down at him and checking the IV taped to his hand.

"Can I see my face?" His cheeks felt numb, and he talked out of the left side of his mouth.

The nurse handed him a mirror. His face was lopsided and distorted, the side with the bandage sagged. And it didn't look like his face at all.

Did he remember a car accident? No, his mind was blank. "Who…who am I?"

"Your name is Henry."

Henry. The name didn't sound familiar, but then

again, his mind was a blank slate. Zero. Nada.

The nurse patted the railing on the side of his bed and smiled. Her eyes were sympathetic and concerned. "You've had head trauma. Things will be fuzzy at first and then clearer." She turned and wrote something on his whiteboard. "You'll get speech and physical therapy when you're moved to the rehab hospital."

Before leaving, she said, "Press the red call button if you need anything."

He didn't know what he needed or even who he was.

Much later, he awoke in a sweat. His eyes popped open, seeing two taillights. He braced for impact, but when nothing happened, he opened them again. The lights were gone, and he was in the unfamiliar hospital room again. The rays from the machinery reflected off the whiteboard where his name and that of his nurse were printed in neat block lettering. His name was Henry, and he was in a hospital, but that was all wrong.

He slowed his breathing and searched his mind for clues. So far, he had Henry and the hospital. The H's were covered.

He drifted in and out of sleep, never fully waking before returning to the images in his brain—all disjointed and scattered. It was as if someone had dumped a bunch of old pictures on the table, and he needed to identify them, but he had no clue.

Later, when he awoke again, a different nurse had her back to him. "Hello?" he said softly.

She turned and smiled. "Hello, we heard you came out of your coma! Can you tell me your name?"

"Richard?" That didn't sound right to him. Ronald? No. "Robert?"

She turned, her mouth pursed and her eyes

frowning. "Is that your middle name?"

"No, I'm…" His gaze drifted to the whiteboard. His name was Henry, but that seemed wrong. Robert was the most familiar. "Robert," he said with determination.

"Hmm. How old are you?" the nurse asked.

"I don't know." He moved his chin toward the chart she held. "What does it say there?"

"Eighteen."

He licked his chapped lips and tried to concentrate. Eighteen, huh? And Henry…The name Henry didn't sound right. It was almost as if he had woken up a different person, but that couldn't happen, could it?

He looked down at his arms—one was wrapped in a cast. The other was resting on the blanket. He squinted at the unfamiliar appendage. That couldn't be his arm, could it? His forearms had been muscular, his fingers long and tapered, not short with bitten nails. This arm had scars on the wrist that looked old and had a tattoo he didn't understand. How does one wake up in a different body?

"Where do you live?" The nurse continued her questioning.

He replied with the first thing that popped into his head. "Green Creek. Is this Green Creek?" Henry asked. He didn't think his name was Henry, but for now, he'd call himself Henry.

"Clearwater." The nurse smiled tiredly, no doubt had a long shift, and had heard every story in the book.

"What…what happened to me?" he whispered. "I remember an accident."

"That's correct. Someone in the wrong lane hit another car, causing a domino effect."

"Did…did the driver of the…."

She shook her head sadly. "No, I don't think so."

He remembered the fog and leaned forward to see out the windshield. The road was one with a gray mist. He should have stopped and waited out the fog, but he continued, anxious to get home.

Now he only remembered the tail-lights and having no time to swerve. The impact was a flash of red-hot pain and then nothing.

Chapter 2

Alison

The weekend was quiet, just Alison and her mother. School started on Monday, so they watched old movies, did the laundry, and read. When she finished reading, Alison put her book down and looked out the window, remembering years past when Rob was alive and how they always celebrated this time of year—the start of school for her and major league baseball playoffs pending for him.

The ritual was to unpack her oversized sweaters, make hot cider, and play their favorite music. They had an eclectic taste: Rob—country, and Alison—vintage rock.

But now, she did none of those things. She sat with her mother, who didn't like cider or either of those types of music. Although it was September, still technically summer in her mind, the trees swayed in the breeze, and a few leaves floated to the ground. She looked at the thermometer—a brisk 62 with fall just around the corner in Michigan. It was her favorite time of the year, and she figured the fresh air would make the thoughts of Rob and all she had lost ease her troubled mind. Alison put on a light jacket and told her mother she was going for a walk, and closed the door behind her.

Alison walked down the street and stopped at the

corner. Did she go left or right, or straight? Left would take her by the house she and Rob had owned, and she rarely drove past Maple Street anymore, but something tugged at her, and she turned left.

The neighborhood had changed little since they lived here two years ago. Some of the houses looked a little care-worn, but that's what time did to everything. Time faded paint and memories. People's faces got laugh and frown lines, and hands got age spots.

The house where Alison and Rob had anticipated raising their child didn't resemble the happiness they had felt at the time. This house seemed to sag on the foundation as if happy memories had disappeared.

The grass was long and hadn't been mowed in a while, and the once vibrant pink and red roses were skeletal and bare. The trim had faded from blue to a dull gray, and the white was sun faded, the color of old parchment paper. Had the house indeed changed, or had her ideal image dulled?

The garage door still had the crack Rob wanted to fix when he returned from the store—but that never happened. The split was still there, and now Alison had a fracture in her heart that no amount of patching could mend. Alison was tempted to run her hand along that crack—the last thing Rob had touched. Instead, she hugged her jacket around her and rubbed her arms. So many hopes and dreams were crushed, pushed aside, and lost forever.

The front door opened, and a woman with a cane stepped out. She looked at Alison and then raised her hand as if the woman recognized her. Alison drew away from the garage and raised her arm and smiled, and called, "Good afternoon."

With some difficulty, the woman descended the steps. "I thought you were someone else!" She smiled sheepishly. "Sorry. Do you live around here?"

"A couple of blocks over. My husband and I used to live in this house."

"Oh!" the woman said, slowing her step. "Where do you live now?"

"I live with my mother."

The woman turned and looked back at the house. "This was your house?"

"Yes, until my husband was killed."

"I'm so sorry," the woman said. "I lost my husband too, but not to an accident." The woman continued her tentative steps toward Alison. "Cancer," she offered. "Cancer slowly eats away at a healthy body, like rust on a car until there's nothing left of the original."

Alison nodded as her eyes filled with tears. "My husband was on his way home from the store. I kissed him goodbye, and a few hours later, he was gone."

The woman gave Alison a look that seemed an eternity. It was the knowing women gave each other when they've lost their man, their soul mate, a part of their heart.

"I don't know if rusting out is better than dying suddenly. The end is the same," the woman finally said and hugged her sweater tightly against the chill.

Alison wiped her nose on her sleeve. "I'm sorry for your loss."

"And for yours." She nodded.

"Rob's been gone two years," Alison said.

"My husband just died last year." She reached out a hand. "My name's Esther. Would you like to come in for a cup of tea?"

Alison looked in the direction of the home she shared with her mother. She really should get home to her. "Thank you, but I better get home to my mother."

Esther looked sad, and her eyes glinted with tears. "Maybe another time."

"Maybe," Alison said with a nod.

Chapter 3

HB

"Here!" Henry's mother put a pamphlet in his hands. Her red fingernails tapped on it as if he couldn't read. "I've enrolled you."

Clearwater Adult Education. Walk-ins Welcome. Henry turned the brochure over and studied the smiling, seemingly excited faces of the students. Would he, could he, exude that much enthusiasm? He seriously doubted it. He scanned the rest of the brochure: Alison Larkin, Teacher. The name caused a stab by the scar on his forehead. The confusion made him shake his head. He had forgotten more than he could remember.

"Don't shake your head 'no' at me, Henry! Either you go to school or get a job!" his mother said, thinking his head shaking meant something else, not just his way of settling his thoughts into place.

HB (only his mother called him Henry, he learned) didn't say anything. If he thought about it, the scar on his forehead, where the windshield had carved into his skin, throbbed and pulsed.

The force of her voice increased. "It starts tomorrow. Get your butt in gear. You're nineteen with three credits to your name, Henry!" His mother wagged a finger back and forth at him, imitating a cuckoo clock.

He didn't want to think about his lack of credits

either. Yeah. Three credits and a vague remembrance of his life before the accident. He went into the hospital E.R. one person and came out another—brain damage, they told him, but he suspected something else, like a craniotomy. He wondered how he knew that. Something on TV? That's why he couldn't remember anything. Sometimes his thoughts weren't his own. The doctor explained it as "head trauma." It could be, but HB remained skeptical.

HB wished he had died in the accident as he now stood facing his overworked and harried mother. He absently rubbed at the scar on his left wrist. He vaguely remembered trying to slash his wrists but didn't know why. Was it a situation like now?

His mother was shaking her finger at him; her face turned down into a grimace. "I've had enough of you sitting around and feeling sorry for yourself!"

That made two of them.

Chapter 4

Alison

Clearwater High School was set back from the road, with several housing developments encircling it on three sides. A blacktop drive led to the school with the football field to the left, and behind that was the softball, baseball, and soccer field. The school was very basic and looked like a box with gash-like windows in the siding, and the green roof blended with the stately trees that flanked the front double doors.

Alison unlocked the door to the trailer housing her classroom and brought in two shopping bags of treats for the students. She instantly recognized the smell of damp, freshly steamed carpeting, antiseptic cleaner, and disturbed dust—"first day of school" smells that would ultimately be replaced by perfume, coffee, aftershave, and dirty sneakers.

She set down her bags with a sigh. The staff meeting would ultimately start at eight a.m., so she would have plenty of time to get things organized before classes officially started tomorrow.

She began by flipping on the lights and threading herself between the rows of chairs and tables, stopping at her desk. A tulip lay across the top, a splash of pink against the dark wood.

Her breath seemed wedged in her throat. Could her

forgetful mother, who didn't drive anymore, have placed the flower on her desk? Somehow, Alison couldn't see her mother devising such an elaborate setup—sneaking out early, meeting the janitor to open the door, and returning home before Alison got up. Highly unlikely. If it wasn't her mother, it must have been Rob who had left the flower. But it was improbable that he had returned from the dead to leave her a flower...wasn't it?

He knew Alison loved pink tulips. And when Rob was alive, he always left her a pink tulip on the first day of school.

With a tentative finger, she touched the stem, pressing to assess its freshness. The flower wasn't wilted; the petals splayed open slightly, the stamen dark against the baby pink. She set down her purse and briefcase, picked up the flower, and inhaled the fragrance.

Ah. Alison's favorite flower.

She looked for something to put it in, opening the cupboard above the coffee pot. A discarded cup with a reindeer motif would have to do. There was a penny in the cup—a penny from heaven?

She smirked as she shook it into her open palm and peered at the date—2013. The year they were married. The engagement ring he had given her was blurry on her finger, and she let out her breath and sagged against the desk momentarily. The book she had read about communicating with the dead had been right. Rob was with her in spirit and wanted her to know.

She straightened, feeling lighter. Rob was still with her, but even with that joyful feeling, tears gathered, making her blink. She sniffed and used tissue from the box on her desk to blot her eyes. Alison took a deep breath and tossed the tissue in the trash. She grabbed the tulip and went to the sink, trimmed the tulip stem and filled the cup with water, and placed it on her desk.

She turned away to survey the empty, quiet classroom. The flower and penny discombobulated her somehow and brought back the sadness of the familiar, painful jab to her gut. She was all alone. She placed a trembling hand over her rumbling stomach, thinking that instead of a tulip, she could've used an egg and cheese sandwich.

She firmly pushed away from her desk, unpacked her shopping bags, and put snacks into a basket by the coffee maker and candy bowls on each table. Then she took a construction paper roll from the cupboard to cover the boards. The students needed some cheer in the room.

After twelve years of teaching, she was on autopilot as she cut the paper to size and stapled it into place. Alison had known she wanted to be a teacher from an early age. She worked to put Rob through medical school, and then when the kids came, Alison would stay home. Her life didn't resemble any of her dreams. She was a single teacher, living in her childhood home with no kids of her own. She had been robbed of her dreams, and she resented it.

She jammed the last staple into place. The bulletin board wasn't her best work—there were gaps and ripples in the paper. She grimaced but was sure no one would notice her sloppy work and began using tacks to secure postings for tutoring sessions, community college classes, and district pamphlets.

She stepped back. The work on the bulletin board did little to keep her thoughts from coming fast and furious—the ones she tried to distance herself from. And she would have kept them tucked away if not for that tulip.

Two years ago, when the sheriff knocked on her door—the lights of his cruiser flashing on the house, across his face—was still fresh, as if it had happened yesterday. She focused on the lights, not his words…accident, white flash, dead, blue flash…

She was a quivering mass on the inside and a block of ice outside. The sheriff's words sliced off a piece of her heart. Instinctively, she had placed her hand on her stomach, sheltering their baby from the sheriff's awful news.

Rob was killed instantly after leaving the grocery store, buying ice cream for her pregnancy cravings. And worse, she miscarried their child not two weeks later. Alison had lost a part of him when the cramping and bleeding started. At that moment, life stopped, the coldness set in, and she threw herself into teaching and helping—a noble cause.

She shook away those memories and forced herself to look at the list of students enrolled and made folders for each. Several students were repeats from the previous year, but one name stuck out: Henry Comstock. The only person to survive the deadly crash that took Rob and Leo's lives.

There were several other new students on her roster. She made folders for them and wondered how they would fit into the class. She'd find out soon enough. And how would she respond to Henry? Would it be awkward? She took a deep breath and vowed to treat him as she would any other new student.

The intercom interrupted her thoughts. "Welcome back, staff! Please report to the library for our meeting!"

Alison glanced at the clock over the door; time to go. She hurried across the parking lot to the Clearwater High School and walked toward the office, passing the showcases of athletic trophies and pictures of past athletic stars. She slowed and looked up at the lopsided smile of her late husband, Robert Larkin, who seemed to be smiling down on her. The state championship trophy he had helped capture sat front and center in the case.

"Alison!" Marilyn called. "I picked up your mail!" Marilyn waved envelopes and loose sheets of paper in her hand.

Alison bid her husband a silent adieu and followed her friend into the library, which was set up for the opening meeting.

Alison sighed before surveying the room and making a beeline for the coffee. With coffee in hand, she turned and greeted others before spotting Marilyn and sliding into the chair across from her.

Most teachers were seated at the library tables, chatting and catching up about their summer. Alison waved to Steve, the principal who had once been Rob's best friend. Never could the three friends have imagined the turn their lives would take fourteen years after they graduated from this same school.

"How was the last weekend?" Marilyn asked, sipping her tea. "I'm sorry to have skipped our weekly shopping trip."

Alison moved her head from side to side. "Quiet. Did a lot of reading. Took a walk. You?"

Usually, on Sundays, Alison and Marilyn went to the thrift and antique shops and then stopped for lunch.

"We went to the beach." Marilyn let out a sigh. "The place was crawling with the last of summer sunbathers and swimmers. The place was a zoo!" Marilyn had teenaged twin girls.

"Sounds fun," Alison said, sliding a copy of today's agenda close and savoring her coffee.

Marilyn frowned at Alison's roster of students. "Won't that be awkward?" she asked, pointing to Henry Comstock's name.

"I've made peace with Rob's death." Alison pulled the roster closer to her and away from Marilyn's prying eyes. "Besides, he didn't cause the accident; that other boy did."

"True. But he was a discipline problem before his accident." Marilyn jabbed at his name with her finger. "Drugs and fights mainly."

Alison shrugged. "Adult education seems to make a difference with those that didn't fit in the regular high school." Alison sipped her coffee before continuing. "Don't you remember that Sarana girl?"

Marilyn rolled her eyes. "Do I!"

Sarana had superglued Marilyn's door on the day of finals so that they couldn't get into the room.

"She was a perfect student for me," Alison said simply.

Marilyn shrugged. She should let Alison decide what was awkward or not.

"You might have a point," Marilyn said, studying the staff meeting agenda.

Alison tucked away the information Marilyn shared and decided to give Henry the benefit of the doubt before she passed judgment.

Something glinted on the floor—another penny.

"You're going to have good luck today!" Marilyn saw her pick up the coin.

19

Alison studied the agenda as she moved the penny between her thumb and forefinger. Either Rob was sending her signs daily, or someone was careless with their money. She hoped it was Rob.

-*Introductions*
-*New curriculum requirements*

Did Steve never change these? Alison suspected he deleted last year's date and put in the current one. Essentially the topics were the same.

"Don't you want to know?" Marilyn asked, interrupting Alison's thoughts.

"Er, what?" Alison pretended to be engrossed in reading the agenda.

"Why, it's your lucky day."

Alison smiled, picturing the pink tulip on her desk. It had to have been from her mother. Alison didn't know how or why, but it couldn't be anyone else. Alison glanced sideways at Marilyn. Had Marilyn been part of the flower scheme?

"Your lucky day. There's a new single biology teacher."

"Oh?" Alison continued perusing the agenda. Most new teachers were young, in their twenties, and fresh from college. Hardly an interest to a thirty-four-year-old woman.

"He's retired Navy, second career. Very handsome!" Marilyn whispered loud enough for several teachers to turn their way. "And single."

Marilyn had already mentioned the single part.

Alison lifted her head as Steve, the principal, stood and asked for their attention. He tapped a microphone, and Marilyn mouthed they'd talk later.

"Welcome back! I trust everyone had a relaxing

summer. Recharged those batteries! We've got over four hundred students registered! This is going to be a good year." The microphone squeaked in protest.

Alison grimaced. Steve said the same spiel every year. He always had high hopes—the cheerleader at the helm.

Steve went on to introduce the new staff. When the biology teacher stood, Marilyn nudged her. "See, isn't he nice looking?"

Alison had to admit he was, but she didn't feel a spark—not like the one she had felt when she had met Rob in high school. She knew he was the one immediately, just by looking at him.

After introductions were finished, Steve asked, "Does anyone have any questions before we begin?"

Alison surprised herself by raising her hand.

"Alison!" Steve pointed, his eyebrows raised in shock. "Mrs. Larkin! Your question?"

Alison suddenly reddened. "I want to thank whoever left the pink tulip on my desk. It was a pleasant surprise. They're my favorite."

Heads swiveled toward her. She glanced at Marilyn, who was either a really good actress or had nothing to do with the tulip.

When no one took credit, she stammered, "I-I assumed it was a welcome back gesture from the boosters?"

Murmurs and whispers. "I didn't get a flower? Did you?"

"You must have a secret admirer, Mrs. Larkin," Principal Steve teased.

She felt a blush creep up from her collar to her cheeks. Alison nodded before giving the room a forced, tight smile and ducking her head, pretending to study the agenda. All the while, her heart raced.

When Alison looked up, she noticed the new biology teacher looking intently at her. He had a determined jaw and piercing eyes.

Chapter 5

HB

HB felt his life was a puzzle, leaving him scrambling to find the pieces that fit together. He had located all the pieces for the parameters and fitted them together for the frame. The inside was another matter, and very few pieces looked like they would connect to create a better picture of who HB was. His life wasn't right, and the medicine and counseling weren't working.

He remembered some flashes—memories, he assumed—of a baseball game. He must have played baseball at some point. He even searched his closet for his baseball gear, but when he searched the top shelf, there was nothing but old comic books, an empty whiskey bottle, the remainder of a joint, and some smelly socks.

He had missed almost a year of school because of the accident, coma, and rehab hospital—he'd never catch up. His mother said he only had a few credits, but he distinctly remembered getting all As and Bs on a report card.

When he looked at his text messages, his friends didn't seem like the athletic or scholarly types—messaging him about drugs and drinking and ditching school.

Then, a couple of days ago, two guys had shown up

wearing low-slung, ripped jeans, leather jackets, and scuffed black boots. He tried to remember their names and looked at his mother for direction, but she had a blank stare on her face as if she'd never seen them before.

When they showed up at their front door, HB forced a smile. "Hey, guys."

"We heard about the accident," a tall blond guy spoke first.

HB touched the bandage on his forehead.

The other boy whistled through the gap in his front teeth. "You're lucky to be alive."

Something wasn't right about this situation, but he didn't know precisely what—besides having memories that weren't his and an unfamiliar body. There had to be an answer.

HB snorted in agreement. "I'm a bit fuzzy still," he admitted.

The paramedics said he was on the verge of death when they arrived and managed to get his heart started, and the bleeding stopped. All he remembered was the bright lights coming faster and faster toward him. He tried to turn the wheel of his car away, but the lights burst into flames as they merged.

The three stood around in uncomfortable silence until the tall guy said, "Well, we gotta go." He patted HB. "See you at school?"

"Sure." Wait. HB shook his head. "No. I'm, um, I'm going to adult ed."

"Cool. Cool." Mr. Gap-tooth whistled.

HB closed the door as they shuffled away. He went into his bedroom and flopped down on the bed and surveyed the walls. Everything was black—the sheets, curtains, and walls, the only color from the heavy-metal posters on the wall. He even had a black tattoo that marched up his arm—YOLO. You Only Live Once—was that supposed to mean something special to him?

HB scanned the rest of his before life: an ashtray overflowing with cigarette butts on the windowsill, the corner of a wall covered with graffiti. He had a dark and angry room. Why was he so angry, he wondered? The room seemed off-kilter with his dreams of baseball and a good report card.

He bolted upright, wanting to escape the negativity, and went into the kitchen for a soda. He took a cola and then flipped on the television to watch baseball. Watching baseball seemed more natural than the black bedroom and the angry feelings it evoked.

The Tigers had a spotty record and lost as much as they won. He doubted they'd be in the playoffs, much less the World Series. He opened the soda and settled back to watch the game.

"Hi, honey, I'm home," his mother called.

"In here!"

She stopped by the couch and swiveled toward the television. "Baseball?"

"Yeah?"

"Since when did you start liking sports?"

Hadn't he always liked sports?

"Dunno." HB shrugged. "I must have started following the teams in the hospital." A plausible explanation, even if it rang untrue.

"Odd," she said under her breath but still loud enough for him to hear. "Good for you."

HB dozed on the couch with the drone of the ballgame in the background, waking to an undercurrent of voices drifting down the hallway. Cautiously, he eased off the couch but stayed out of sight so he could listen to his mother's conversation. Was she talking to his father?

His father looked ill at ease when he visited the hospital and twisted his hat while sitting by HB's bedside. HB also remembered his mother calling him a "good-for-nothing jerk" when he left. No, she probably wasn't speaking to him.

HB peeked around the corner. She had put the phone on speaker while she did her nails. HB assumed she thought he was still napping.

"Will he ever be the same?" she asked.

"Head trauma takes a while to heal, if ever." HB recognized the carefully worded voice of his therapist. The funny man who wore sweaters with a tie.

He heard her gasp. "If ever?"

"I need to be honest with you. That's a possibility. Henry was in a debilitating accident and sustained a concussion and trauma."

"But he's so different now!"

"He might always be different," Dale, his therapist, said.

"Have you counseled anyone else who came out of the hospital as a different person?"

There was a pause. "Once," Dale said.

"Were you able to help him?"

"No." Dale cleared his throat. "He kept saying he had a new soul."

"Hmmm."

HB frowned. How did someone get a new soul? Was it like getting a heart transplant?

"I'm sure Henry will improve over time," Dale said.

"I actually like his new personality." His mother

laughed.

Still breathing shallowly, HB turned and tiptoed back to the couch and faked sleep, his mind turning over and over. Sure, he knew something wasn't right, but a new soul? Did he have a new soul?

As he lay there, he dozed. His dreams were vivid and of being someone else. While not as scary as monsters under the bed—just baseball uniforms and a batting cage and a rogue baseball smashing into his forehead—thinking he was someone different terrified him. And what scared him more was that the feeling stayed with him even after waking up.

Chapter 6

HB

HB drove to his former high school. Once past the gate, if he turned left, he'd be in the large parking lot in front of the building, and to the right and around back was a trailer with the sign, ADULT EDUCATION, WALK-INS WELCOME with an arrow pointing the way. A boy with long hair ran wildly at HB's truck.

How had the boy recognized the new truck the insurance money had paid for?

HB stopped and lowered the window. The boy was one of the two guys who had stopped by previously. Mr. Gap-tooth.

"H, I need some shit!" His words whistled through the gap in his teeth.

HB's mind froze. "I don't have anything." A pencil in his pocket, but he didn't think that was what he meant.

The boy frowned. "But you...always do."

HB touched the scar on his head. "Don't remember." And that was a fact. "Sorry."

"Oh?" The boy turned away with shoulders slumping, and HB continued to the adult education trailer. He draped his arms over the steering wheel and pressed his head to his hands. What had that boy meant? His request seemed familiar, yet it wasn't. What kind of shit? Drugs? Yeah, drugs, he suspected. His mind was still foggy, and he couldn't recall all the details of his life before the accident.

He was parked behind a blue Subaru with 4EAEA on the license. The plate caused him to pause and squint at the number and letters—it meant something to him, unlike the YOLO on his arm. For a brief moment, he got excited. 4EAEA meant something! But what?

His inability to pull the meaning from his brain was frustrating.

He exited his car and walked past the Subaru, looking in the windows at a pile of papers on the front seat and a gas station cup in the holder. An older man walked up the steps ahead and held the door.

"Thanks, man," HB said.

"Welcome."

Once inside, HB saw four women seated at one of the tables, huddled around, looking through pictures on someone's phone, laughing, and pointing. Which one was Alison Larkin, the teacher, he wondered.

He glanced around. The room appeared to be a typical classroom—round tables and plastic chairs. Had he expected something different for an adult-ed setting? He hesitated by one of the tables in the back.

A woman turned. He was sure she was Alison and studied her curly blonde/brown hair, which reminded him of Meg Whatshername. Another frustrating aftermath of the accident—things he should know but couldn't recall.

"She looks like someone, doesn't she?" a petite girl whispered behind him.

Turning around, he saw a freckled face smiling at him.

"Hi"—she thrust her hand to his—"I'm Tiffany—

but people call me Tiff!" She bounced on her heels.

"Uh," HB stuttered.

"Ah!" Tiff snapped her fingers. "Meg Ryan!"

"Huh?" HB knitted his brows.

"Alison Larkin. Ms. Larkin looks like Meg Ryan!" Tiffany exclaimed.

"Oh right," he said, "Meg Ryan. The actress."

HB rubbed his neck as he approached the Meg Ryan look-alike. "Are you Alison?"

"Yes, I'm Alison Larkin, the teacher."

She looked too young to be a teacher, but she wore her age well. With her out-of-control hair, upturned nose, flouncy hippy skirt, and blouse, she was beautiful, and he couldn't help staring. Her friendly, familiar smile drew him closer. When he realized he was looking at her intently, he nodded and dropped his head. Then reality hit him. Could she be the wife of the man who died in the car accident? Rob Larkin?

"Who are you?" Alison held out her hand.

"Henry," he mumbled before sitting.

"I'm sorry." Alison came over to him. "I didn't catch your name." Her floral, citrusy perfume enveloped them both, and for some reason, his apprehension seemed to dissipate.

He nodded and looked up. "Henry Bingham Comstock." He swallowed. "HB."

She froze. Her eyes widened at the realization he was part of the accident—*the* Henry Comstock.

He cleared his throat. "If this is too awkward having me here…"

She shook her head, but her eyes glistened with unshed tears, and she forced a smile to her lips. "You weren't the one who caused the accident," she said softly.

She straightened as if pushing those thoughts away and said, "How many credits do you need to graduate?"

She casually leaned against the table as they talked.

He was acutely aware she was close by the smell of her perfume. His scar twinged, and he dragged his thoughts from her fragrance to her question and said with a grimace, "A bunch." He liked Alison's clean, open face and friendly, attentive eyes.

"I see."

"I've only earned three credits." He sighed.

"Oh." She nodded.

"I missed a lot of school after the accident, and I think I was a screw-up there." He moved his head toward the high school building on the other side of the parking lot.

She gave a slight shake of her head, and a switch seemed to turn on, and she began to speak again. "You'll have your work cut out for you, but I've had students with zero credits succeed," she said, nodding as she talked.

HB exhaled.

"How old are you, HB?"

"Nineteen, almost twenty."

"You can always go back to the regular high school because of your accident?"

Her statement was more of a question, and HB knew he couldn't leave her class. Alison—Mrs. Larkin—seemed caring and compassionate, and he wanted to stay until he finished his GED.

"Nah." He shook his head. "I won't go back. I want to be here. I want to be with you." He coughed—he couldn't believe he had just said that.

Alison's cheeks turned pink. "Okay," she said, quickly turning away from him to pull out a booklet and a pencil from a nearby cabinet. "I'm going to give you some pre-tests to see where we need to start you."

HB took in the other students and what they were doing. Some students were already working out of books and had folders open before them. None of the other students were given a test.

Alison smiled. "We do things a little differently here," she explained, watching him look around. "We don't have lessons, and I don't instruct the whole class on subjects." She nodded toward the group of women still talking and looking at pictures. "They were here last year and know what they need to do. I'm going to test you so we can start you out where you need to be and not repeat things you already know."

HB nodded. "Okay. That sounds good."

"How are you at math?" she asked.

"Dunno."

She pointed to the directions.

"Sounds easy enough." HB opened the booklet and began working on the numbers.

While his mind settled, he absently rubbed his forefinger over his thumb, a habit he didn't know he had until now.

Alison stopped by his chair again and raised her brows. "Questions?" she asked, her eyes on his fingers.

He stopped and put his hands on the table. "No, why?"

"Uh." She absently chewed at her lip. "My husband used to rub his fingers like that, usually when he was thinking or figuring something out."

"Oh?" HB looked down at his fingers. Is that what

he was doing—signaling he had questions? "No, I think I know what to do."

She nodded and continued down the row to the next student.

HB returned to the test, but several times his mind wandered back to the teacher's face with the sprinkle of freckles on her nose, making her seem younger than she actually was. He forced his mind back to the test each time his thoughts meandered away.

He glanced up at the clock. Two hours passed before he reached the end. He closed the booklet with a sigh.

"Ali, I'm done."

She jerked up her head. "What did you call me?"

His mouth hung open at her question. "Uh," HB stuttered. "Sorry." He didn't know why he had called her Ali. "I don't know why I assumed you were called Ali."

"No," she said, gently shaking her head. "My husband called me that."

"Uh, sorry," he said again as he handed her his papers and jogged out the door. As he left, stopping by the Subaru license plate again—wondering why 4EAEA needled his sub-conscience. What did it mean?

He couldn't get the plate out of his mind as he drove past the student body parking lot when someone waved him over.

HB lowered the window. A boy with a shaved head and a tattoo on his neck leaned in. "How you doin'?" he asked. "You got anything?"

"Uh," HB said, "who are you?"

"Funny," the boy said with a smirk. "You got anything?" he asked again.

HB moved aside his hair to show the boy his scar.

"Um, cool scar," he said. "But, uh, I meant, do you

have any shit for me?"

"Pardon?"

The boy stepped back and studied him. "Did you just say 'pardon'?"

"Yes, I didn't understand your request." HB's face was blank.

"You really are messed up in the head," the boy said, his eyes narrow and confused.

HB sat looking at him.

"So you came out of the hospital with a different personality or something?"

HB knew the boy was teasing him but answered, "I guess." HB eased his foot from the brake as the boy shoved his hands in his pockets.

"Sorry," HB mumbled, rolling up the window. He flipped on the stereo and drove.

Driving home, HB replayed the encounters with the boys before and after school. Their requests made it seem like he had been a drug dealer. He couldn't imagine selling drugs to students. Wait a minute—he was a student himself.

At home, he picked up the bong and syringes under his mattress and sniffed a baggie of something he found stuffed in a drawer—marijuana. It might've been legal in Michigan, but this drug paraphernalia confirmed his suspicions—he had been a druggie in school. In the bottom nightstand drawer, he found an assortment of pills. He shoved it all in the trash.

Druggie no more! He put his hands on his hips, giving a firm nod.

Later in the early hours of the morning, HB bolted upright from a sound sleep with sweat beading his brow. The words "Forever and ever, always" ran through his

brain. What did those words mean and why? 4EAEA—
Alison's license plate.

Chapter 7

Alison

Alison was thinking about HB. Of course, she was—she was correcting his test. He was good at math even if he had only earned one math credit in the three years he was a student at Clearwater High School. She had flipped through his folder: troubled kid, missing school, detentions, suspensions…She had other students who didn't fit the "typical high school student norm" and had done well in the adult education setting.

HB reminded her of a young Andy Gibb—a singer and younger brother of The Bee Gees—her idol when she was a kid. He had a lean, lanky body, with curly blond-brown-ish hair that hung over his eyes until he shook it away, revealing expressive brown eyes that hinted at mischief, but were also searching and caring. His body would someday fill out, making him an incredibly sexy man women would want.

Calling her Ali was a common mistake. Others tried and stopped when she didn't answer. So why did this morning's incident bother her so much? There was something familiar about the kid. Perhaps she had taught an older sibling of his?

She guessed it was a sore spot because Rob called her Ali. The pink tulip brought all the memories back and opened the emotional wound of his death. Ali and Rob.

Rob and Ali. High school sweethearts, married young, full of plans for medical missions to foreign countries, having children and taking them to the big amusement parks in Florida and Ohio. They envisioned a fantastical marriage, her teaching, and Rob on his way to becoming a doctor with at least two children, a pool table in the basement, and a swing set in the yard.

All that vanished by the actions of one inexperienced new driver who drifted over the center line in thick fog, killing both the driver and Rob instantly and leaving HB with brain damage and scars. The accident wasn't HB's or Rob's fault. She let out a long sigh. Life could be so unfair at times.

Now Ali lived with her mother so she could pay off Rob's medical school bills. Even dead, his debts followed him.

****

Later, when Alison got home, she couldn't wait to share the tulip incident with her mother and gauge her reaction. Had her mother left it? They had so little to talk about these days, her mother forgetful and often living in the past—sometimes thinking Alison was her dead sister, Penelope.

Alison unlocked the door of the cute little cottage her father had built for her mother when they were newlyweds, the same house Alison had grown up in. The place hadn't changed much from her childhood—blue couches and chairs, an antique sideboard, and needlepoint pillows—blue was her mother's favorite color, and it showed.

She smelled something delicious when she stepped inside. Her mother had made soup. She lifted her nose and followed the aroma to the kitchen. "Smells good,

37

Mom! What kind did you make?"

"Is that you, Penelope?"

Alison didn't answer and waited a couple of beats for her mother's mind to catch up as she set her purse and briefcase on one of the chairs.

"It's Alison."

"What did you say, dear?"

"I said, the soup smells good. What kind did you make?" Alison took the top off the pot and breathed deeply. It smelled like chicken noodle.

"The only kind your father will eat." Alison kissed her mother on the cheek, which brought a smile to her mother's pale, lined face.

Of course. No use correcting her. Daddy had been dead since Alison finished college—twelve years earlier. He hadn't been around to walk her down the aisle, her mother doing the honor. And Penelope had died thirty years ago. Alison had only vague memories of her aunt.

"Sit," her mother commanded.

They sat at the kitchen table—rolls and soup, perfect after the "welcome back" luncheon the Boosters held for the teachers.

"How was the first day?" her mother asked.

Alison moved her head from side to side. "The typical first day—meetings, bulletin boards, checking my roster. I have eighteen enrolled so far this year."

"That's good, isn't it?" her mother asked, squinting at a piece of celery in her soup.

"A good start." Alison nodded. "They come and go." She gestured with her spoon. "This is good!"

"Used a rotisserie chicken, added broth and vegetables—hardly gourmet, but your father likes it."

Alison noticed the third bowl in the spot where her

father used to sit. Sometimes Alison felt her father's presence or thought she saw him in the distance, walking briskly along, but when she got closer, the man didn't look remotely like her father. The same way she thought she saw Rob sometimes.

"Dad has good taste." She lowered her head.

"You're thinking about something, I can tell," her mother said.

Alison made a face. "It's nothing. I found a pink tulip on my desk when I entered my classroom."

Mother chuckled. "Rob!"

Alison chewed her lip, unsure of how to respond, saying, "Of course."

"Alison, you need to get on with your life. Find a boyfriend. Go out with friends. What about that nice girlfriend you have from the English department?"

"Marilyn." Alison took a bite of chicken. "We go out every Sunday morning shopping and to lunch."

"I mean at night."

Alison shrugged. "Maybe." Alison stood, changing the subject. "I'll clean up if you want to watch television."

"I'm reading a good book! I'll get back to that," her mother declared, leaning on her cane and moving slowly to the living room.

Alison watched her mother's stooped, retreating back as she gathered the dishes and took them to the dishwasher. She mentally clicked through the scenario in her brain of finding the tulip. They were out of season, so someone took the trouble to track one down. But who? If not Rob or her mother…then who? A chill slid up her spine.

She turned the lights off in the kitchen and headed

for her bedroom and sat at the little writing desk she had had since she was fourteen or fifteen, and picked up Rob's framed photo. She loved that picture of him. He was looking straight at the camera, his dark hair cut across his forehead, eyes twinkling with an unspoken joke or secret, his right brow higher than the left, making him look continually surprised.

Alison was the one surprised that she was the girl he wanted. The picture had been taken right after they graduated from college and were engaged to be married. She touched the frame, her finger pressed to his chest, his heart. She had loved him at first sight. They sat by each other in social studies, where she would sneak glances at him while the teacher lectured. He caught her looking and winked. That wink was the gravitational pull to him.

She put his picture down and prepared for bed. She'd distract herself by reading the book she had found on one of their shopping trips—*How to Communicate with Your Lost Loved Ones*.

Marilyn had pointed a thumb at the book and quirked an eyebrow. "Let me know if that's any good."

Alison felt Rob's presence in bed with her, just a feeling of disturbed air, but she could have sworn he had been next to her. She thought she smelled his aftershave in the bathroom. This book confirmed her suspicions his spirit was still hanging around.

She thought she had heard him answer the questions in her head. Where had his spirit gone after he died? The book said they hung around making sure their loved ones were okay before leaving. Was that what happened?

She fingered the book jacket, studying the star-shaped light and a ghostly transparent angel on the cover.

The author was a minister and spiritualist—an interesting combination, Alison thought.

When her eyes closed again, she reluctantly tucked the book away.

****

Alison's dreams were always the same, with Rob reaching for her hand and mouthing something she couldn't quite understand. She thought he said, "I'm coming home."

He had been on his way home from helping coach the JV baseball team at the high school when the accident happened. He had called her from the field and said, "I'm on my way home." That was her last conversation with him as she put the final touches on dinner in anticipation of seeing him soon. She waited and wondered as ten minutes stretched to twenty and then an hour. She phoned the coach. "Have you seen Rob?"

"Why no, he left the same time I did."

"He's not home yet." The realization chilled her, and she gripped the table to keep from falling.

"He said he was stopping at the store for you. Ice cream."

She had a knot in the pit of her stomach—it didn't take an hour to go to the store.

And then the sheriff arrived at her front door with the hang-dog expression of wanting to be anywhere but at her house. She knew something terrible had happened before he even began to speak. "No!" she had cried.

It was because of these dreams she bought the book. Alison tried to remember them, but the images were fleeting and fluttered away just as her mind shifted from sleep to wakefulness. Damn. What was he trying to tell her? It was as if he was reaching for her hand from beyond the grave.

She wasn't sure what to believe after reading the spiritual communication book. She had thought she had glimpsed him several times at the baseball diamond. But when he turned, it was Coach Nelson, who looked nothing like Rob. Rob was six foot two, with the build of an athlete and a full head of thick, brown hair—Coach was an aging athlete with a bald head hidden under a ball cap.

She was always disappointed when her vision of Rob morphed into someone else. Someone who didn't look anything like him. Was it a way of coping?

Alison missed Rob so much. Was her mind playing tricks on her? The pink tulip—Rob always gave her one on the first day of school, but how could that be?

Chapter 8

HB

It had been uncharacteristic of him to break into a building and leave a pink tulip. Only a force stronger than him urged him on. But the compulsion spurred him forward. It was something he didn't have the willpower to stop. He suspected it had something to do with the new soul in his body. It was the soul that made him do it. Yeah, that's right. The new soul made him do it.

A single tulip was hard to find—and expensive!—in their tiny town.

He went first to one store then another, only to be told, "They're out of season."

"But I need one for a very special lady," he had insisted.

The clerk raised her brows at him. "I can do a pink rose."

"Nope, has to be a tulip." He shoved his hands deep into his pockets to hide his clenched fists.

"We'll have them for Valentine's Day." Many months away. "Try Adele's?"

Adele's Nursery was out of the way, and he grimaced.

"Sorry, the best I can offer," the clerk said.

He went to Adele's and bought the flower at an inflated price that would take a chunk out of his budget.

But it couldn't be helped. She was close by now, and he had to let her know—he was returning to her.

Chapter 9

Alison

But life wasn't all depressing. Alison and Marilyn
continued their weekly shopping trips to thrift, antique,
and vintage stores in and around the West Michigan area.
They had an established routine. They spent Sunday
mornings shopping and finishing with lunch. Marilyn
called it her "sanity" time away from her family and
students. Since Rob's death, Alison needed these sanity
trips even more so.

This morning, Chelsea, the owner of the Robin's
Nest, waved as they walked in, "Hullo! We've got some
wonderful new finds in!" She spoke with a softly slurred
Scottish accent that was brisk and welcoming at the same
time. Alison smiled and returned her wave.

Marilyn said, "I do hope they have something for me
to wear to 'back to school' night."

"I'm sure they do," Alison said, raising her brows
and asking, "Can you show us your new clothes?"

Chelsea eased from behind the reception desk that
held the old-fashioned cash register. "Right this way!"

Alison and Marilyn followed Chelsea to the clothing
section at the back of the store, passing dishes, crystal,
paintings, dollies, and assorted books as they went. After
they checked out and tried on the new clothing, they'd
spend time browsing these sections too. But first things,

first.

Chelsea had styled several of the new clothing pieces on yellow and aged dressmaker dummies. One dummy had a silk blouse with long ties and a red skirt with embroidered blue and pink flowers. And on the other form, a flowery dress that Alison thought would look lovely on Marilyn. Marilyn ran her fingers over the fabric. Alison could tell her friend was already envisioning wearing it. "That would look nice on you."

"You think?" Marilyn asked, scrunching her face in contemplation.

"Yes."

"And I can see you in that," Marilyn pointed to the red skirt.

Alison stood back, considering. "And that blouse?" she asked, unsure.

Marilyn moved her lips as if deciding what to say. "Reminds me of basset hound ears all floppy and sad." Marilyn chuckled.

"But you like the skirt?" Alison asked.

"It'll look great with a different kind of blouse."

When they finished shopping, Marilyn bought the flowing dress in peach and turquoise and Alison the red skirt before going next door to the café that was known for its homemade soups and breads.

When seated, Marilyn asked, "So how's Henry Comstock doing in adult ed?"

Alison buttered her roll and took a bite, and thoughtfully chewed as she thought about what she knew about Henry "HB" Comstock so far. She swallowed before answering, "He's very bright. He aced the Algebra I test and started on Algebra II."

"You don't say?" Marilyn said, looking doubtful as

she added sugar to her iced tea.

"He seems like a nice guy," Alison said. She liked him a lot.

"Is it awkward having him in class?" Marilyn gestured with her spoon. "You know…with the accident and all." She began eating her soup.

"No." Alison shook her head as she thought about her answer. "He was impacted by it too."

"True," Marilyn said.

Alison had also wondered if the accident would be a problem, but HB was such a nice guy they got past that sticking point rather quickly. She ended up shrugging all thoughts of HB off as she began eating.

Chapter 10

HB

"So, how are you, Henry?" Dale, the therapist, sat on an uncomfortable-looking chair with legs crossed, revealing multi-colored checked socks.

"HB, please," he said, not taking his gaze off those socks.

HB wouldn't be caught dead wearing multi-colored socks, looking like something an old-time golfer might have worn, but they seemed perfectly normal on Dale. HB sank into the overstuffed chair, glad that he—the patient—got comfortable seating and not the other way around.

Dale was an older man who wore striped sweaters and a ring in the shape of a cross on his right hand. A churchy kind of person, HB concluded, and a worthless hour out of his day.

HB slumped in his chair, crossing his arms. When HB had first come home from the hospital, he had to see the therapist twice weekly, then once a week, and now, once a month.

"All right, HB." Dale clasped his hands together, his ring slightly glinting. "Get me caught up. What's been happening since we last spoke?" Dale's hands picked up the notepad and pen behind him and set it in his lap, ready to write down anything profound Henry might utter.

"I know you talked to my mother." HB scowled.

"True." Dale nodded his head but didn't elaborate.

"I overheard you."

"Uh huh." Dale cleared his throat.

"Can I meet the other patient that had a similar experience to mine?" HB leaned forward.

Dale uncrossed his legs and leaned forward too. "I'll have to ask him if he'd be willing to speak to you."

HB was curious about the other person who had woken up from a coma a different person.

They both stared at each other in silence. HB uncrossed his arms and forced a thank you from his lips. Dale spoke as if there was never any awkward pause between them.

"But in the meantime, fill me in on what's been happening with your life."

"Going to school." HB shrugged.

"And how is that?"

When HB thought about school, his mind naturally went to Alison, and he brightened and sat straighter.

"It's different than regular school," he said. "We work at our own pace."

"How will that be for you?" Dale paused. "Can you motivate yourself to get the work done?"

He wasn't sure why that question was asked, but his mind returned to the unfinished homework he found in the graffiti-covered backpack. With a slight nod, HB confirmed, "I can."

Dale raised a brow and gave HB a look he couldn't read.

"I can," HB repeated.

HB thought it better to suck up to the man and make

his life sound hunky-dory. Oh shit, there he went again, sounding like his grandfather. Hunky-dory. Not a phrase he would ever use, was it? And then he was talking to the kid at school and said, "pardon"! When had he ever said that before?

"Good. Glad to hear you're getting on with your life."

HB wondered if he could share with Dale that he felt a bit like a stranger in his own body. Was that a symptom of a concussion? Yup, he remembered the conversation his mother had with the doctor. A concussion could lead to personality changes. Shit. Maybe he was stuck with the body of a nineteen-year-old with an older man's mind. Had Dale's other patient experienced something similar? HB sure hoped the other patient would be willing to speak to him. HB felt as if he were on a desert island with no one to talk to.

Dale leaned forward as HB considered his options. "Anything else?" Dale was always asking questions that HB felt compelled to answer.

But HB decided to keep the dreams and strange thoughts to himself for a while longer. He was dreaming of a baseball field with a ball spiraling ninety miles an hour toward his head. Even when he put up his hand, it drilled through his fingers and caught him square in the forehead. Everything exploded in red, dripping like paint on a lens, but he knew it was his blood.

"I don't think so. Things are still a bit fuzzy around the edges."

HB inwardly laughed at his words again. Not the words he would normally use. "Fuzzy around the edges?" Something else his grandfather used to say. HB would have responded with something vulgar and downright rude.

HB squinted at Dale.

"It all takes time. Concussions and head trauma can leave you sick with headaches, loss of memory, and even personality changes." Dale looked down at his notes before saying, "Still, you're making great progress for someone who sustained those kinds of injuries." Dale tapped his pen on his notebook.

HB felt the jagged scar on his forehead, the flesh still puffy and smoother than the regular skin. He didn't think he was making good progress but had nothing to compare it to.

When HB returned home, his mother was waiting to pounce on him. "What'd he say? Are you getting better?"

He vaguely remembered his parents arguing about the medical bills when he was in the hospital. His father wasn't paying his fair share, and it showed on his overworked mother's face.

What HB wanted to say was he was getting worse, he felt like the old HB was slipping away and being overrun by a new foreign being, but that would only make it so he'd have to see Dale longer, which he didn't want to do.

"He says I'm making progress," HB said.

His mother, with a look of relief, sank back on the couch, turned up the volume, and returned to the show she had been watching. HB watched her and the television images for a few seconds before going to his room where he shut the door and leaned against it, studying the blackness all around him. This would have to change, he thought. It was just too depressing to be in this room.

He opened the door. "Can I paint my bedroom?"

51

His mother poked her head around the doorway to the family room. "What color?"

"Something light. I hate all this black!"

Her brows first rose and then her face settled into a smile. "Of course! I think there are paint cans in the garage."

HB went into the garage and began taking down cans to see if there were any colors he liked: black, white, yellow, and blue. There was a can of medium blue paint—a soothing color. He'd paint his bedroom Marine Blue. He brought it in and showed his mother.

"What made you change your mind?" she asked.

"I hate that black room."

"Me too," she said with a sigh, smiling.

Chapter 11

Alison

It had been a long day. Alison had several new students that needed testing and wanted Alison to sit by them as they worked through the test to determine their placement. Every time she left them to help someone else, a hand shot up in the air. After the testing phase, she hoped they could work by themselves.

Alison pinched the bridge of her nose, massaging to ease the tension between her brows, and put down the pen she used to correct papers. Lately, her mind had been on HB. There was more to HB than he revealed, but maybe she hadn't been asking the right questions. She just saw the tip of the iceberg. Perhaps, his head trauma had rendered him utterly different from the boy Marilyn described. He seemed nice and a hard worker, and there was something familiar about him. Most of her students had hard luck stories, teens having babies, dropping out for who knows what, quitting school to help with the family finances. HB's complex life story was different from his natural innate intelligence. He'd finish his GED in no time.

She yawned and pushed her thoughts of the other students aside and put the papers in her briefcase and prepared for bed, said goodnight to her mother, and gratefully crawled under the covers. She looked at the novel face down on the nightstand but reached for the thrift shop book about spirit communication.

She opened the thin book and began reading where she had left off.

Chapter Three — Walk-ins

A walk-in is a New Age concept of a person whose original soul has departed their body and has been replaced with a new, different soul.

That sentence caused Alison to stop. Rob's soul could be in a different body. The concept scared yet fascinated her. How would she know?

Would there be a clap of thunder or a flash of insight? Did people with different souls wear the letter *S* on their foreheads?

****

The following day, Alison stopped by the bakery and picked up a cupcake for Wayne's birthday. She had gotten into the habit of giving birthday cupcakes, and the students enjoyed them.

She carefully unlocked the door, balancing the cupcake so it wouldn't get smushed, flipped on the lights, and walked between the tables toward her desk at the front.

Cindy was the first this morning, swinging her purse onto a table and getting her work folder. She grinned at the cupcake. "A birthday today?"

"Yes, Wayne's." Alison looked up. "So, how are you today?" she asked.

"Good!" Cindy yawned. "The baby kept me awake. Cutting teeth."

Alison made a clicking sound with her tongue. She had never experienced a teething baby before. She had longed for a child, but she kept the desire tucked away and didn't take it out to examine very often, and she wasn't about to today. Now at age thirty-four with no boyfriend on the horizon, motherhood would be difficult in the usual way. She had thought of freezing her eggs but rejected that. She wanted the father to be Rob and no one else.

"My husband and I could use a date night, but his mother flatly refuses to babysit at night. Doesn't like to drive in the dark."

Alison smiled and was surprised when she said, "I'd be happy to babysit for you one night."

Cindy raised her brows. "Really?" She took out her folder before asking, "What about your mother's care?"

"I think she would be okay by herself for a few hours." Alison left her home all day long while she worked.

"That would be wonderful!"

They agreed on a time and night before Cindy began to work on math.

Next, Samuel came in, yawning widely. He blinked and smiled at her. Alison knew he worked at the factory, third shift, and probably had just left work an hour or so before. She nodded matter-of-factly at him and brought him a cup of coffee. He thanked her and sat at a table by himself to work on English, chewing absently on his pencil and alternately sipping his coffee.

Wayne, wearing his customary Tigers hat, sat close to the heater and rubbed his hands together to warm them up. He looked up at Alison and smiled sheepishly. "Arthritis." He shook his tin box of mints at her. "Want one?"

"No, thanks. Maybe later." She picked up the cupcake in a clear plastic container and placed it by

Wayne. "Happy birthday!"

He grinned. "I might save it."

Next, HB came in, pulling up his slouchy jeans, and gave Alison a smile and a slight tilt of his head. He tapped on Wayne's shoulder as he walked by and gave him a thumbs-up over his Tigers hat.

"HB, I corrected your pre-test. Would you like to go over it with me?" Alison asked.

She motioned to the chair by her desk. "Would you like some coffee?"

"No, thanks." HB fumbled in his pack for an energy drink, popped it open, and took a swallow. "I think I like these." He turned the can around and frowned at the ingredients.

She cleared her throat and began, "You're quite good at math. I think you can test out of Algebra I and go directly to Algebra II."

He remained quiet but seemed to think over what she said, his eyes flickering.

"Would that be okay with you?" she asked.

He was searching for his voice. "Uh, sure," and cleared his throat. "Yes, I'd like that. So I don't have to work through all the problems?"

"No, you'll get credit for taking and passing the post-test."

"So I have four credits, not three?" he gave her a shy smile, and Alison felt her stomach flutter. She was happy the news made HB happy. "Sweet deal." The smile brightened his face.

She indicated a seat near the front of the room for HB to take the post-test. He began and rubbed his thumb with his forefinger, the same way Rob had. Alison watched until he noticed her expression; he smiled at her and returned to work. She felt her cheeks flush that he had caught her staring at him. She busied herself with something else. When HB finished, he brought it to her. "Would you like me to correct it now?" she asked.

"Could you?" he said in a hopeful tone.

"Of course."

She corrected his almost perfect test. "You aced it!" she announced.

Several students clapped.

"You're joking, right?" he asked.

"Nope, I never joke about good news." She handed him the Algebra II book. "Let me know if you have any questions." She moved her head toward Cindy. "She's working on Algebra II, also."

HB struggled out of the chair, pulled up the waistband of his jeans, and sat by Cindy.

"I think you two might want to work together," Alison said. "You're a bit ahead of him"—she nodded at Cindy—"but he'll be able to catch up, I'm certain." Alison winked at HB.

When Alison was sure they would work well together, she bent over her desk and began correcting Wayne's essay.

Around 11:00 a.m., Alison usually took her lunch with Marilyn in the teacher's lounge and unofficially closed adult education. Ushering students out, she smiled when HB brushed past, saying, "See you tomorrow!"

Alison checked her mailbox, took the announcements, and went into the lounge to reheat her soup from the night before, nodding and greeting others already seated around the lounge area. Marilyn was sitting with the new biology teacher. Alison remembered his face from the opening staff meeting.

"Alison!" Marilyn called when Alison took her soup from the microwave. "I want you to meet Mark. Mark Hutchins."

Alison forced her lips to smile. She had wanted to discuss HB, but matchmaker Marilyn had other ideas. Mark was attractive, with a bit of salt in his otherwise dark hair. She took his outstretched hand. "Mark, nice to meet you."

"Alison teaches adult education," Marilyn said. "But she used to be in the trenches with us."

"Nice to meet you too." He had a white, toothpaste commercial smile. "That soup smells delicious. Chicken, noodles with vegetables?"

"Yes!" Alison exclaimed, warming toward him.

"One of my favorites."

"My mother served it for dinner last night."

Mark cocked his head at her. "You live with your mother?"

"Oh, yes," Marilyn said and patted Alison's hand. "Alison here takes care of her mother."

"Very commendable. That's got to be tough," Mark said.

Alison gazed into his eyes and found them unsettling—large dark pupils that seemed to be flickering with agitation.

She continued eating her soup in the companionable silence that followed. Marilyn ate her yogurt, and Mark unwrapped a sandwich and poured a packet of Dura-sterone into his water and gave it a good shake.

"What's that you put in your water?" Marilyn asked.

"Helps with my workouts," Mark said.

Marilyn raised her brows. "I wonder if it might help me do a workout?" She laughed.

Mark quirked a brow and patted his stomach. "It's helped me achieve better results at the gym."

Marilyn laughed again. "So I actually need to go to the gym?" She picked up the packet, analyzing the ingredients. "Is it a steroid?"

"Sort of," he said.

The casual way he answered Marilyn made Alison uneasy.

There was a knock on the door. "Mr. Hutchins?"

Mark pushed back from the table. "Please, excuse me." Mark gathered the rest of his lunch. "I'm helping Ken with his homework. I'll talk with you again?" he asked, his gaze stopping on Alison. Then he turned to Marilyn, smiling at her.

"Yes," Alison said, picking up her spoon. "I eat in here most days."

"Good." He moved his hand in a gesture that reminded Alison of a salute, but not quite, a hard habit to break, she reasoned. "I'll look forward to seeing you." His eyes bore into Alison's, before saying, "Tomorrow."

"So?" Marilyn asked, leaning forward expectantly. "What'd you think?"

"I don't like that he takes steroids." Alison puckered her lips.

"Not that!" Marilyn gave her an incredulous look. "Mark! He's very handsome." She nudged.

"Hmm," Alison said. She had noticed, but not in the way Marilyn imagined. "I don't know. Seems nice." His casual use of steroids bothered her.

"I told him about you," Marilyn said conspiratorially.

"Marilyn…"

"Can't fault me for trying." Marilyn shrugged.

59

"I don't know if I'm ready," Alison said.

"Come on. It's been two years."

"I know."

Marilyn touched her arm. "You just had a funny look when he was here. You like him, don't you?"

"I don't know him." Alison sat back with her arms crossed. She still couldn't get past the use of steroids. When Rob coached baseball, he harped on the players not to use them because of what they did to their body.

Marilyn reached behind her to throw away her yogurt and napkin. "I'm going to have you both over for dinner."

"Marilyn..." But Alison could tell by the far-away look on Marilyn's face that her mind was already on the menu for the "set-up dinner."

"If I were single, I'd go out with him," Marilyn said with a wink and another wink.

Alison wasn't sure at this point.

The next morning, Alison had two surprises. First, HB came in with a bunch of wildflowers for her. "Why thank you. What are these for?" she asked.

"You're the nicest teacher I've ever had. And I passed the algebra test." He broke into a smile.

Alison felt her face flush, turned away, and found a vase in the cupboard, filled it with water, and put the flowers front and center on her desk.

Then, Mark, the new biology teacher came in, looking around like he expected something different.

"Hi," Alison greeted him.

"Nice flowers," Mark said, waving a hand over them.

"A student gave them to me."

Mark turned to survey the room, and HB gave him

a smile and a small wave.

"Teacher's pet, huh?" Mark asked jokingly, but the humor didn't reach his eyes.

HB shrugged.

Mark turned to Alison. "I just wanted to apologize for leaving so abruptly at lunch yesterday," he said.

Alison raised her brows. "No need to apologize—a student needed you."

He backed away. "See you at lunch today?"

"I'll be there."

Wayne raised a hand, and Alison went to help him, nodding to Mark when he opened the door to leave.

Chapter 12

Alison

"It's all set," Marilyn said when Alison joined her for lunch—no greeting, just Marilyn's clasped hands and shining, eager eyes.

Alison set down the tote that held her sandwich and apple. "What is?"

"Dinner?" Marilyn gave her an incredulous, wide-eyed stare.

Alison frowned. "What are you talking about?" She rubbed the bridge of her nose. She had so much on her mind.

"I'm having you and Mark over for dinner, silly. Does Saturday night work for you?"

Alison wanted to protest, but Marilyn knew her all too well. Alison would be home on Saturday night watching TV with her mother or reading. Dinner out would be a nice change.

"Let me check. I promised Cindy I'd babysit for them one night." She crossed her fingers that the babysitting gig would be on Saturday night.

"Cindy?" Marilyn moved her mouth in contemplation.

"A student. I'll get back to you." She felt ambivalent about Marilyn's match-making.

As it so happened, Cindy wanted her to babysit on

Friday night, making Alison free on Saturday for dinner at Marilyn's. Why wasn't she more excited? She had crossed her fingers that the babysitting gig would be on Saturday night.

On Friday, Alison arrived at Cindy's apartment and was greeted by a tiny human that could only be described as a cherub. Ben Junior was chubby, with a dimpled cheek, soft blond hair, and eyes that twinkled with mischief. He carried around a ball and kept throwing it and running to retrieve it. Cindy and her husband, Ben, had a budding ball player on their hands.

Cindy hugged her. "You're a lifesaver! We won't be gone long." Before they left, Cindy showed Alison where Ben's diapers and bottles were kept and what Alison would need to do to put him to sleep later.

The next evening, Alison was met at the door of Marilyn's house, where a different evening would unfold. She had parked behind an unfamiliar brown SUV in the drive.

Marilyn and her husband lived in a craftsman-style bungalow with their twin girls.

Alison liked the twins with their reddish-auburn hair and freckles, and they reminded her of Pippi Long-stockings.

"The twins are at a sleepover, so we'll have a chance to talk without the drama of fifteen-year-olds. We get enough of that at school," Marilyn said, to which Alison nodded and gave her a pained smile.

Alison wasn't sure what or how she felt about Mark. He hadn't given her a tingle like when she thought of Rob. But maybe if she got to know him, she'd feel differently.

Alison sniffed. "It smells wonderful in here!"

Marilyn gently pushed Alison toward the living room, where Mark was already seated talking to Marilyn's husband, Emerson, a police officer in Clearwater.

"Hi, everyone." Alison gave a small wave before sitting in the chair Marilyn indicated.

"Wine?"

Alison smiled. Just what she needed. She scolded herself, why so nervous? It was dinner—plain and simple, nothing else.

Emerson turned from Mark to Alison. "How've you been?"

"The usual. Busy now that school's in session and with my mother's care." Her mind went back to yesterday when her mother had accidentally left the iron on. It had tipped over, burning a black outline onto the carpet. She wasn't sure how long she would be able to leave her mother alone during the day.

"You look a million miles away," Mark said, leaning toward her, his elbows resting on his knees.

"Just thinking about my mother leaving the iron on." Alison snorted. "One of these days, I'm afraid she'll burn the house down."

"My father almost burned down the kitchen after my mother died. Left a candle burning by a curtain. The neighbors called the fire department when smoke billowed out of the window. We finally had to put him in a senior apartment complex where someone came in twice a day to check on him. He hated it."

Alison couldn't picture her mother anyplace other than home. She'd be lost and fearful. "My mother would also hate it."

"My dad missed his shop and tinkering in the

garage, but all the widows made him food, and he put on ten pounds!"

Alison smiled, picturing a line of old ladies, each holding a casserole dish.

Marilyn handed her a glass of wine, and Alison sipped at it, peeking at Mark under her lashes. So far, she had enjoyed getting to know him. Not a "love at first sight" but learning about each other as friends. "What did you feel when you put him there?"

"Really crappy, but I was still in the military and was moved around a bit. My job wasn't conducive to caring for an elderly person."

Alison held the stem of the glass and circled it between her fingers. "I'm not sure how we'd do financially if I didn't work."

"A tough decision to make," Mark agreed, shaking his head.

"Dinner is served," Marilyn said, and they all went into the dining area to eat.

After dinner, Mark walked her to her car. "Do you think we could have dinner sometime?"

Alison smiled and blinked. "What do you call what we just did?" She rubbed her arms against the nighttime chill. Fall was fading.

He laughed and tilted his head back. "I mean, just the two of us."

She surprised herself by saying, "Sure." He had revealed himself to be a nice guy during dinner tonight. Maybe they'd have a good time on their own, and she could learn more about him.

Chapter 13

HB

HB thought about taking money from his mother's purse but knew that was wrong. Since she worked at the bank, all the bills were arranged in order, and she always knew exactly how much she had. He thought he remembered taking money from her before but couldn't recall the outcome. There was a dull roar in his ears from his conscience.

His mother came into the room, her coat slung over her arm and picked up her purse.

"I need some money," he mumbled but gave her a beguiling smile.

"I'm glad you asked this time"—she smirked—"instead of just taking it." She unzipped her purse. "What do you need it for?"

"Gas." He threw up his hands. "Lunch."

"I'm thrilled you're going to school." She handed him a twenty.

"Thank you."

"Do you think you can get a job?" she asked tentatively, giving him another smile.

"Um." He bit his lip.

He could get a job, he guessed, but would it interfere with school? He thought about the flexible schedule and the free time he spent watching television or playing games.

"I'll look into it," he promised.

HB drove slowly past the Moonglow Inn. It was sporting the same sign that had been there for years—a carving of a golden moon and the inn's name—Moonglow. A sign on the door read: "Help Wanted. Inquire Within." A job would allow him to have his own money and not rely on his mother for gas or lunch. He knew the Moonglow Inn.

He parked, smoothed back his hair, and went inside. It was still as he remembered it: red cushions and red/gold wallpaper and candles on each table.

"Can I help you?" a voice called from the back.

"Here for the job."

"Oh, yes." A woman came hurrying out from the swinging doors, and he knew instantly that was the kitchen. Was it because he heard pots and pans clanging or some other reason?

"Any experience?"

He frowned and looked around the dining room. Yes, he remembered taking the plates off the tables and piling them in the big gray tubs by the kitchen door.

"Yes, I think I worked here?"

She frowned. "I don't remember you, and I've been here for over ten years. Maybe you worked at Tote's Tavern?"

"You don't remember me?" He pushed aside his bangs. "I was in an accident and forgot some stuff."

"That's a nasty scar on your forehead, but, sorry, I don't remember one of our workers in an accident. I'm sorry."

HB continued, hoping she would take pity on him. "Kid hit a car head-on. The domino effect. Windshield did this."

Her expression turned to concern, and she pursed her mouth. "You poor thing!"

"Put me behind in school, but I'm going to adult ed to get my diploma," he said.

"Good for you!"

He knew he had won her over by telling about his accident.

"So, you're ready to clean tables and bus dishes?" she asked.

He looked around. It couldn't be that hard to take dirty plates to the kitchen and wash them. HB put his hands on his hips and stuck his chest out. "I'm ready."

He hoped his face revealed his enthusiasm. "Take the dishes off the table, put them in the bin over there." He pointed. "Just scrape and rinse and put in the dishwasher."

"That's right," she said. "Now the job is for about fifteen to twenty hours weekly at minimum wage. But sometimes the waiters share their tips with the bussing crew."

"That sounds good."

"Sometimes we're slammed with customers, and it's a mad house. Can you work under pressure?"

"My middle name!" He grinned.

In a pinch, he could pour water for the customers. He nodded vigorously. The pitcher of ice water was around the corner by the clean dishes. How did he know that? He shook his head. If he hadn't been a dishwasher, he might have eaten here many times.

"Do we still wear black pants and white shirts?" he asked.

She raised her brows. "Why, yes, we still do! I don't

know how I missed having you work here."

He shrugged.

"Well." She eyed him. "When can you start?" She pulled a pencil from behind her ear and wrote in a small notebook she had in her pocket.

"Whenever."

"Let me get some information, and you can start training tonight. How does that sound?"

He felt he knew the job already.

When HB told his mother about the job at the Moonglow Inn, she held out his arms to study him. She put a palm on his forehead, pretending to take his temperature.

"Did I have a job before?" he asked. "You know, before my accident."

"Nope, you've never had a job." She frowned.

"I remember working there."

"Nope," she said again. "You never worked at the Moonglow Inn."

"I clearly remembered the setup and how things were done and wearing black pants and a white shirt."

Even now he remembered the bread plate to the left, two spoons and a knife on the right, glasses to the right, and the napkin folded like a hat on each plate.

"We went there a couple of times for lunch, but you never worked there," his mother said, clearly confused by this revelation.

"Strange. I feel as if I had."

"Did you work there and not tell me?" his mother asked, her face as perplexed as he felt. "That sounds like something you'd do." She chuckled.

"Could be." He pursed his mouth and studied the tip of his sneaker. Why these weird remembrances?

His mother patted his shoulder. "I'm proud of you for taking the initiative for a job." She pulled him in for a hug.

"Hmm." He squirmed out of her grasp, still thinking about what he remembered about working there. It was clear, but instead of lamenting, he said, "Maybe the accident knocked some sense into me?"

She gave him another quick hug. "I like this new Henry!"

Much to HB's surprise, and his mother's, he kept going to adult education. Even though he was working, he attended daily, scheduling work around classes. He attended, not just for the credits but because he liked the easy way Alison acted around students. She wasn't so much the teacher but the orchestra leader, keeping them all on the same tempo and key.

"So, Henry, how is class?" his mother asked as she frowned into her morning coffee.

"Already earned a credit." His revelation made him stand straighter.

His mother's brows rose sharply.

"Yeah, I've already earned my Algebra I credit." He felt himself grinning.

His mother inhaled sharply. "I didn't think you liked math?"

"I took a test and passed."

"Really?" his mother asked, putting her elbows on the table, her hands clasped together over her now cold coffee. "Just like that?"

"Just like that." HB poured himself some cereal with milk.

"So what's the difference?" She got up, putting her cup in the sink.

He was different from what he had been before the accident, but he answered with, "The teacher."

HB went daily to see Alison and hear her say, "Good morning." And when she walked by, the faint scent of citrus and flowers followed wherever she went. He definitely had a growing crush on her.

His mother looked at him sharply. "Tell me about the teacher?"

"Ali is a great teacher."

"Ali?" his mother sniffed.

"Alison. It's none of the Mr. or Mrs. stuff in adult ed."

"I see. Ali, huh? She young?"

He didn't think he knew her age, but he blurted out, "Thirty-four."

His mother's mouth made a slight *O* shape. "Will I meet her at the open house?"

He gave a strangled chuckle. "Open house? I'm in adult education, not kindergarten!"

"Well," his mother said, covering her embarrassment. "Good to know you already passed algebra!"

Chapter 14

HB

HB went to see Dale as scheduled. Dale began, "I talked to Ashton about speaking to you and sharing his experiences after his accident."

HB sat forward and waited for Dale to continue.

"His situation sounds remarkably like yours. New personality. New memories." Dale raised his hand. "Now, I don't believe in that stuff, but I think you should talk to him."

HB wasn't exactly sure what "I don't believe in that kind of stuff" meant.

They had their regular session, and when finished, HB thanked Dale, took Ashton's number, and called from his car. They were going to meet for coffee on Friday. Finally, some answers!

On Friday, HB entered the coffee shop and scanned the tables for someone who looked like an Ashton. A heavy-set guy raised his hand, and HB walked toward him. "Are you Ashton?"

The man nodded. He didn't look like an Ashton to HB.

"I'm HB."

Ashton moved his head. "You sounded much older on the phone.

HB shrugged before they shook hands, and Ashton

nodded to his cup of coffee and said, "Can I get you something?"

HB waved his hand. "I'm good for right now." He waited for Ashton to begin.

Ashton cleared his throat and took a sip before asking, "So you're seeing Dale?"

Not a question, really, more about establishing the facts.

"Yes, I was in a car accident and have lost most of my memories," HB said, playing with a forgotten napkin on the table.

Ashton nodded as HB talked.

"I was told I had a bad concussion and it would take time to heal and my memories should come back. But they haven't, and I remember stuff from somebody else. Dale said you experienced something similar."

Ashton was quiet and moved his mouth like he was considering his words. "I felt like some alien had taken over my life. Before the accident, I wanted to kill myself, but after, I didn't. I wanted to live and be with Greyson, as his significant other." Ashton held up his coffee mug before taking a sip. "I discovered I was gay." Ashton fingered his cup, now on the table. "I believe I have a walk-in soul in my body."

HB frowned. "What is that?"

"As I understand it"—he swallowed—"if a person is unhappy with their life and trying to end it, there can be a switch." He swallowed again. "I think that happened to me."

HB's mind went into overdrive, considering the possibilities. He didn't want to be gay. "Do you know who you switched with?" he asked, wanting the answer but not wanting it.

73

"I'm not sure. Some names popped into my head, and of course, preferring guys to girls was a huge change for me."

"So you went into the hospital as a straight guy and came out gay?" HB asked, incredulous.

"I know, hard to imagine, but it's true."

"How do you know a different soul entered your body?"

Ashton blew out his breath. "It took some sleuthing. But it made sense after I read about it."

People write about this stuff? HB wondered. It must be pretty hush-hush if he hadn't heard about it before.

"I tried to commit suicide, and I remember a voice asking me if I wanted to trade places."

"Trade places?" HB asked. "How?"

"My soul for his."

HB sat back, stunned. "I don't understand."

"A soul isn't attached to one body. It can go from body to body multiple times if necessary."

HB felt his mouth gape open and quickly closed it. "So I could be driving down the road, and someone could switch souls with me?" It sounded silly, and although he wanted to believe Ashton, he didn't.

"No," Ashton interrupted. "Not like that. I made the decision to leave this earth by killing myself. You have to want out of your current life."

"Hmmm." HB put a finger to his lips. "Did Dale tell you that?"

Ashton shook his head. "No, I went to see a woman in Grand Rapids that was a past life regressionist, and she was able to figure out the situation. She was able to make me relax and then asked me questions about what I was remembering."

"Do you think she could help me?" HB leaned forward.

"She might." Ashton fiddled with his pants pocket. "Here's her card." Ashton handed HB a thick piece of cardboard that read: Dr. M.P. Sims, Counselor, Minister, Spiritual Advisor, with the address of her office in Grand Rapids, Michigan.

HB took the card and studied the name—Dr. Sims. "I don't remember anyone asking me to switch with them."

"You don't always remember," Ashton said. "I read a book about walk-in souls."

"Walk-in souls," HB said, slowly turning over the words as if looking for clues.

"That's what it's called," Ashton said with a nod of his head before picking up his phone. He scrolled down, looking for something. "Here." He turned the phone around so HB could see the cover of the book. "This is the book that explained how walk-ins work."

HB frowned and took note of the title and the author. He'd search for it later.

This was all so new age and confusing. Was Ashton hallucinating? Was he on drugs? HB studied him. Not likely. Ashton looked professional, he wore nice clothes, and his hair was short and neatly combed. He didn't look like a druggie with his clean-cut style, but professional people also took drugs.

Chapter 15

Alison

After the students had left, Alison gathered up her things and drove home. She opened the door, calling, "Mom! I'm home."

There was no answer, but Alison detected a burning smell—like a scorched pan. She hurried to the kitchen. A pan with what looked to have been tomato soup and vegetable beef was black and crusted over. Alison turned off the burner and removed the pan. When it had cooled sufficiently, she figured she'd throw it away.

She tried her mother again. "Mom?"

"In here." Her mother sounded far away behind a closed door.

Alison found her mother in the bedroom, surrounded by a mound of clothing. "What are you doing?" And why did you leave the stove on? she asked silently. Would chiding her mother do any good?

"Gads!" Her mother sniffed the air. "Did you leave the stove on? I smell something burning."

"Not me. I just got home from school."

Her mother frowned. "Did your father leave the burner on again?"

"I don't know, but I turned it off."

"Thank goodness you arrived when you did!" her mother pouted. "Your father is getting so forgetful!"

Alison chose to ignore that comment and instead pointed to the clothes on the bed. "What are you doing?"

"Making room for your father's things."

"I see." She purposefully kept her voice neutral.

Alison backed away. Her mind turned over all the possibilities for her mother's care. She couldn't imagine putting her mother in a home. But if Alison didn't work, could they live on social security? Alison doubted it. She'd have to quit teaching to watch her mother 24/7. She wished she had siblings she could share the task with. Once again, Alison thought that if Rob hadn't died, they could have easily taken care of Mom...

She stepped back into the kitchen and looked at the black, sooty pan with vegetables blackened on the bottom, all the liquid boiled away. If she hadn't gotten home when she had, would she have found the kitchen on fire?

Mark said his father had caught the kitchen curtains on fire. They had reversed roles with their parents. Alison filled the sink with water and put the still-smoking pan in to cool down so she could throw it away.

What to do about dinner? She fixed a plate of crackers and cheese and went to her bedroom to correct papers.

Chapter 16

HB

HB scratched his chin while searching the hall closet for his baseball bat and glove. Where had he put them? When he cleaned his bedroom in preparation for painting, he had moved the furniture and cleaned out the closet, and there was no sign of the sports equipment. The only unsettling things were the drug paraphernalia and depressing blackness.

Next, he went out to the small detached garage next to the house and shoved aside the door that covered the opening. Neither he nor his mother parked there, and it was filled with boxes of ornaments, a lopsided Christmas tree from years past, a red wagon, bicycles with flat tires, and a plethora of tools on a warped bench. There was one bulb that glowed weakly in the gloom.

Where was his sports equipment? As he searched, he moved aside dusty boxes and walked through sticky cobwebs that made him shiver. He sneezed as he reached for a box labeled "etc"—old black and white pictures of long-lost relatives he couldn't identify.

"Henry?" he heard his mother call.

He shook off the dust and exited the garage. The afternoon sun made him shade his eyes against the glare.

"What are you doing in there?" she asked, her brows rising.

"Looking for my bat and glove. Do you know where they are?"

His mother squinted at him. "Baseball?"

"Yeah, I thought I'd go to the batting cages and work on my form."

She was silent as she listened but folded her arms over her chest as if she didn't believe him.

"Do you know?"

"I don't remember you having baseball equipment." She turned toward the garage and refolded her arms.

"I could have sworn I played baseball." He put his hand on the garage's rough surface.

"Not that I can recall."

He'd have to use his earnings from the Moonglow to buy some equipment and see the therapist Ashton suggested.

HB bought an inexpensive bat and glove at the local big-box store. He had tried to break in the glove as he watched the Tigers, but the leather was unyielding and didn't bend to his hand as it should to catch balls. It would have to do for now.

HB drove to the baseball field and the batting cage on a day he didn't have to work. He parked, got out, and looked at the cage and the pitching machine. The machine held ten balls and could be programmed to throw a combination of pitches. His fingers twitched in anticipation, and he could almost hear the whack of the ball against the bat.

From a bucket in the cage, HB loaded baseballs into the machine and selected a low pitch to start. He stood back as the machine shot out the first ball. His bat hit the ball and sent it into the net.

"Pretty good," a voice said behind him.

HB exhaled quickly. He hadn't realized he wasn't alone. The ball shot from the machine and grazed his arm.

"Sorry I startled you."

HB turned to find Coach Miller standing behind him, scratching his bald head before replacing his Clearwater Baseball cap on his head. HB hurried back to turn off the machine so it wouldn't continue pitching balls at him.

"I hope it was okay for me to come here and use the machine," he told the coach.

"That's what it's here for." Coach studied him intently. "Do I know you? Are you a student?"

"I am," HB said.

Coach seemed surprised but pleased at the same time with the way his eyes widened. "Good—I hope you go out for baseball."

"I mean," HB stammered. "I'm an adult student. We can't play sports."

Coach seemed to deflate some and said, "Oh, that's too bad."

"I'd love to help though if I can," HB said, surprised he had made an offer.

"Now that's an idea," Coach said. "We don't start anything official until after Christmas, but some of the guys do conditioning all year."

HB nodded as Coach talked. If he helped, he could work out with the team.

Chapter 17

HB

Alison sat next to them and explained polynomials and radical expressions. HB had figured it out, but Cindy was still struggling. HB probably could have explained it to Cindy, but having Alison next to them was pleasant, and he kept sneaking peeks at her from under the hair that flopped over his forehead.

"Thanks, Ali…" He stopped abruptly before adding the "son" to Ali. He didn't know why but he wanted to call her Ali. He needed to call her Ali. Maybe she had been a counselor at the *Y* program when he was younger. Perhaps she was Miss Ali then? Somehow though, he didn't think that was where they had initially met.

Or, had he experienced something like what had happened to Ashton? If he had a new soul, did it have a connection to Alison?

Alison was looking at him oddly again, her eyes familiar with deep pools of brown and gold shades—an interesting, unique combination he loved.

He continued looking sideways at her, studying the silver earrings that dangled like fishing lures from her ears and how she tucked her hair out of the way. He was similarly focused on the smattering of freckles across her nose, her brown hair highlighted with red and gold.

"HB?" Alison asked. "Did you understand?"

What had they been talking about?

"I-I think so?"

"You don't sound sure," she said.

"Maybe you should explain it again." He liked having her close, her perfume light and citrusy. He hit his forehead with his palm. "I still have trouble focusing sometimes." A plausible lie, one quickly explained. However, he didn't know exactly why he was thinking of her freckles and hair and not math. He had the sense of déjà vu, the situation repeating itself, and perhaps it had, but he didn't know where or when.

"Oh." Her mouth opened when she realized he was referring to his accident. "Of course."

He reached out to where her hand was on the edge of the book and squeezed her fingers. "Thank you." They stayed that way momentarily until she pulled away and tucked it in her lap.

"I'm getting used to the new me. I feel like someone else woke up in the hospital."

He had thought about what Ashton had shared, but it was implausible, and he needed time to wrap his mind around the concept of a new soul entering his body.

"That must have been so frightening!" Alison's eyes, compassionate and concerned, were like deep pools he could drown himself in. This time she reached out and lightly touched his hand. Not an uncommon gesture for her, but it felt more intimate than friendly.

"I guess." He shrugged. It wasn't frightening exactly. He just felt disjointed and off balance. It was hard to explain.

After going through the steps to solve the problems again, Alison excused herself and went to help another student, leaving HB bent over his work.

Much later, at almost the end of the day, Alison leaned over the desk to see what he had done and said, "Let's take a break from math." She gave him an imperceptible nod. "I need to assess your writing skills."

HB closed his workbook.

"I'd like you to write an essay about a situation." She placed several sheets of lined paper on the desk with a pencil. "Any situation that shows courage. It can be about anything. Rescuing a kitten from a storm drain. Stopping a robbery. Anything. It can be true, or you can make it up. You decide."

HB sat back, folded his arms, and closed his eyes, thinking. He wasn't a hero when the three cars smashed together—he was a victim. He searched his brain for memories floating around. He remembered something about an amusement park. Not just any amusement park. Cedar Springs in Ohio. A favorite for many midwestern people. He had been a hero when he saved a child when the Ferris wheel malfunctioned. They were stuck at the top while the wind coming off Lake Erie was getting stronger, pushing the seats while they waited for the fire department to come and rescue them. He could write about that.

He had been there, he couldn't remember when, but he knew the details. They were laid out like a comic strip, scene one, scene two, and so on. Cedar Springs and a child stuck at the top, one seat from them. She was crying and screaming.

In his mind, he was there, many years before, in the chair behind her, the wind rocking violently, making the little girl's light frame fling back and forth as she screamed for her mother. "I want my mama...Mama!"

As HB watched, the child struggled out of the

restraining strap and wiggled to a kneeling position, hanging onto the bar as the seat swung, pushed by the gusts coming off the lake, almost tipping the girl out to plummet to the ground far below. "Mama!"

"Can't you do something?" his girlfriend screamed.

He couldn't see her face, but he knew she was his girlfriend.

"Sit down! Pink shorts!" he commanded as he eased out of his seat, holding onto the arm that held the seats together and climbed up to the girl whose chair was pitching and shifting. He had helped his father paint their two-story house. Heights didn't bother him.

"Hey! I'm coming to get you in a jiffy. Take a deep breath and hold steady," he commanded.

The little girl's tears stopped, and the redness on her cheeks faded a bit. He climbed hand over hand to reach her, carefully placing his feet between the metal bars holding the support together. One false step and he'd be hurtling toward the ground below. He didn't look down, only at the little girl. He reached her seat and held out his hand. "Carefully take my hand," he instructed. She reached out with shaking fingers and grasped his. He guided her hand to the bar, folded her fingers around it, and then went for her other hand and did the same.

In the distance, he heard the whine of a siren. And a fire truck came into view. "See! They've come to rescue us." He pointed to the red truck. "You okay?"

The little girl nodded, her knuckles white as she gripped the bar.

"What's your name?"

"Jani."

"That's a nice name."

The fire truck parked below, and the crowd pushed

back as the ladder was raised and reached their seat.

"I'm scared," Jani whispered.

"A fireman is climbing up to get you." HB touched her arm. "See?"

The fireman's head popped up next to them. "No need to worry. We'll get you down."

He pushed Jani toward the man with a red helmet. "This is Jani," HB said. "She's first." He winked.

"Well, Jani. I'll strap you to my body, and we'll climb down together. Do you think that would be all right?" the firefighter asked.

She sniffed, wiped her nose with her hand, and nodded. HB helped her into the fireman's arms, where she was strapped to his chest, and slowly they made their way to the bottom.

Only then did he dare to look down where people cheered and waved.

The ladder rescue was repeated until everyone was off the stalled Ferris wheel.

"You're a hero!" his girlfriend said.

"Nah!" But secretly, he felt proud of himself. But a hero? He guessed so and liked the admiration in her eyes. Way to score points!

"You are! She would have fallen if you hadn't helped her sit down and be calm."

Presently the newspaper was there, asking questions and taking pictures.

Yes, he'd write about being a hero at Cedar Springs and rescuing the girl. The girl's parents hugged, cried, and thanked him. "You saved our baby!"

With a look of concentration, HB began to write. The rescue images clicked through his brain, and he wrote about each scene.

Chapter 18

Alison

Alison read HB's essay with a feeling of déjà vu. She remembered that incident at Cedar Springs. HB must have read about it, too, since he would have been a tiny tot. The *Clearwater Journal* ran a story about it on the tenth anniversary.

HB's paper was short but well-written for someone who had only completed freshman English.

She closed her eyes and massaged her nose and thought back to Cedar Springs—a large amusement park on Lake Erie, a favorite of Clearwater folks for as long as she could remember. Alison's parents had taken her there as a child, and then she went with friends when they were old enough to drive.

With her eyes closed, she pictured the entrance, the sounds of excited voices, and the squawk of the gulls swooping in for dropped pieces of popcorn or candy. Music weaved its melody in and around the excited squeals of children and bells and buzzers from the games. The smells of hot dogs, burgers, and popcorn combined with hot concrete made a satisfying aroma. Yes, she remembered Cedar Springs and the feeling of the wind pulling back her cheeks as she rode the Blue Flash, her body jerking forward and back and sideways with each twist of the track.

She would never forget that incident on the Ferris wheel. It was as if it happened this morning. In her mind's eye, she saw her knuckles trying to burst through her skin as she held on to the bar for dear life. The breeze coming off Lake Erie turned persistent, adding to the rocking and swaying of the wheel. From her view, the seat seemed to be held by a thread, stretched beyond endurance, ready to release its burden at any second. She ached for the child and what she knew Rob would do to save the little girl.

Calls from the little girl's frantic mother jabbed her stomach, and her palms turned sweaty as she watched the girl swing back and forth in the seat, ready to fall. She didn't want to think of what might happen if Rob didn't reach her in time. Instead, she concentrated on Rob's slow progress inching along the arm that held each section together. The wind was a pesky finger, poking and prodding his precarious hold on the metal. She imagined the metal was cold and stinging. No, she had never forgotten the scared feeling and how brave Rob was. She had already decided she loved him, but his heroism cemented their bond. She would always love him. Thus, her license plate: 4EAEA—Forever and Ever, Always.

She opened her eyes. Cedar Springs vanished and she finished correcting the essay. HB got an A, and she was sure he'd be happy with that. She wasn't playing favorites. He had done A work.

Something nagged at her. A detail she had overlooked. Did it matter? Yes, he mentioned the little girl wore pink shorts. There were only a handful of people who knew that detail.

Chapter 19

Alison

Alison handed the corrected essays back one at a time, giving each student a word or two of encouragement even for the most atrocious ones which she had given C- grades. These students had been beaten down during their educational careers, and it was her job to encourage the most reluctant ones so they would finish their GED or adult education diploma. She saved HB's for last. Cindy was thrilled with her B++ and smiley face. When Cindy received her paper, she looked up and grinned at Alison, waving the paper. Alison had mouthed back, "You did a good job."

Funny what some students responded to. Alison could have put stickers on the papers and pretended they were all elementary students—young and old alike were encouraged and heartened by her smiley faces and added pluses.

Alison stopped short of HB's chair. She nervously smoothed back her hair and felt heated around the collar, suddenly her throat closed and nothing came out. His essay had touched off so many memories of Rob. Rob in high school. Rob as a hero. Sure, she had examined them before, but they still brought back a pang. She cleared her throat with some difficulty.

HB looked up and frowned at her. "Is...is

everything all right?"

His question flustered her. "I-I was thinking of something. Sorry I startled you." She realized she was standing in the middle of the aisle—immobile, clutching his paper, wrinkling the edges. She looked at his essay and thrust it toward him. "Is this a true story?"

"Yup!"

"Oh." She had been sure he would tell her, he made it up after reading about the tenth anniversary. His answer further discombobulated her.

Turning the paper over, a slow smile spread across his face at the A. "Thanks!" He waved the paper, flashing his A.

"Uh…" Alison awkwardly gave him a pat on the back. "You earned it," she said as he kept grinning.

Something in the essay didn't sit well with her, or maybe it was that the details were spot on. Anyway, she gave him a forced smile and continued down the aisle toward her desk. At her desk she turned. "What color did you paint the house?"

He frowned and paused as if considering her question. "Blue. We painted the house blue."

Rob had helped his father paint the house. He had climbed to the second story on a rickety ladder—heights didn't bother him—brandishing the blue paint.

****

HB turned over the essay and smoothed out a wrinkled edge where Alison had clutched it. He had never been much of a writer before, but suddenly he was better at everything. If what Ashton had shared was true, HB came away a better student. But he chalked it up to the relaxed atmosphere and working at his own pace, not a new soul in his body.

When he had turned to see her standing behind him, his essay in her hands, the last one of the pile, she wore an expression he swore he had seen before. No, not while in class. He knew that expression—one of dumbfounded confusion—although he couldn't recall the occasion.

It was this confusion that bothered him—the knowing, but not knowing. Once he had worn two different tennis shoes, both running shoes. It felt as if he had a snowshoe on one foot and a ski on the other. Both shoes good for the snow, but very different. That's how his memories seemed to go.

HB stopped his remembrances. Little by little, he was discovering something he hadn't known about himself. He thought he had been someone else before, or was he thinking about Ashton? As weird as it sounded, could he have been someone older who had loved Alison? It was funny. He remembered things from before his body had been born.

"HB?" Cindy asked.

And all at once, a sudden wind blew through his mind, forcing all those thoughts away in a swirling mass.

"Will you help me with algebra?" Cindy asked.

"Uh…" He looked down at the essay and then up at her earnest expression. "Sure."

A grin split her face. "Good. I hated to bother you. You were a million miles away."

He tapped the scar on his forehead. "Sometimes I confuse myself."

"Oh sure." She tapped her own forehead. "I keep forgetting."

Chapter 20

Alison

Alison's mind played cruel tricks on her. It had happened many times since Rob's death. She thought she had seen Rob, but he walked behind a tree or a building, and the person who came out on the other side didn't look like Rob. The last time was the baseball coach. Her emotions took the roller coaster to the top, and just as suddenly, they were headed vertically down, her heart lodged in her throat—a cruel trick.

And now, she thought she had seen him again, behind the cars in the parking lot. She longed to cry out, "Rob!" and wave her arms so he'd see her, but she knew better. Still, she held her breath and waited. The person morphed into HB, threading himself between cars, making for the door. She dropped her arms.

"Good morning," HB said.

She opened her mouth to speak but, startled, turned away instead.

"Did I say something to offend you?" he asked, stepping around her, so they were face to face.

She could have told him…what? That she thought he was her dead husband? That was utter nonsense, and she knew it.

"Oh, nothing. Sorry. A lot on my mind." She massaged her temples. "I thought you were someone else for a moment."

He nodded. "I think the same thing." HB pretended he was holding a ball and made the gesture of pitching it.

Alison's breath caught momentarily. She had seen that gesture before. Rob used to pretend to throw the baseball.

"Do you play baseball, HB?"

He stopped and appeared to be thinking about her question. "I don't know. I could swear I did, but I'm not sure." He touched the scar on his forehead. "I went to the batting cages, and…it came back to me. So I guess the answer is yes."

"I know you're confused," she said.

"You have no idea." He slowly shook his head. His thoughts collided into a mishmash of memories.

She didn't respond, just rubbed her arms like she was cold. HB took a step toward her as if to hug her, then stopped before going inside and joining Cindy at the table. Did she want a hug? Yes, she did.

Alison closed the classroom door behind her, leaned against it, and willed her breath and heart rate to return to normal, but still, the pulse in her neck vibrated.

She needed something to get her mind off Rob. Maybe she should take Mark up on his dinner offer and get out more often and not dwell on the past.

Chapter 21

HB

HB took the can of medium blue paint, draped the furniture with old sheets, and began to repaint his bedroom. He was in the middle of the wall when his phone vibrated in his pocket. He put down the paintbrush and squinted at the caller ID. Ashton. "Hey!"

"Hi, I haven't heard from you and thought you might have more questions," Ashton said.

"I know. Sorry. I've been busy with school and work." And painting his bedroom blue instead of the godawful black. He paused and scanned the half-black, half-blue bedroom. It already looked one hundred percent better.

"Any thought about seeing Dr. Sims? She was very helpful."

"Ummm." HB rubbed his head. "Is she real expensive?"

"A little," Ashton admitted and told HB the cost for an hour.

HB chewed his lip. He'd have to spend a big chunk of what he had saved. HB didn't want his mother to pay for a meeting with a new-age-type person about having a walk-in soul. Did he want to know or not?

"I'm still considering it," he finally said.

"Call me if you need help," Ashton said.

"Thanks!"

HB fished the business card for Dr. Sims from his wallet. Should he call, or shouldn't he? He moved the card between his fingers, leaving behind some blue prints. He wiped his hands on his jeans. What harm could seeing Dr. Sims do? He'd spend some of his savings on a quack or learn more about what Ashton had confided.

He let out his breath and called, hoping he wasn't throwing his money away.

Chapter 22

Alison

Mark seemed surprised and pleased when Alison, prodded and pushed by Marilyn, said she would love to go out to dinner with him. Hopefully, Marilyn would get off her back about dating him. Plus, it broke up the monotony of watching old movies and reading on Saturday nights.

Mark picked her up at five thirty, and she introduced him to her mother, Irene. Mark kissed Irene's hand, and she had a surprised and delighted look on her face.

They opened the door to leave, and Alison was glad she had brought a sweater. It was definitely chilly, and she could see the beginnings of autumn all around her by the copper and red leaves on the trees.

"You kids have fun!" Irene waved her hand at them as they walked to Mark's SUV and headed to the town of South Haven, about forty-five minutes away from Clearwater.

From May to September, most Michiganders avoided those towns—so touristy—but in October, the town had settled after the frenzy of warm weather activity and hunkered down to recharge their batteries and cater to the locals.

Mark had made reservations at a quaint little restaurant called Louie's with dark, rich paneled walls and a fire blazing at one end. A bell chimed on the door when they arrived. Tantalizing smells greeted them as they waited for the hostess to seat them. Mark took a brochure about things to do in the area.

They were seated by the fire, and Alison rubbed her hands together.

"This is nice, Mark!" she exclaimed, looking at the bottle-lined walls and the candle on the table.

"Have you ever been here?" He smoothed out the brochure on the table.

"No, but I've heard about it. I've just never had a chance to come here."

Come to think of it, Marilyn had mentioned it in passing, and now they were here—probably Marilyn's suggestion. But if Marilyn hadn't pushed, Alison would probably be watching black and white TCM with her mother. She unfolded her napkin and put it in her lap.

"I asked around for recommendations, and this was Marilyn's suggestion."

"Marilyn." Alison shook her head as she picked up the menu. "Of course," she said, smirking, and a waiter filled their water glasses and explained the specials. Everything sounded delicious.

"She means well," Mark said.

Alison tilted her head in agreement. After studying the menu, Alison ordered lasagna and Mark, the spaghetti. Chianti for her and a dirty martini for Mark.

Over drinks, Mark asked. "Do you like to do any of these things?" He pointed to the pictures on the brochure. Even upside down, Alison could read it.

"Biking sounds like fun."

"Hmm," Mark grunted. "What about golf? Are you a golfer?"

She shook her head. "Never got the hang of it."

"Me either." Mark chuckled. "I'm too impatient to chase after a little white ball. I like basketball. Fast action!"

"I can't say I'm much into sports, really. My husband coached, played, and watched baseball."

"Now, that's a boring game!" Mark said with a snort and slapped his hand on the table lightly.

She had to agree with him, but the conviction in his words about "boring" needled at her. To each his own, she thought. And besides, Rob loved the sport. So what if it was a little slow?

The waiter brought their dinners. She was happy to leave sports behind, and tactfully, she changed the subject after tasting her food. "Delicious." She motioned with her fork. "How's the spaghetti?"

"Tasty. Perhaps a bit more garlic and oregano are needed, though."

Alison was sure restaurants had to walk a tightrope between too many spices in a dish or not enough.

"Marilyn probably told you about me. Some which is likely embellished!" she said, using her fork to emphasize her words. "I don't know much about you except you're divorced and ex-military," she said.

He smiled. "Fair enough. You should know more about me." He took a sip from his drink, held up the glass, and swirled the liquid, biding his time. "I retired after twenty years in the Navy. I was married then, and we have twin daughters."

"How old are they?"

"Seven," he said.

"You're so lucky!" she replied.

"I bet you wished you had kids of your own," Mark

said.

She hung her head, studying her lap for a moment. "I had a miscarriage after my husband was killed."

"I'm so sorry, Alison." He reached over the table for her hand. "I bet that was rough."

He had no idea. She smiled at him. "Please, tell me more about your life before you moved here."

"Very well," he continued. "We traveled and lived all over the world."

"How interesting." She had only lived in the Midwest, but she and Rob had gone to Paris for their honeymoon. They had dreamed about traveling to more exotic locations, but sadly that never happened. "What places were your favorite?"

"I liked Japan. My wife liked Hawaii."

"Both those places sound wonderful," Alison said. After their honeymoon, they had medical school bills and bought the house—so there wasn't much left for expensive vacations. She wanted to travel, but it was out of the question with Mom. "Do you miss it?"

"Both too expensive," he said, "and claustrophobic!"

"Never been to either place," Alison said, so it was tough to judge his statement.

"I was married to a woman I met in the Navy. What a mistake that was! She was from Michigan and wanted to return when I retired." He paused as if considering what to say.

Alison nodded for him to go on.

"I suspected she was seeing someone else even before we moved to Michigan. She was secretive about whom she was texting and talking to. Just a feeling." He stopped when the waiter asked if they wanted a drink refill. Mark nodded yes, and Alison put her hand over her glass, indicating she was fine. Then he muttered, "I should have married her sister."

"Pardon?"

"Nothing." He waved his hand, meaning he wasn't going to repeat his statement.

Alison took a bigger bite of her lasagna. "Good restaurant choice," she changed the subject. "The spices are just right."

"Glad you like your entrée."

Even if he thought the seasonings were wrong, Mark ate his food with gusto, swirling the noodles, sauce, and meatballs expertly with his fork before taking a bite. After swallowing, he said, "I'm glad we found this place."

"Tell me about your daughters?" Alison asked.

"They moved to Houghton when their mother left me," he said with bitterness.

"Houghton! That's about as far away as you can get!" A city in the upper peninsula of Michigan, another place she had never visited but knew about.

"Exactly. Thank you. My lawyer said she couldn't leave the state, so she picked the farthest spot she could think of."

"I'm sorry. That must be horrible for you. Do you get to see your girls often?"

Mark shook his head sadly. "No, it's a long drive and an expensive plane flight. My pension and teaching salary only go so far. Our divorce gives me most of the summer and every other Christmas and Spring Break."

They ate in silence while Alison considered Mark's circumstances. She understood better the hurt expression she often glimpsed on Mark's face.

"A penny for your thoughts?" he asked

"Just comparing our differing circumstances to single-hood," she said.

"Both stink," he said, taking another bite of a meatball.

"So true." She had been devastated when Rob died, but Mark's wife chose to end their marriage and move away. She imagined he was mad and felt betrayed. Betrayed and sad were different emotions.

"I like this place," Mark said when dinner finished. "This could be *our* place!"

"That's sweet, but let's see how things unfold."

"Of course." He looked disappointed but tilted his head in acquiescence.

She could tell he was lonely, but having a special place was moving too fast for her.

She reached over to touch his hand, but he grabbed his drink, gulped it down, and signaled for another while averting his eyes.

Alison declined another glass.

After dinner, he drove her home, and Alison was glad she lived with her mother and didn't invite him in. She did allow him to kiss her—nothing. She didn't feel the tingle of desire with Mark like she had when Rob first kissed her.

Oh, they had a nice time, and she felt relaxed from the wine. She had liked Mark, except something seemed off about him. Emotions were simmering just below the surface which made her feel anxious. But hey, that's why people dated, wasn't it? To get to know each other better, right? At least, that's what she told herself.

After Mark drove away and Alison said goodnight to her mother, she went into her room to prepare for bed.

Her eyes immediately rested on her briefcase. Inside were papers and essays to correct. Her mind returned to HB's essay and the similarities between what she and Rob experienced in high school on the Cedar Springs Ferris wheel and what HB had written about. She guessed it could have happened to HB, also. There had been a write-up about the new safety features the park had installed after their ordeal, but things happened after ten years, didn't they?

Alison wished she had kept a copy of HB's essay. There was something he had written that only they, meaning Rob and Alison, had experienced and knew about. None of the newspaper articles mentioned that fact. But why did it matter? HB wasn't Rob. Rob was gone. HB couldn't fill his place even if Alison felt a pull toward the talented, likable nineteen-year-old. HB didn't seem like he was nineteen. His birthday was soon, and she would bring him a cupcake to mark the occasion.

HB had a steady gaze with knowing eyes that belied his age. He was what Alison's mother would have categorized as an "old soul." A person in a young body with experiences far beyond his years. Of course, he would react that way. He had been in a bad accident that made him forget his identity by erasing part of himself.

It was just a coincidence HB had guessed what had happened on the Ferris wheel. That was it, a lucky guess. And the house paint color? Many people had blue houses, probably one of the most requested colors after white or tan.

She needed to start over and tell HB she liked his essay and not be weirded out by the déjà vu feeling.

Chapter 23

Alison

On Monday morning, Alison caught Steve at the mailboxes that lined the teacher's work area. "Hey!" Alison said, absently wiping her sweaty hands on her pants. She had been thinking about HB and the essay all weekend and wanted to get Steve's take on the weird vibes she was receiving.

"I have HB Comstock in adult education." When Steve started to speak, she lifted her hand. She had heard all about his bad-boy image from Marilyn. "He's quite smart. He aced the Algebra I test and went right into Algebra II." She looked at Steve's surprised expression and added, "I was warned by Marilyn, but he's been wonderful. He's a good writer, too."

"You don't say?" Steve frowned at a flyer taped to the wall about travel for teachers.

"We have a different atmosphere out there." She moved her shoulder toward the back of the school and her adult ed trailer.

"True," he said, still looking at the things on the wall.

"He wrote an essay about the Cedar Springs rescue. Do you remember that?"

"Of course, the big news in little ol' Clearwater." Steve leaned his shoulder against the wall as they talked.

"Why did he write about that, you suppose? Brownie points with the teacher?"

"Steve, that was a long time ago." Alison chewed her lip. "I wonder where he got that information."

Steve narrowed his eyes as if thinking.

"Did we go to school with any of his relatives?" Alison asked.

"Don't think so. I've met his mother several times. Not the father."

"I wish I would have kept his essay. He was spot on in some of the details."

"Good imagination?"

A teacher walked by with a cup of coffee, and both Alison and Steve smiled and nodded to them.

"Could be. Would you talk to him?" Alison asked.

"I could, but what would I say?" Steve grimaced. "Are you a psychic or something?" He shifted feet as if he was uncomfortable.

She chuckled and then shrugged. "Is he?" She chided herself for even thinking that. "No!" She shook her head. "That I told you what a talented writer he was and ask him about the Ferris wheel rescue."

"I suppose I could. I didn't realize there were two such incidents. I wonder why the paper didn't write that up and compare the two?"

"I don't know, but I'm a little creeped out by the whole thing." She shifted her feet as tingling vibes crawled up her spine.

Steve patted her shoulder. "Don't get excited. I'm sure that sort of thing happens all the time. Let me read the paper, and then I'll talk to him."

"I'll get it back from him."

Steve was summoned to the counseling office,

leaving Alison to shuffle through her mail, still pondering how HB knew details that weren't reported to the general public. Or was it, as Steve suggested, an overactive imagination? Maybe, just maybe, Alison needed to get on with life and not live in the past.

Alison left the office and went back to the adult education trailer and asked HB for his paper so the principal could read it.

"Really?" he asked, clearly puzzled.

"I told him what a talented writer you were."

HB raised his brows, shrugged, pulled it out of his notebook, and handed it back to her.

Chapter 24

HB

HB awoke to his mother coming in and opening the shades. "Happy Birthday!"

He sat, rubbed his sleep-encrusted eyes, and squinted at her.

"Did you forget?"

"I guess." He yawned and stretched his arms up over his head.

"Shall we celebrate tonight?"

He could have sworn his birthday was in the spring.

"Sure," he said, struggling out of bed before going into the bathroom for a shower.

When he exited the bathroom, hair still dripping, his mother sipped her coffee and gave him an expectant look before dipping her chin toward the brightly colored package on the table.

"I can't believe you forgot!" she admonished.

He shrugged.

"Is Chinese okay for your birthday dinner?"

"Anything is fine." He took out a bowl and poured in cereal and milk.

"Aren't you going to open it?" she asked after placing her empty cup in the sink.

"I thought I'd wait," he said.

"No, go ahead!" she said, making a sweeping

motion with her hand.

HB opened the box with two new shirts and a hoodie. "Thanks!" He kissed her on the cheek.

"Do you like them?"

"I do." He held up the blue one.

"Yes, blue's a good color for you," she said, gathering up her purse, lunch, and coat for work.

****

Later that same morning, Alison had brought him a cupcake. He remembered she gave cupcakes to all her students on their birthday.

"What's this for?" he asked.

"It's your birthday, isn't it?"

He shrugged. "Yeah."

Cindy punched HB's arm. "You didn't tell me."

"It's not a big deal."

"You're twenty?" Cindy asked.

"Yeah." He nodded and fingered the clear plastic around the chocolate with vanilla frosting cupcake from the local grocery store. "It looks delicious. Thanks, Ali," he said.

HB noticed the strangled look on her face when he called her Ali and remembered her telling him that's what her late husband had called her too.

****

Soon, Alison was in the swing of things, helping students, grading tests, and reading essays. HB and Cindy were working on math, whispering and pointing to problems on a page when Principal Steve walked in. Steve! She had forgotten she had asked him to talk to HB.

HB turned and saw who it was. His old friend, Mr. Principal. The realization caused him to stop and consider who he was exactly. How did he know he was an old friend? Something intrinsic?

And now Principal Steve had stopped next to HB and Cindy. "Can I talk to you?"

HB looked around. "Me?" Principal Steve was looking at him.

"Yes."

HB looked at Alison. "Is it okay if I go to the office?"

"Sure."

Cindy grinned at HB. "I promise not to eat your cupcake."

"What's the occasion?" Principal Steve asked.

"My birthday," HB said.

Steve nodded.

"I don't go to the high school anymore," HB said, his words tripping over each other. "Am I in trouble?" He followed the principal out the door, across the parking lot, and into the main building.

"No, I just wanted to ask you a few questions."

It felt like he was in trouble, but part of him knew the principal was a friend. But he couldn't recall all the details of why he thought so.

As they walked down the main hallway, HB wondered what the principal could want with him. If it was something bad or happened before the accident, he could always say he didn't remember because of his concussion and head trauma.

HB's steps slowed in the main hallway. There were cases of trophies, pictures of past athletes, former student leaders, and other awards. He stopped and studied a picture of a guy with dark hair and kind eyes. The guy was holding up a trophy.

Principal Steve stopped next to him. "Do you know who that is?"

HB blinked.

"That guy." He pointed.

HB squinted. He recognized him, but how? "I don't know." He shrugged.

"He was my best friend and Mrs. Larkin's husband."

HB stepped back but couldn't take his eyes off the picture. He had a memory of that particular day. They had won the state championship over the weekend, and the photo was taken for the paper on Monday when they returned to school.

When the principal motioned for him to follow him to the office, he did so reluctantly. He just wanted to study the good-looking boy holding the trophy and sporting a lopsided grin.

HB remembered the principal's office with its metal, uncomfortable chairs and an uninspiring desk. HB sat in the offered chair, his tailbone pressing against the back, waiting for whatever was going to happen.

"Ms. Larkin says you're doing quite well and have become a very focused and committed student."

Had the principal dragged him out of class to tell him that? He shrugged and moved his head noncommittally.

"So what's the difference this year?" Steve laughed. "We spent a lot of time together before your accident."

HB studied the man with nondescript brown hair and glasses, who wore a red and blue striped tie, trying to remember being in the principal's office. He realized he couldn't remember, and an awkward silence ensued. He thought he recognized the principal wearing a baseball uniform and cap, but the man was in his thirties, so that would have been impossible, wasn't it?

The principal leaned forward, waiting for an answer. What was the question exactly? Adult education. "Uh, Alison treats us differently."

"I see. You call her Alison?"

Alison. Ali. He preferred to call her Ali. It felt right somehow.

HB nodded. "She wants us to call her by her first name, so it's more like a college setting and not high school."

"Right." The principal tapped his chin. "So that's made a difference?"

"I think so. I don't remember regular high school being so informal." HB moved aside his bangs to bare his scar. He pounded his fist on his knee. "I remember random things about before."

Steve whistled. "That scar looks bad."

"They tell me I'm lucky to be alive." HB paused. "Can I ask you something? It's totally off the wall."

"Shoot."

"Did you play baseball at Clearwater High School?"

The principal chuckled and moved his head toward a panoramic picture of the baseball team on his wall. HB assumed it was a current team, but when he studied it further, the uniforms were out-of-date. Had he seen the picture before? He must have if what the principal said was true. HB had spent a lot of time in this office before his accident.

"Yes, I was on the team when we won the state championship. I played with Alison's husband, Rob."

HB narrowed his eyes, his thoughts scattered and disjointed. Then a memory of lifting a giant trophy and parading around the school with the prize.

"Ms. Larkin—Alison—said you are a talented writer and wrote about something that happened to you at Cedar Springs."

HB swallowed. Why was everyone questioning his essay? "It was nothing. I saved a kid when the Ferris wheel got stuck at the top. She was scared, so I climbed over to calm her down."

"And when was this?"

"I was a junior, I think. Like I said before, I'm a bit fuzzy about some of the details."

"So this happened just a year ago?" The principal leaned his forearms against the desk and gave him an intense stare. "You must have been a celebrity!"

"I don't remember." He rubbed at his temples, trying to clear his head.

"What else don't you remember?"

HB sat back and looked at the ceiling. "I have all kinds of random thoughts."

"Give me a for-instance?"

"I remember a camping trip where our quad broke down, and we had to walk about fifteen miles to the main road."

The principal coughed. "W-where was that?"

"I think maybe in Ludington? A hunting area around there?"

"Who was with you?"

HB concentrated. "My best friend, I think."

The principal took a sip of water and used his fist to tap his chest. "Something similar happened to me."

"Really?" HB sat straighter and leaned closer.

"We were deer hunting," the principal added.

HB didn't remember killing a deer. The plaque on the principal's desk read: STEVEN CHANSON,

PRINCIPAL. Funny, HB thought, his best friend was named Steve.

"Your name is Steven?" HB asked.

"You never knew that before?"

"I guess not." He frowned at the nameplate.

"Tell me more about the camping trip," the principal said.

"I thought we, er, I mean I, was going to die. We got stuck out in the woods about fifteen miles from the campground and had to walk back, but you twisted your ankle, and I helped you along."

"Me?" Steve gasped. "You said 'you.' "

HB frowned at him. "Uh, sorry, I meant someone else. My brain, you know." HB pointed to his head and gave a slight laugh. "It short circuits sometimes."

"Understandable." The principal nodded. "Anything else?"

HB noticed Principal Steve's face blanched some while they talked.

"We each had two water bottles, but I gave mine to you—someone." HB corrected himself and gave an infinitesimal head shake.

Again Steve, the principal, coughed and pounded his chest but didn't comment. Finally, Steve took a deep breath. "Okay, then," he said. "Just wanted to talk to you about the dramatic turn-around in your demeanor in school."

"My mom says the accident knocked some sense into my head."

Principal Steve chuckled. "Well." He hesitated. "Keep up the good work!"

HB stood and started to leave the office, but he turned back to see an indescribable expression on the principal's face: disbelief, concern, and maybe alarm. HB nodded to him, and Principal Steve rearranged his face to a neutral expression.

****

Alison's head lifted when the door opened later the same day. Steve came in.

"Can you step out for a second?" he asked.

Alison held her sweater closed as they stood on the small porch that led to the trailer. "What's the matter?"

"Nothing." Steve looked shaken and pale.

"There has to be something the matter. You're as white as a sheet, Steve."

"Er, the kid's psychic," Steve said as he chewed his bottom lip.

Alison let out her breath. "How so?"

"He remembered the hunting trip when Rob and I got stranded in Ludington."

"Oh, gosh! How did he know that?" She frowned, thinking back to the story Rob and Steve told her when they returned.

"I'm not sure, but it gave me the willies. I hadn't thought about that in years."

"Me neither," Alison said, tightening her grip on the sweater.

"He must know someone who went to school with us." Steve stared off into the distance.

"Did you share that story?" Alison asked.

He grimaced. "I don't think so. Rob and I were embarrassed by our stupidity at the time. I think only the three of us knew."

And now, apparently, HB knew too.

"There has to be some explanation," she said.

Steve blew out his breath. "Could be. I'm not sure.

112

I don't exactly have the time to chase down the source of that story."

"I understand," Alison said as Steve began edging down the steps. "We might never know."

"It's not important, is it?" He stopped at the bottom and faced her, his hands holding the railings as if for support.

She had the feeling spiders were crawling up and down her spine, she did a mental shake.

"You're probably right."

****

Later as she locked the door after the students had left, Mark stopped her in the parking lot. "Alison!"

"Hi." She turned around.

"Haven't seen much of you since dinner."

"Been busy with students and papers and Mom," she said, lifting her bulging briefcase so he could see the papers inside.

"Have a drink with me! I've meant to go to the Moonglow Inn for happy hour."

"Let me stop home and check on Mom. I'll meet you there in an hour?" She looked at her watch. "Four thirty?"

"It's a date."

"No, I'm buying drinks since you paid for dinner."

"I'll never turn down an attractive woman's offer to buy!"

Alison drove slowly out of the parking lot, passing the baseball field as she did. Already students were practicing pitching, throwing, running, and sliding. She slowed and then stopped when she saw a familiar figure watching from the periphery of the field—HB. He held a ball in his hand and raised it in a pitching stance as if he were going to throw the ball. She shook away the feeling of déjà vu—Rob had played on this field in high school and then coached when they moved back after medical school.

She eased away from the baseball field and drove home, where she found her mother crying. Alison rushed forward and put her arms around her mother. "What's wrong?"

"I've been calling Penelope all day, and she doesn't answer. I think she's mad at me."

Alison patted her mother's back. "She's probably out shopping. Why don't you come with me and meet a friend from school for a glass of wine." She handed her mother a tissue. "You'd like to get out of the house, wouldn't you?"

Her mother hiccupped and nodded.

"Dry your eyes. Put on some lipstick, and we'll go to the Moonglow." She hoped the mention of her parent's favorite place to dine would cheer her mother up, but her mother looked at her blankly.

"Moonglow?" Her mother's brows shot up. "A new place?"

"I guess you could say that." The restaurant had several owners over the years.

Mark had a table and looked surprised when Alison, holding her mother's arm, arrived at the table.

"Mark, you remember my mother, Irene?"

"Oh, yes!" He took her mother's hand and squeezed lightly. "I can see where you get your beauty."

Alison glanced at her mother, who blushed and put her palms to her cheeks. Mark pulled out the chair for her and helped her sit.

"My!" Alison's mother said. "When you said a

friend, you never mentioned this handsome fella!"

The waiter came to take their order. Mark had a beer, and both Alison and her mother had white wine.

Alison's mother looked around. "Is this a new place?"

Mark raised his brows as if to say something but didn't.

"It's under new ownership," Alison said quickly. Moonglow had been around when her parents were dating and was also Rob's first job when they were in high school.

"I like it," Irene said.

"Mark only moved here a couple of months ago. He teaches Biology at the high school," Alison said.

"You don't say. Alison teaches there too!"

"Yes." Mark smiled. "That's how we met."

"You know that's where Alison and Rob met too," Irene said with shining eyes.

"Rob?" Mark asked.

"Oh, dear. She has a husband, you know," Irene said.

Alison nudged Mark's shin with her foot.

Mark nodded. "We'll be friends then."

Irene patted his hand. "You'll like Rob."

"I'm sure I will," Mark said in a soothing voice.

"Thank you," Alison mouthed. He had been kind to her mother, giving him extra brownie points in her book. Her uneasy feelings about him were evaporating. She paid the bill and squeezed his fingers, thankful he had taken her mother's mind off her dead sister, Penelope.

"That was delightful!" Irene exclaimed. "What nice friends you have!"

115

Chapter 25

Alison

When the students arrived the following day, Alison was determined to speak to HB about his essay—the similarities between the two incidents were eerily alike. Would she tell him she had witnessed her boyfriend rescue a child at Cedar Springs too?

She sat with HB at one of the unused tables and handed him his paper. "I liked your essay," Alison said, her finger tracing a scratch across the laminate top. She paused, let out her breath, and continued, "How did you know about that accident at Cedar Springs?"

"I was there."

She let out her breath. "Yes, you said that."

Alison did the mental math. That incident took place over fifteen years ago. How could he know unless he had been there? Had he been on another seat and watched what happened ahead of him when he was a boy? The questions continued running through her head.

"I see," she said as a way of pausing and trying to collect her thoughts and next words.

"Is everything okay?" he asked, peering at her and frowning. "The principal asked me the same questions."

"Just remembering something similar happening to my boyfriend and me." A simple explanation and the truth. "I guess your paper brought back some memories."

Better to be honest and not be weird about the situation.

"I'm sorry I upset you." He lightly touched her arm. "My memories seem to be someone else's and not mine at times," HB said, with a shake of his head. "My accident and all."

His hunched shoulders made him look lost and afraid.

She believed his accident had caused trauma in his life, physically and mentally. Her life was changed also. She had a lifetime of memories that were all her own and not someone else's.

He was sincere. His eyes wavered a bit as he chewed on his lower lip. Alison wished now she hadn't reacted this way. Maybe having HB in class was too much, digging up memories of Rob and the accident that killed him. HB was, after all, injured in the accident too.

"It's very confusing." He sniffed. "It's unsettling not knowing what is real and what isn't."

She smiled at him and squeezed his fingers. Perhaps she held them a little too long, but she believed him and felt the pain he had been through.

Chapter 26

HB

HB tilted his head but remained quiet. When had he experienced the incident at Cedar Springs exactly? With his brain not firing on all cylinders, he couldn't remember how old he was or who he was with. It was a girl. He remembered sitting by a girl—his girlfriend, he thought. He didn't see her face clearly, only her hands with orange-pink polish with sparkles on her nails.

He clearly remembered that incident, even if other things were blurry. The questions from Alison and Principal Steve made him feel uncomfortable and emotional. He had the urge to kiss Alison but knew that was wrong, so he jumped up. "I've got to go!" He reluctantly pulled his fingers away from Alison's hand.

"You just got here," she said.

"Work. I forgot. I have to go to work." This wasn't true. He had the sensation the air in the room was suddenly gone and he rushed outside gasping for breath while clinging to the railing for support.

He left to wait for his shift at the Moonglow Inn to start. Alison's questioning made him feel unbalanced and dredged up feelings he couldn't name exactly. He just didn't want Alison doubting him when he knew in his heart he had been the teenager on the Ferris wheel.

He remembered the sheer terror of clutching the

cold steel with his bare hands and not looking down at the ground far below. He kept his gaze on the little girl with pink shorts, standing and rocking on the seat, which was ready to tip her to the ground. The crowd gasped as her teddy bear fell from her flailing hands, a brown dot below.

"Hey!" he yelled. "Sit down, Pink Shorts! I'm coming for you."

She had turned and looked as he climbed carefully out of their seat, keeping his eyes on the pink shorts, his hands gripping the bars holding the giant tinker-toy ride together. The calls of encouragement from the gathering crowd below made him square his jaw and edge closer to her. And there was encouragement for him as well. "Steady! You're almost there. You're doing great!"

It wasn't a scene he had made up. He had been there. He had turned back to his girlfriend and given her a thumbs-up, and she gave him a smile he could never forget even after head trauma. The smile said she loved him and admired his courage.

The fire truck arrived as he reached the girl. He sat holding her as the ladder was raised, and a fireman climbed up and helped her down first and then him. Nope, there was no way his mind had conjured up that scene. He had been there, with the smells of popcorn, hot dogs, cotton candy, and sun-blistered pavement.

Now he was back on the tan couch, the air filled with a touch of spice from his mother's room freshener, not the fish and seaweed smell from Lake Erie. He yawned and went into his newly painted, blue bedroom for a nap and to wait until his shift at work started. Maybe he should take a few days off adult education until this was old news. He hated to leave Cindy in a lurch with math and wished he hadn't shared that story.

When HB returned from his shift at the Moonglow, his mother was still awake and watching television.

"How was work?" she asked, her feet propped on the coffee table and a bowl of popcorn by her side.

He liked working there, and it kept him busy. "It's good." He paused. "Can I ask you something?"

"Of course."

"Do you remember when I saved that little girl at Cedar Springs?" Asking the question made sweat pop out on his forehead.

She muted the television and frowned. "Saved somebody? Cedar Springs? No."

"I was cutting school and went there with my girlfriend. It was a big deal. The newspaper interviewed me."

His mother looked like she had been punched and was speechless.

Surely she would have remembered? He continued with his questions. "I wrote a paper about it, and now everyone is asking me about it."

"I honestly can't recall." She absently chewed on her lip as he waited. "Why don't you ask Dale when you see him?"

Not Dale. HB had Dr. Sims's card. Dale had introduced him to Ashton, who told him about Dr. Sims.

He tipped his head, not agreeing or disagreeing with his mother. Instead, HB went to the computer to research the incident.

LOCAL KIDS ARE HEROES

Two local teens skipping school saved a little girl on the Ferris wheel at Cedar Springs Amusement Park in Sandusky, OH. The park is a favorite for many midwestern families. Two Clearwater teens were stranded when the Ferris wheel suffered mechanical difficulties and stopped midway through the ride. An unaccompanied girl was frightened and tried to get out of her seat when Robert L climbed to her side and comforted her until they were rescued by the fire department.

Chapter 27

Alison

"What do you think of reincarnation?" Alison asked Marilyn after their weekly shopping trip, and they were now enjoying lunch.

Marilyn shrugged and stabbed at her Cobb salad, spearing some lettuce and ham. "Interesting concept that's not embraced by western civilization."

Alison studied her salad but so far hadn't eaten much. She didn't think what she had questions about was reincarnation exactly.

"Why do you ask?"

"I had a student write about something that happened to Rob and me."

Marilyn moved the salad around in her bowl and selected a hard-boiled egg. "Maybe you have a friend in common?"

Alison doubted she and HB had a mutual friend outside class. "I'm not sure about the reincarnation part. More like one mind took over another."

Marilyn frowned. "Someone has a new brain?"

"No." Alison sat back and studied the ceiling as she thought back to what she had read in her book on spiritualism and communicating with the dead. She shook her head vehemently. "It was called something else in the book."

"Are you talking about a soul transfer?"

That wasn't what the book called it, either.

"Do you consider it silly of me to think one of my students has Rob's spirit in him?"

"Who's the student?" Marilyn asked.

"No one you'd know." She knew what Marilyn thought of HB, so he remained nameless.

Marilyn pushed aside her salad, picked at a piece of sourdough bread, popped it in her mouth, and chewed slowly, her eyes narrow in concentration. "I wouldn't discount it exactly. But—and don't take this the wrong way." Marilyn tilted her head. "Are you sure you're not looking for ways to communicate with Rob, that you're grasping at straws?"

Alison exhaled. "You're probably right." She took a sip of her iced tea. "I miss him so much!" She stabbed her salad.

Marilyn reached over and grasped her hand. "How's it going with Mark?"

"So-so." She put down her fork. "He's not Rob."

"Alison…" Marilyn squeezed her hand. "No one is going to be Rob."

"True." She picked her fork back up and continued eating.

"Give Mark a chance. He's a nice guy. I sat by him at a meeting last week, and his ideas were thoughtful and right on."

She hadn't been open to a relationship with him. There was no soda tingle in her veins like when she saw Rob, even after all their years together. A relationship needed the pull of attraction and common interests, but she didn't feel that with Mark. "You might be right." It was going to take some major convincing to give her heart to Mark.

Chapter 28

HB

Dr. Sims's office was located in Grand Rapids in an office building with many other professionals. HB fought the traffic from Clearwater on 97 to Grand Rapids, one of the bigger cities in Michigan. It was a noisy place where horns honked, and tires squealed, so different than quaint, old-fashioned Clearwater. But he remembered living in a big city at one time. Or had he? Another unfamiliar memory, yet, not.

He followed maps on his phone, arrived at her building, and studied the list of accountants, doctors, and financial planners listed by the elevator. He found her name and office number, took the elevator to her floor, and followed the signs.

He wasn't sure what to expect from someone who did regressions. What exactly was that? But Ashton had sworn by her help to figure out his faulty memories.

Could she help HB? Would she help him reveal something spooky and unreal?

He stood before her door, hesitantly touched the handle, and let his breath out. It would be easier to chalk everything up as head trauma, but he grimaced. He couldn't let this go.

HB opened the door and stepped inside. So far, nothing was alarming about this office. For all he knew, he could be at the dentist. The waiting area had chairs and magazines—typical and non-threatening.

A door to his right opened, and a woman stepped out. "Hello, can I help you?" she asked.

"I've got an appointment with Dr. Sims."

"I'm Dr. Sims," she said and extended her hand.

HB didn't know what he was expecting. Maybe someone that wasn't so average looking? Dr. Sims wore a pinstriped pantsuit and a pearl necklace. Hardly the new-age guru he was imagining. He wiped his hand on his jeans before shaking hers. "I'm Henry Comstock. Call me HB."

"HB, nice to meet you," she said and motioned for him to follow her into an inner office. She sat behind her desk and moved her hand for him to take a seat on the couch. She had a folder on her desk, which she squinted at before speaking.

"So, why are you here, HB?" she asked.

"I met Ashton."

"Oh!" She clasped her hands. "How is Ashton?" she asked. "I haven't seen him in a couple of years."

HB raised his brows. "He's fine, I think. His story is different than mine."

Dr. Sims moved her head slightly as he talked.

"But parts are the same. He went into the hospital one person and came out another."

"Yes, he's the first walk-in I've ever encountered in my practice," Dr. Sims confirmed.

"He mentioned a walk-in, but I'm not sure what that is."

Dr. Sims swiveled around in her chair to face the wall of bookcases behind her desk. She tipped her head back as she surveyed the titles. She selected a slim volume and handed it to HB. "This has the best description I've seen."

HB turned the book over in his hands. *Walk-Ins, Indigo Children, Star People.* He looked up and shook the book. "These are all real things?"

"Yes."

"I've never heard anything about Indigo Children before."

"Probably not. I don't think you're an Indigo child, but you may have a walk-in soul."

"How do I know?" He looked at the book and then up at her and swallowed. Did he want to know? Life was less complicated when he was just another person with head trauma or a concussion.

He motioned with his chin toward the book. "If it's real, why don't more people know about it?"

"Why do you think, HB?"

"It seems far-fetched."

"Exactly. The medical community wants facts, not something murky and unclear like a soul-switching body. You can't exactly see a soul, so it's like religion—you have to have faith it exists like there's a God or Buddha, etc." She paused and looked at him. "God is another intangible thing that millions of people believe in." She got up from her desk and sat on the couch.

"So…so, what's the difference?" HB asked, running his forefinger over his thumb.

"You tell me?" she asked.

"I'm remembering things I don't think I've done in this body." He held his arms wide. "I think I was someone named Robert."

"You have a name?" She leaned forward. Her face registered surprise.

"I think I'm Robert Larkin. His wife is my adult education teacher."

"Interesting. I don't think Ashton knew the name of his soul, but you do?"

"I guess." He shook his head. "It all started when I wrote an essay about something that happened fifteen years ago." He let his breath out loudly. "That's when things started to get strange."

"It sounds like you have much of this figured out already." She frowned. "Why do you need to see me?"

"I don't want to sound like a psycho when I tell Alison I'm her dead husband. She's my teacher, after all."

"And you don't think there's another explanation?"

"Head trauma?" he asked, parroting Dale and the other specialists he had seen.

"You don't sound sure."

"I'm not. That's just what they told me in the hospital, and Dale keeps saying."

Dr. Sims nodded and clasped her hands around one knee. "We can do a regression, and I can try to ask some questions and see what your subconscious will reveal. Would you like to do that?"

HB studied the ceiling tiles as he grappled for an answer. Did he want to know, or didn't he? "Do you use hypnosis?"

"No, I have you visualize a relaxed state and then encourage you to remember events."

HB pursed his mouth. That didn't sound bad. "What if I'm Robert?"

She moved her shoulders. "Then you are."

Even if he learned he was Robert, would it change anything? Alison was the teacher, and he was her student, not her husband. And what would Alison think if she knew? Kick him out of class? Guess he was being a jerk? What?

"Oh, okay," he said slowly, "let's do it." He hoped he wouldn't regret this decision.

"Do a regression?" she asked.

"Yes, if that's what it's called."

"Let's set another appointment, and we'll see what we learn."

Chapter 29

Alison

"Gads, you're quiet this evening," Alison's mother commented over dinner. Alison pushed away the weird concoction her mother had served her—beans with bacon soup and chicken with pasta stars. Not one of her mother's better combinations.

"I guess I'm not good company." She toyed with her napkin and wondered what she should share with her mother. "Do you remember when Rob and I went to Cedar Springs, and he helped rescue that little girl?"

"Of course. It was the front-page news, and Rob was a hero. So?" Alison's mother, Irene, grimaced at her soup too.

"So?" Alison blew out her breath. "One of my students wrote about it."

"One of Rob's friends?"

"No."

"No?" her mother asked.

"No."

When Alison didn't elaborate, her mother frowned, no doubt forgetting the topic, and asked, "Would you like seconds?"

"I haven't even finished this yet, Mom." Alison pushed away her bowl.

Had HB somehow found the story and decided to

embellish it and make it his own? But somehow, Alison didn't think that was the case.

Alison stood and began gathering the dishes, and her mother drifted back to the living room and her favorite chair by the window.

Was Rob trying to send her a message through HB? The book talked about walk-in souls. She re-read that chapter. Depressed people who wanted to kill themselves could let their souls leave and find another body. Was Rob depressed and thinking of suicide? What about Leo, the boy who caused the accident? Had he wanted to end it all? He was a popular, smart kid in high school. Probably not. Then that left HB. Before the accident, he was a troublemaker at school. Did he want to die? Would he remember what led up to the accident and his emotions? When she had a moment, maybe she could ask him. Would it be awkward for her to ask, "Were you depressed and contemplating suicide before the accident?"

On Monday morning, somewhat refreshed from the weekend of correcting papers and caring for her mother, she stood at her desk and greeted her students as they staggered in. Alison stood by her desk and checked off students. And when finished, she scanned the classroom. Her eyes focused on Cindy and the empty chair next to her. "No HB today?"

"No," Cindy said, then scrunched her mouth. "I miss his help on math."

"I wonder if he's sick?" But Alison instinctively knew he was upset about her reaction to his essay about the Cedar Springs rescue.

"I'm going to text him," Cindy said. "I need help with these problems." She stabbed her workbook with her finger.

Alison glanced at the clock. Only ten minutes had passed. "I'll help you." Alison went over and answered Cindy's question, and when she looked up, Wayne raised his hand, and Alison went to him, leaving Cindy to her Algebra II problems. Before bending down to look at Wayne's work, she glanced around the classroom. Cindy was frowning and raised her hand again. With a sigh, Alison realized she needed to talk to HB and apologize for how she reacted to his essay. Would he understand why she had acted the way she had? His face had betrayed his inner turmoil when she questioned him. And she definitely wouldn't ask if he was depressed and thinking about suicide.

"Any luck reaching HB?" she asked Cindy.

"Nope, he never responded."

Alison knew she needed to talk to him. So after work, she'd drive to his house and apologize. And besides, she missed him too.

When the last student finally exited, Alison slumped back in her chair, exhausted. HB, she realized, was a big help in the class, especially in math, and she missed his presence, but more than that, she missed him. She turned on her computer, looked at HB's enrollment form, wrote down his address, and left, closing and locking the door behind her.

She was familiar with HB's street. Rob's mother had lived on Chestnut Way before moving to a senior apartment complex as her health began to worsen.

Alison pulled into HB's driveway, parked behind his truck, and sat for a moment, rehearsing what she would say. After turning several scenarios over in her mind, she decided the best way was honesty.

She turned off the car and walked to the front door and knocked. When there was no answer, she rang the bell. It resonated deep in the house, echoing off the walls, and then there was the tread of heavy feet before the lock turned on the front door.

"Ali! Alison!" HB opened the door, his face marked with sleep indentions from the pillow and his hair. "What…what are you doing here?" His sleep pajamas were slung low, exposing his stomach.

"I need to apologize," she said, feeling her cheeks warm as she stared at his bare midriff.

He swung the door open. "Would you like to come in?" And hoisted up his pajamas and tightened the waist.

She nodded and stepped over the threshold. The house was small but neat, with a profusion of artwork on every wall.

"What do you need to apologize for?" he asked, nodding for her to sit on the couch.

She sat on the edge of the sofa and cleared her throat. "All the weirdness surrounding your essay. It upset me because it brought back memories and Rob's death." She shook her head. "I didn't handle it well, and I'm sorry."

He looked at her and was quiet. Then his mouth worked as if tasting the words.

She concentrated on breathing evenly. "My boyfriend and I were in a similar situation many years ago. I didn't realize it had happened twice. My boyfriend became my husband who…" She held out her arms. "Was killed in the same accident that hurt you."

"I'm sorry I upset you," he said. "I should have written about something else." Again he paused, and his mouth moved as if he were rehearsing what to say. "The funny thing is…" he stated and shook his head. "No, not

133

funny," he said, shaking his head. "My mother said it never happened."

Now it was Alison's turn to move her mouth in contemplation.

"My mother and I didn't have the best relationship before my accident, so I figured I didn't tell her."

He seemed to gulp in the air and continued. "I'm totally confused. I talked to my shrink, and he said it's common for the brain after trauma to have memories that never happened." He looked at his feet. "He also said sometimes people come out of comas speaking a different language."

"Hmm." This wasn't exactly like that. As ridiculous as it sounded, she asked, "So you pretended to be Rob? My Rob?"

"I don't know if he was your Rob or not." He looked at her, wondering what she was thinking. Her head was cocked a little to the side and a brow raised.

"So I guess I made up the story and thought I was Rob." He was quiet again. "Even the principal..." HB paused. "I remembered being with him and walking back to camp." He shook his head, his hair falling over his eyes, and pushed the locks aside. "Now granted, we didn't have a good relationship when I went there before. I was always screwing up, and he was always suspending me. I guess I remembered something that happened to him and me."

Alison opened her mouth but the words wouldn't form. "Ah," she managed to utter. Had Rob been able to channel his spirit through HB in some way? How did that happen? Was Rob trying to reach out to her through HB? This whole situation was getting harder and harder to understand or make sense of.

He sighed and slumped forward, resting his elbows on his knees with hands clasped together.

She didn't know how to respond and nodded, but she didn't fully understand. A concussion did all this to HB?

"I went into the hospital one person, and now I'm different." HB had a peculiar look on his face, and Alison thought he was hiding something, but she didn't know what.

"That's got to be confusing." She grimaced. "It was as if you and he switched places." Under her breath, she said, "As if that could actually happen."

He may have sensed her words because he shrugged slightly.

She continued, "If I'm confused, I'm sure it's far worse for you." She struggled to stand. "I'm so sorry. I hope you'll come back to class. Cindy and Samuel miss you. We all do!"

"You too?" His words hung in the air.

Before she could stop herself, she answered, "Of course!"

"I'll be back tomorrow," he promised.

She bit her lip and gave a quick nod. "I'll see myself out," she said.

She ended up sitting in her car before backing out. She noticed the curtains moving slightly. He was watching her. She let out her breath, backed down the drive, and drove home, feeling somewhat better but thinking strange, convoluted thoughts.

Imagine waking up and being a different person. No, she couldn't imagine thinking foreign thoughts. No wonder HB had the air of someone older and wiser. He could be her contemporary, not just a student.

Chapter 30

Alison

Alison arrived early the next day, anticipating seeing HB when he returned to school. Someone parked an unfamiliar car nearby. Perhaps an eager new student? Alison walked over to the car, and a woman lowered the window.

"Are you Alison?" she asked.

"I am. Can I help you?"

"I'm Jani," the woman said.

"Jani?" Momentarily Alison couldn't remember how she knew Jani.

"I'm the girl Rob rescued at Cedar Springs," she reminded her.

"Of course!" Although the woman's features were unfamiliar, her eyes were still the same startling icy-blue color.

"We moved to Muskegon, and I wanted to look you up since we were so close now." Jani lowered her head. "I wanted to tell you how sorry I was to hear about Rob's death. I should have reached out sooner."

Alison reached through the window and squeezed Jani's hand. "Thank you. Would you like to come in?" She motioned her head toward her trailer classroom. "I'll make some coffee."

"Sure." Jani got out and followed Alison into the

classroom. "I always wondered what happened to you," she said. "I asked around and was told you work here."

"Everyone knows everyone in a small town."

"I bet you're a great teacher."

"I try," Alison said as she busied herself, making coffee and opening the shades. Alison frowned as she took two mugs from the cupboard. Why had Jani chosen this time to reconnect after fifteen-plus years? "Cream or sugar?" she asked, and Jani indicated she didn't take those.

Alison put cream and sugar in her cup, swirled it together, and tapped her spoon before bringing the coffee over, sitting opposite Jani, wondering what she wanted.

Jani sipped her coffee and let her breath out. Alison waited.

"I read about Rob's death in the newspaper. I meant to reach out sooner, but…" She trailed away. "I got busy. I've got my kids now."

Cedar Springs seemed to be on everyone's mind these days. They spent a few minutes chatting about Jani's family and her husband's new job in Muskegon.

Jani looked at the clock and stood. "I have to go now."

Alison nodded as she heard a car door slam in the parking lot. "Thank you for coming."

Jani dipped her chin and headed for the door as HB came in. They stopped and looked at each other.

"Are you…" Alison heard HB say.

"Who?" Jani asked.

"The girl from the Ferris wheel?"

"How did…" Jani choked. "Who are you?"

"I'm…never mind…"

Alison couldn't hear HB's reply, only Jani retorting,

"I've got to go!"

How had HB recognized Jani when Alison hadn't? The eyes were the same, but she was all grown up now.

Cindy came in as Jani ran out. Cindy frowned at the person racing by her before hugging HB, exclaiming, "Partner!"

Alison hoped to talk to him alone, but there wouldn't be time as students began streaming into the room. And, too, there wouldn't be any time to ponder the interaction between HB and Jani. A lucky guess on both of their parts?

"I told you I would come back, and here I am!" HB held his arms out as if to hug Alison, stopping short and rubbing his hands together. "Good to be back! I've got more credits to earn." He slapped the nearby table.

Alison laughed and squeezed his arm— momentarily stunned by the shock that zinged through her at touching him. His presence and smile lightened the room. She didn't want to ruin the day's mood by thinking about Cedar Springs and the particular sequence of events that made her question and doubt what she believed spiritually. She told herself people did not return to this earth after they were gone.

HB pulled up a chair and straddled it as he leaned forward to help Cindy, and soon Samuel joined them. "Let me show you how to change that into the second power."

Alison snuck looks at HB when they were busy working on algebra. Could he have channeled Rob somehow, or was it wishful thinking Rob had come back to her in another form? She felt chills as she considered the ramifications. Sure, she had read about such things in the alternate spiritual book. Some believed such things, but she never considered herself one of them, but now…now she was questioning conventions she had thought were universal.

After an hour of watching HB help everyone with math, Alison said with a laugh, "Who's the teacher here? You or me?"

"You were busy, so I helped him. No biggie."

"Thank you. You are such a kind soul, HB."

He shrugged and flashed her a smile before turning the chair around and sitting down to his work.

"You know, I'm proud of you for earning a math and an English credit in the first month of school!"

He gave her an "aw shucks" grin before dipping his head.

Alison went back to correcting papers with a feeling of buoyancy.

When class ended, and only Cindy remained, Alison stood and stretched. It had been a good day with HB back in the fold. Her thoughts were interrupted by Mark coming in. Only Cindy remained, and she gave Alison a sly smile. Alison didn't have time to interpret what Cindy's smile meant.

Cindy winked at Alison while gathering up her things to leave. Alison wasn't sure what she felt about the handsome Biology teacher. It was flattering to have his attention, but something about him didn't sit well with her. Probably his divorce. Until he reconciled his feelings about his ex-wife, there was little chance of him and Alison having a relationship.

Mark had stopped by to chat after school on several occasions before he helped with ROTC drills.

Cindy nodded to him, and he held the door open so she could leave when a bird flew in and perched on one of the tables. An ordinary blackbird with iridescent purple-black feathers. He cocked his head as if studying them and ruffled his wings.

"Sorry!" Cindy said.

Alison approached the bird, which regarded her with beady black eyes. When she got closer, the bird flew up and perched on the clock, watching Alison flap her arms, its head tilted to one side regarding her antics.

"Gotta go," Cindy said. "The sitter is waiting," and she let the door close.

"I've got a better idea," Mark said, taking off his ROTC cap. "You distract him, and I'll catch him."

Alison waved her arms and fanned the air with a forgotten piece of scrap paper on one of the tables. The bird flew off, perched on her desk, and began pecking at the crumbs left of her breakfast muffin.

Mark crept forward, cap in hand, and as the bird took off, he caught it in his hat and, with a swift movement, broke the bird's neck and tossed it in the garbage can. "No more bird!" he declared.

Alison thought she had heard the faint crack of the bird's fragile bones. What an insensitive thing to do. Was this something he had learned in his years in the military? Was life devalued? She wanted the bird outside, not dead in her garbage can. At this point, she felt like gagging.

"Are you all right?" he asked.

"You...you killed it!" The lump traveled from her stomach, lodging in her throat.

"I thought that's what you wanted me to do."

"No, shoo it outside." She looked up at him with tear-filled eyes.

"It would have made a terrible mess in your classroom." He patted her shoulder and said, "I'm sorry.

I wouldn't have done it if I knew it would upset you so much."

She pulled away and nodded but wasn't sure that would have been the case. Couldn't they have left the door open and shooed it toward the opening? Mark didn't have to break its neck! The crack of fragile bones still filled her ears.

She didn't want to see it in her garbage can either. Suddenly she felt cold and nauseous. "I've got to go home."

"You look a little pale," he admitted.

"I've got to go!" She gathered up her things and headed for the door, afraid if she stayed, she'd vomit.

"Dinner Saturday?"

"No, I have plans." But she didn't.

He followed her to the door. "Are you upset about that bird?"

She flipped off the lights, locked the door, and hurried down the steps to her car. Mark kept pace. "Are you upset about the bird?" he repeated.

"Yes, yes, I am." Alison covered her face with a hand. "I think I'm going to be sick!"

She got into her car, started the engine, and drove toward home, her stomach in a knot. She didn't like the casual way he had killed that helpless creature.

Was it his years of military training? Or had he been stripped of his compassion for others because of his contentious divorce? She couldn't put her finger on her reservations about him. Something didn't feel right, but if someone had asked her to explain her feelings, she couldn't.

She pulled into the driveway, stepped out, and vomited into the lilac bush.

She slowly took the steps into the house and used her key to open the door. Her mother was sitting on the couch and frowned when she came in.

"Gads, you're pale!" her mom said. "Are you feeling well?"

"I think so. Something happened at school."

Later as Alison sat on her bed and prepared to sleep, she avoided thinking about the dead bird and replayed the interaction between HB and Jani. How had he recognized her when Alison hadn't? Or a lucky guess? Or…the following supposition was beyond weird. Was HB somehow Rob? The notion terrified yet excited her. If only it were possible. She yawned and switched off the light. As she stared into the darkness, her mind refused to quiet itself to sleep even though she was tired. Her body relaxed, but her mind galloped from one memory of Rob to another.

Chapter 31

Alison

The following day, Alison unlocked the door to her classroom somewhat cautiously and flipped on the lights, and her attention went immediately to the pink flowers on the desk. Air caught in her throat, and she gasped. Pink tulips, but as she got closer, they were unopened pink roses that resembled tulips from a distance.

She reached a tentative finger to touch them but pricked her finger on a sharp thorn. That's why she didn't like roses. They were beautiful but also pain-causing. She sucked her finger and stooped to smell them, but they were hot-house flowers with no scent. Disappointed, she stepped back.

She heard the door open and knew it was Mark.

Alison turned and watched him stride toward her.

"I've come to tell you how sorry I am." He spread his arms wide and gave her a shrug and a smile. "Please, let me take you to dinner and make it up to you. I'm a guy. A clod. We think nothing of killing spiders, birds, bugs, and snakes."

He looked so remorseful, and she laughed. "O-okay."

"Good! Because if you said 'no,' I would camp out here until you said yes. And you'd make me miss my

Biology classes!"

Maybe she should give him another chance. She was being overly-sensitive. He was trying to make amends.

Before he left, they made a date for Friday night at the Moonglow Inn. "I'll pick you up at six?"

She nodded as he exited, and her students began to arrive.

The first thing HB said was, "Nice flowers."

She was quiet as she looked at the blood on her finger from the sharp rose thorn.

"Are you all right?" HB asked, leaving his table and coming to her side and bent down to look at the blood bubble on her finger. "Thorn?"

"Yeah."

"You don't seem very excited about them." He nodded to the bouquet on her desk. "Most women like flowers."

She shrugged.

"I know you like...tu...lips?" He frowned.

"How did...you..."

He tipped his head back. "I don't know how I knew." He raised his shoulders as if in resignation. "Lucky guess. We live in Western Michigan. There's the tulip festival in Holland."

"I do like them," she said and moved her finger with the blood toward her mouth.

HB grabbed her hand. "Don't do that. You can get bacteria from your mouth in the wound." He took a tissue and wrapped it around her finger and gently pressed it. "Keep some pressure on it, and the bleeding will stop." His hand stayed on hers.

She laughed. "Are you now a doctor and math-whiz, HB?" She moved her hand, but he kept the pressure on her finger.

He stood. "I guess."

"Thank you," she whispered and reluctantly slipped her hand from his. She liked holding his hand. She gave him a sideways look. She didn't have the same reaction to Mark, she realized.

Cindy entered next and made a beeline to Alison's desk. "Someone has a secret admirer."

"Not true," Alison said. "From a friend." She moved the vase to an out-of-the-way place on the counter.

Cindy gave Alison a raised brow. "I bet I know who they're from."

HB nudged her, and Alison saw him ask, "Who?"

"I'll tell you later," Cindy whispered back.

Alison shrugged and bent over her desk to mark students present and then stood and began to pass back papers, not wanting to talk about Mark or the flowers or the reason for the flowers.

Chapter 32

HB

HB's second meeting with Dr. Sims was the next week, and he was anxious to get that behind him. As he drove the forty-five minutes to Grand Rapids, he absently rubbed his forefinger on his thumb and wondered what a "regression" with her entailed. What if he found out he was an axe murderer?

Dr. Sims had said it wasn't hypnosis. Then what could it be?

He parked, went in, and entered the office.

Dr. Sims greeted him. "HB, come in." She laughed. "I promise not to bite!"

He shook away the apprehension and gave her a lopsided grin. "I'm a little nervous, I guess."

"Understandable." She motioned for him to sit on the couch in her office. "Get comfortable, stretch out, and close your eyes."

HB did as she instructed.

"Now I want you to think about a place that makes you feel relaxed. The beach. A place in the woods. A favorite vacation spot. Anything that makes you think relaxation."

HB scrunched his mouth and remembered a trail that meandered in the woods behind their house with a small brook that burbled and splashed over rocks and sticks. A peaceful place with running water, the soft whispering of trees, and the chirps of birds.

"Are you there now?"

"I am," HB said.

"I'm going to ask you to find the long dark tunnel in front of you. Do you see it?"

HB frowned. His mind was on the brook and the bird chorus, not a dark tunnel, but he saw the blackness. He nodded; he had found it.

"Now, I want you to move slowly toward the light at the end of the tunnel."

He opened his mouth to protest that he didn't see the light, but finally, he did. A tiny pinprick of yellow that got bigger as he moved forward.

"Let me know when the tunnel ends."

HB moved cautiously along in the dark, wanting to hold his arms out in front of him so he wouldn't run into anything, but nothing was impeding his progress, and he kept going. The light progressively got brighter, and he squeezed his eyes shut. He stepped out of the tunnel and saw a house below him. "I've reached the end of the tunnel."

"And what do you see? Can you describe it?"

"It's a house. Blue. Two stories."

"Do you know whose house it is?"

"Mine, I think."

"What can you tell me besides the house is blue? Do you see people?"

HB heard voices before he saw their figures. "There's a boy on a swing."

"Who is that boy?"

"Me. I'm about seven years old."

"What do you look like?"

"Dark hair, and I'm wearing a baseball jersey."

"I see. Do you play baseball?"

"I must." Yes, he played baseball.

"Okay, let's fast forward a couple of years."

HB seemed to soar over the field and looked down on the players standing at the bases. He recognized the in-town park's baseball field. A game and he was pitching. He remembered his signature move of stepping back with his left foot and then lunging forward, his upper body level with the ground as the ball hurtled toward the batter. And he still had dark hair, but he was older now, maybe eleven or twelve. "I'm pitching at a baseball game."

"What is your name then?"

HB frowned, stymied by that question. Who was he? The name was on the tip of his tongue, but the vowels and consonants refused to arrange themselves into a name. "I don't know."

"Are you HB? Or Henry?"

"No, I don't think so." Those names rolled off his tongue easily and without effort.

"Could you be remembering things as this other person?"

"I guess my thoughts feel familiar." He remembered vaguely why he was here, watching and remembering the scenes below him. "How is that possible?"

"I'm not sure how the phenomenon happens. Let's continue and move forward. Tell me what you see?"

HB was in the school gymnasium, filled with balloons and streamers. He recognized the gym with the old wooden bleachers, the athletic flags with the year and sport in bold letters, and a banner welcoming the class of 2004.

"Are you still with me?" Dr. Sims asked.

He mumbled his reply. The scene made him happy and sad—but Dr. Sims continued talking and asking questions, leaving him no time to reconcile what he was feeling.

"What's happening now?"

"A dance. I'm taking my girlfriend to the Christmas dance."

"And who is your girlfriend?"

HB tried to see her face clearly, but it was blurry and distorted. The name was on the tip of his tongue but wouldn't reach the area of his brain to say it. Suddenly he knew it was part of his cerebrum. "I don't know her name." But he knew the details of the brain.

And he recognized her perfume—floral and citrusy at the same time. Her scent was so close it tickled his nose. Even with all those bodies with their woody aftershave and hair gel, the only thing he was attracted to, like a bee to honey, was the floral/lemony embrace of his girlfriend.

"Let's move forward again."

He didn't want to leave her. The girl had her arms wrapped around his neck, and his nose was buried in her hair. No, he didn't want to leave. "Do we have to move on?" He wanted that dance to last forever.

"Yes, we do." She was quiet as he moved to the next scene.

"What do you see?" Dr. Sims prompted.

A big auditorium stretched out before him, and the smells were far different from the dance: books, papers, chewing gum, dirty sneakers, a hint of sweat, and an undertone of bleach and strong cleaner. There had to be hundreds of students facing a board and a man wearing a white jacket over his shirt and tie. A college class of some sort. "Um…a college class, I think."

"What kind of class?"

He couldn't see the exact words on the board, but the book on the desk in front of him was about anatomy. He was in some sort of biology class studying the human body. "Anatomy."

"Would you like to stop now?"

"Yes, please. Yes." He wanted to return to the dance and the smell of her skin and drink in the feeling of contentedness.

He also felt a profound sadness. It would have been better if he had been an axe murderer, not a boy in love.

Chapter 33

HB

After meeting with Dr. Sims, HB was glad his
mother was working late. He sat in front of the TV,
muted baseball game, and thought about the things he
had found out about himself. Or rather the person he had
once been. Ashton's story certainly seemed possible.
Was it possible that Rob's soul had switched with him at
the accident scene? And if he was Alison's dead
husband, how would he tell her? He absently rubbed his
thumb over his forefinger. What to say to her? "Hey, I
think I'm your dead husband!" No, that would never fly.
He felt he should ease into that discussion and reel her
in. Even then, it would be a stretch.

HB drove to school the following day, feeling sure
Alison figured into his remembrances somehow. He was
sure she was the girl at the dance whose face he couldn't
see clearly. HB watched Alison covertly as he and Cindy
worked together. The algebra was easy, and he could do
the problems and peek at Alison at the same time. He
wanted to share his regression.

When Wayne raised his hand, Alison got up from
her desk and walked past them to where Wayne sat.

HB froze. The perfume. The lemony/floral aroma
followed Alison and seemed to circle his head.

Cindy frowned at him. "Are you all right? You've

got a peculiar look on your face."

"I do?" he asked.

There was no time to talk to Alison privately, so HB did the next best thing—he'd go to the high school library and peruse old yearbooks. When HB stepped into the library, the librarian frowned at him.

"Can I help you?"

"I'm, um, from, um, adult education," he spat out.

"Okay." She leaned forward expectantly.

"I'd like to look at the old yearbooks from 2003 and 2004."

"Oh?" she raised her eyebrows. "Anyone or thing, in particular, you're trying to find?"

He shrugged. "Maybe. I don't know."

She pointed to a far wall and to the very bottom shelf and a long line of yearbooks starting with the first year the school was in existence—1957.

HB sat on the floor, pulled out the 2003 book, and scanned the index looking for pictures of the Christmas dance.

"You can't check those out," the librarian said, and HB gave her a thumbs up.

It had been many years since he had looked at this yearbook. The book was familiar even if it had been more than fifteen years since he had looked at the names and pictures and remembered his time at Clearwater High School.

He slowly turned the pages with the images in black and white but could read the small print. There was the same picture Principal Steve had on his wall; next to it was a photo of the principal with his arm around a dark-haired boy. The same boy he had seen dancing with the girl in the red dress.

HB continued turning the pictures slowly until he came to the section on dances and events. Once there, he found a picture of Robert Larkin with his girlfriend, Alison Steele. He couldn't discern if her dress was red or not, but his face was shadowed by hers, and she had her arms around his neck. This was the exact image he had seen with Dr. Sims.

He checked his watch. He needed to get home and to change for his shift at work. He'd come back another day and look at the yearbooks again, but giant goosebumps stood out on his arms. Ashton had woken up a different person. And the same thing happened to him—he had someone else's soul in his body. He was sure he had Robert Larkin's soul.

****

Alison met Mark at the Moonglow. He had a table and ordered red wine for her—even though she preferred white.

She pointed to the glass. "Is this for me?"

"I know you like white, but red is better for you."

"I see." She took a sip—too bold for her and set it aside. Mark had a martini.

"I also took the liberty of ordering you the lasagna."

She squinted at him. "I'm capable of making my own choices, you know?" She felt more than slightly miffed at his presumptuousness.

"Just trying to be helpful." He shrugged and held his arms out with a hopeless look.

Like killing the bird?

"I want you to know I'm planning a trip over Thanksgiving to see my girls."

"That's nice." Why had he told her that? She frowned at her wine, already thinking this dinner was a bad idea.

Mark started complaining about work before their food arrived. "Half my class left early for a football game!" he scoffed. "We need to run the schools like the military. Precision. Order. And respect for authority. I could shape that place up. Steve is a pansy! Don't you think?"

She had her own opinions about what was necessary at school, which didn't resemble Mark's.

"Did you know Steve and I went to high school together?" she said.

"Hmm." Mark took a long swallow of his drink. "Are you going to finish your wine?" he asked.

"Red wine gives me a headache."

"I wish you would have told me that!"

If he had asked, maybe she would have. She rolled her eyes.

He raised his arm. "Waiter!"

The waiter walked by, burdened by a tray of food.

"She needs a different wine when you have a chance!"

The waiter nodded as he continued with his load to a table of four.

HB came out of the back and began cleaning a table. Alison waved to him, and HB looked surprised to see her and came over, wiping his hands on a towel.

"I didn't know you worked here!" she said, genuinely happy to see him.

HB nodded to both of them, but his eyes never left Alison's. "Can I talk to you for a minute?"

Alison leaned back, surprised at his request. "Sounds serious."

"School talk on Friday night?" Mark forced a

chuckle. "Can this wait until Monday?" He asked, his eyes narrow. He was clearly perturbed by the intrusion of HB on their dinner date but trying hard to cover it up with a smile.

Alison held up her hand. "We were just talking about school." She felt her ire rising. "What's the difference?"

Mark sat back, seemingly surprised by her words. "Okay. Okay."

"Sorry," HB mumbled. "I guess I can wait until Monday."

"Are you sure?" Alison asked, tugging HB's sleeve.

"Yes," he mumbled again.

She turned to Mark. "I could have spoken to him for a minute." She crossed her arms.

Mark rolled his eyes and gave another tight smile. "If you insist."

"My students aren't typical, and many have insurmountable obstacles that kept them away from school," she said.

"Who's fault is that?"

"Clearly not his doing," Alison said, feeling her face flush and irritated, making her words short and direct. "He was injured in an accident."

HB had already backed away and was headed to another table to clear the dirty dishes.

"HB?" she called. "What is it?"

"No, he's right." HB straightened and put the remaining plate in the tub of dirty dishes. "We'll talk on Monday."

"You're sure?"

"I am."

Alison returned to their table. The waiter stopped

155

after unburdening his tray. "What would you like to drink?"

"Chardonnay. House."

The awkward silence continued.

"A penny for your thoughts?" Mark asked, breaking the silence.

Alison felt her cheeks get red with her annoyance at Mark. If she were honest, she'd say she shouldn't have come on this date. Being with Mark made her feel like she was walking on eggshells. But she responded, "Oh, I'm just remembering when my husband used to work here." She gripped the edge of the table. "We always came to the Moonglow before formal school dances."

"We had a favorite spot too when I was in high school—The Embers." He shrugged. "I wonder what happened to that place?"

Alison was quiet as he waited for him to continue, wishing fervently she was at home in her bathrobe with a good book.

"My ex-wife and her sister went to Clearwater High School. I wonder if she ever ate here."

"I bet she did," Alison said.

Alison's gaze followed HB covertly as he went about his duties, removing dishes, wiping tables, and sometimes pouring water. She wondered what he had wanted to talk about and wished, no, she needed to be truthful with herself, wished HB was sitting across from her having dinner.

Alison took a sip of her wine, definitely better than the red Mark had ordered for her. Mark tasted the second martini and made a face. "I thought I asked for a dirty martini?"

She didn't drink martinis very often, so she wasn't

an expert, but she didn't remember him asking for a dirty one either.

He waved his hand to get the server's attention and handed him the glass when he came. "I asked for a 'dirty' martini."

"So sorry, sir, I'll ask the bartender to make another."

She took another sip of her wine—it was perfect, crisp, and slightly sweet while Mark cleared his throat and gave her a penetrating look.

"You are lovely, Alison."

"You're funny."

They sat in silence until the waiter brought a new martini, which Mark declared was marginally better than the first.

Awkward and stilted, Alison asked Mark to finish telling her about his military experience—not that she cared, but the conversation was lacking. She moved the rest of her lasagna around the plate.

"There's not much to tell." Mark put down his drink. "The military is disciplined, but I learned a lot about leadership and motivating people. Comes in handy in the classroom."

Alison didn't comment but moved her head to encourage him to go on.

"I did several tours in the Middle East."

"Oh?" Alison set her fork down.

"Yeah, I was behind a vehicle that tripped a hidden mine. One of my good buddies died. I was pretty messed up when they found what was left of him."

Alison shuddered, imagining a body torn apart by the force of a grenade or landmine.

"I've been fighting PTSD. It sometimes wakes me

up at night, and I can see the vehicle blown apart. I relive it again and again."

Was that what she saw behind his eyes, the horror of war, or something else?

"I cannot imagine what that would be like." She reached over and squeezed his hand. "I'm so sorry."

"Thank you, Alison."

She withdrew her hand, and they finished eating in relative silence. Her annoyance at him seemed to evaporate, and she was genuinely sorry for what Mark had experienced.

Alison placed her fork and knife on her plate, indicating she was finished, and Mark waved his hand and called, "Check."

"Please, Mark, let this be on me."

"I asked you out, so I'm going to pay," he insisted.

"Next time," she said, if there was even a subsequent date. She wasn't sure if a relationship with Mark was worth pursuing.

"We'll see," he said.

Her thoughts exactly about treating on another date.

She watched as Mark figured out the tip, wrote the amount, and signed his name. His tip wasn't even ten percent, so she'd leave something on the table for the waiter, server, and HB. She remembered Rob's excitement when the servers shared their tips if it was a good night. Unobtrusively, she reached into her purse, withdrew a ten, and placed it under her napkin for HB to find.

Chapter 34

Alison

Mark insisted on following her home to make sure she was safe. She wasn't sure why. Clearwater had very little crime, and she could drive the quiet streets from the restaurant to home. Was it indeed to make sure she was safe? Or did he have an ulterior motive?

When they arrived at Alison's house, Mark parked behind her and walked her to the front door, which surprisingly was unlocked. Mark leaned forward as if to kiss her when Alison felt a rising panic at finding the front door cracked open and unlocked.

She ignored Mark's embrace. "Mother!" She began running from room to room, calling for her mother. Mark followed her in, asking her what was wrong.

"The front door!" she yelled at him. Alison even knocked on the closed bathroom door and asked, "Mother? Are you in there?" No answer. She opened the door, but it was empty. She ran down the hallway to the bedrooms. "Mother!"

In her mother's bedroom, they found her slumped sideways in her chair. The book she had been reading had fallen to the floor, the pages fanning from the spine. Alison rushed to her mother and shook her. "Mom?"

No response. Alison grasped her mother's cool-to-the-touch hand. "Mother! Oh, my gosh!" She grabbed a blanket from the bed to warm her. "She's cold!"

"I'll call 911!" Mark said, taking out his phone and putting it on speaker.

"911. What's your emergency?"

"I need an ambulance. We have a woman who's not breathing."

"Hurry!" Alison pleaded, wrapping the blanket around her mother's shoulders.

"Your address?" the operator asked.

Alison breathlessly told her.

"We're on our way."

"Please hurry," Alison said again, "She's all I have!"

Frantically, Alison continued shaking her mother and feeling for a pulse simultaneously. Nothing, only the blood pounding in her temples.

"Mark!" she cried. "Can you do something?"

"Let's get her on the floor, do mouth-to-mouth and see if we can get her breathing again."

Alison grabbed her mother's hands. "She's so cold!"

Mark picked up her mother and gently laid her on the floor.

Did Alison remember how to do CPR? Her mind was awash with thoughts crashing over and around each other. While she tried to get her thoughts straight, the room filled with the suffocating sound of Lake Michigan waves pounding the pier—a furious wind sending the water higher and higher. She put her hands to her temples, willing the noise to disappear. Mark began breathing into her mother's mouth and pressing on her chest.

"Breath," Alison silently said. "Please breathe, Mother!" she sobbed. "Don't leave me!"

They were interrupted by hammering on the front door. Alison struggled to stand, but her legs wouldn't hold and melted into the floor.

"I'll get it." Mark jumped up to let the paramedics in. Alison heard the footsteps and Mark saying, "This way."

Alison rested her head on her mother's chest. "Oh, Mom! Please don't go. I need you!" She felt for a pulse on her mother's wrist again—nothing. Maybe she should have continued CPR? Paramedics filled the bedroom, and Mark helped her to her feet while an EMT checked her mother's pulse.

"Maybe you should wait in the other room?" Mark said.

"No! I want to stay with her."

One of the paramedics put a stethoscope on her mother's chest. He moved first to one spot and then another, listening. Maybe he could hear if the roaring in her ears would stop. He couldn't hear mother's heart over the waves!

Another paramedic pulled out a defibrillator.

"You should wait in the other room," the youngish paramedic said. He looked vaguely familiar.

Mark put his arm around her and led her into the living room. "No!" she cried. "I want to stay!"

"They want you to wait here." Mark tightened his grip and guided her from the room.

"What are they doing?" She tried to wrench herself from his grasp, but he had a vise-like hold on her arm. As Alison swiped at the snot running down her face, fresh tears swelled. "No!"

Mark led her to the chair, helped her sit, found a box of tissues, and instructed her to blow her nose.

Alison stopped blowing when the muffled sounds coming from her mother's bedroom changed to a more frantic tempo, with a low undercurrent of buzzing bees. She concentrated on the sounds and wondered what they were doing.

Alison slumped into her mother's favorite chair and picked up the ball of yarn her mother had used to knit a blue and white sweater. Alison stroked it with her finger, the strands crisscrossed in a never-ending ball.

Alison heard the faint wheels squeak as they pushed the gurney with her mother down the hall to the front door. "Where…where are you taking her?" Alison gasped.

"I'm sorry," the youngish one said.

Alison remembered him as a student many years ago when she taught English. Craig McCarthy.

"The coroner's, Ms. Larkin."

Alison jumped up and flung herself onto the gurney, holding tightly to her mother.

Mark gently pulled her away and wrapped his arms around her.

"Will you stay with her?" The paramedics nodded to Mark.

"No…no…there's…" Alison shook her head. Marilyn. "I'll call my friend, Marilyn." She fumbled with the phone.

"I'm happy to stay," Mark said.

"No, you've done so much already. I think I'd like to stay with Marilyn."

"We're going to leave," Craig, her former student, said.

Alison sat still until the ambulance left—it seemed like forever. She hoped they'd take good care of Mother.

Mark called Marilyn and explained the situation, and she arrived ten minutes later. "If you're sure you'll be okay, I'm leaving. Seeing my girls." He was apologetic and looked unsure.

"Thanks, Mark." She had appreciated him being with her when she found her mom. She didn't know what she would have done without him.

After the door closed behind him, Alison sobbed, "Oh, Marilyn, Mom's gone."

"I know, sweetie. I'm sorry." Marilyn sat next to her and pulled her into an embrace. "Your mother was such a nice person. I know you'll miss her." She, too, swiped at the tears on her face.

"She was my whole life," Alison wailed. "What do I have now?" Alison shook her head, still cradled against Marilyn. She couldn't imagine a world without her mother. Even with dementia, her mother continued to nurture her. An innate sense, a hormonal drive, something Alison would never experience. Alison sensed it in Marilyn. Slowly she pulled away from Marilyn and reached for another tissue—the one in her hand now a soggy lump.

"You have your job and friends. You'll be fine. We'll help you get through this," Marilyn said.

If only Rob were still here. He'd know what to do and say. Now she had no one. A lonely place to be.

Alison managed to get through Thanksgiving with Marilyn and her family. Sitting at the table, trying to remember what she was thankful for. She wanted her mother and Rob to be with her. Only an empty void stretched out as far as she could see. She still wanted them, but that wouldn't happen.

Chapter 35

HB

It had been four days off because of Thanksgiving.
HB bounded up the steps to the classroom, wanting to
see Alison and share what he had learned from Dr. Sims.
But he frowned at the woman standing at Alison's desk.
As if reading his mind, the woman said, "I'm Kate
Yarbrough. I'm covering for Ms. Larkin during her
bereavement leave."

HB looked at Cindy with raised brows. She
mouthed, "Her mother, I think."

Had Alison lost her mother?

They worked in silence, his mind imagining how
Alison was coping. How would he feel if his mother
died? He'd be lost even though she drove him crazy
sometimes.

As he and Cindy worked, a picture of an older
woman popped into his head. He knew instinctively she
was Alison's mother. Or was he thinking about his
grandmother? Or was this another of Robert's
memories?

Suddenly HB had the urge to go to Alison and
comfort her. But first, he needed to know where she
lived. He remembered a blue and white house with a big
front porch. He left the class thinking of driving around,
looking for the place in his memory. He went to her

home as if he had been doing it all his life. He parked behind her Subaru—the one with 4EAEA.

He sat for a moment and thought about what he would say to Alison. He'd say he was sorry and tell her he was Robert. No, scrap that. That probably wasn't a good idea. She had already had one emotional upheaval in her life and didn't need another. He got out and walked to the front door and tentatively knocked. From inside, he heard the faint sound of a television, a door closed, and footsteps.

Alison opened the door. She was wearing jeans and an old Central Michigan sweatshirt, her face devoid of makeup. She looked about twelve years old with red-rimmed eyes and blotches on her cheeks from crying.

"HB?" she gasped, clearly surprised to see him. "What are you doing here?"

He shifted his feet. "I came to tell you how sorry I am about your mother."

"Thanks."

"I can't stay long."

She nodded, swung the door open, and stepped back.

He followed her to the couch, where she moved aside a pillow and blanket. "Sorry for the mess. My friend Marilyn has been staying here to keep me company, but she's at school today."

Nodding, HB took a seat and clasped his hands.

"How...how did you know where to find me?"

A plausible lie? "Cindy."

Alison nodded.

He surprised himself by blurting, "Does your license plate say, 'Forever and Ever, Always'?"

"Why, yes, a favorite song of ours. How did you guess?"

"I like his music too."

A silence settled over them, not uncomfortable, but one of friends enjoying being with the other—without words. Alison broke the silence. "Would you like some coffee?"

He could probably use some caffeine.

"Yes." Before she turned away to make coffee, he caught her hands in his. "Is there anything I can do to help?" He squeezed lightly.

She let out a sigh and slowly shook her head. "My mother had most of the arrangements made. She planned everything when Daddy died."

HB followed her to the tiny kitchen with a well-scrubbed linoleum floor. He watched as she put coffee and water in the machine and pressed the button. Soon the aroma of brewed coffee filled the air.

"I don't know exactly what you're going through," HB said as they sat at the small square table with a lacy tablecloth and a small vase of flowers.

Alison poured two mugs of coffee and took the creamer from the refrigerator. She looked blankly at the mugs. Not seeing the sugar, HB went to the cupboard for the bowl.

"How...How did you know where the sugar was?" Alison gasped.

How did he know? "I guessed it would be by the coffee pot." But was that the truth? He knew—he was Rob.

He fixed Alison's coffee the way she liked it. When he finished, she took the spoon, swirled the cream and sugar into the coffee, and tapped the spoon against the lip of the cup. Alison had an indescribable, dazed look on her face, one of surprise, disbelief, and something else he couldn't identify at the moment.

"Is there anything you need?" he asked. The coffee wasn't half bad with sugar. He liked it. Why had he thought he didn't like it?

She looked down at the table before responding. "I wish I had more time with her, with Mother."

He let her talk.

"I knew she struggled and I even toyed with placing her in assisted living." She paused and swallowed hard. "Is that why she was snatched from me? My thoughts about her care?"

"Nah," he said. "I don't think that's how it works."

They finished their coffee in silence.

"Are you okay being alone?" he asked, clearing his throat.

She nodded and pressed her finger beneath her eye as if blotting out a tear. "Marilyn is staying with me for a couple more days." She blew out her breath. "There are all sorts of arrangements to be made."

HB picked up their mugs and placed them in the sink while Alison continued talking.

"I have my moments and wished my husband was with me. He'd know what to do and the right things to say."

He came back to the table and took her hands in his. "Would it help if I told you something about Robert?"

She blinked at him. "What can you tell me?"

"I think maybe I have Rob…" He was interrupted by a knock on the front door. "I'll get it. You stay here."

It was a flower delivery for Alison from the teachers at school.

"Who sent those?" she asked.

He put the flowers on the table.

"Your friends at school." He glanced at his watch before folding the blankets and throwing away the crumpled tissues on the table, and generally cleaning up the place. "You sit and relax. I've got this." He washed up the few dishes in the sink and set them aside to drain.

After about half an hour, he said, "I've got to get to work." He wouldn't be able to tell her about Robert's soul, but perhaps now wasn't the right time to spring it on her—besides, would she even believe him?

"Thank you, HB. I appreciate you and am so glad you walked into adult ed on the first day of school."

He patted her shoulder. "Me too." Then squeezed it before leaving and driving to work.

Marilyn returned shortly after, and Alison told her to go home. She needed to be alone to think about Mother's death.

****

Later, before bed, Alison pulled out her book on ways the dead communicated with the living and began reading. She had her father, Rob, and now her mother on the other side. Could she communicate with them? Was it a two-way street? She wanted to tell her mother how much she missed her. On some intrinsic level, Alison knew her mother would know. She had been a dutiful daughter, trying hard to please. The only thing she couldn't give to her mother was a grandchild.

She began reading the chapter about Walk-Ins. *A walk-in is someone who didn't go through the birth process but instead asked permission from a new host body if they would switch places.* Alison frowned and wondered how such a thing was possible. Could she go up to Marilyn and ask her if they could change souls? She couldn't imagine a scenario where she would ask that question. There had to be more to it than that. She continued reading:

This usually happens when a soul is unhappy with its earthly body or wants to leave. The souls make a pact to switch places and agree to continue to follow the other's known worldly habits: walk the dog, take the kids to swimming lessons, and do their job.

Alison smoothed down the page. Surely, there was some sign of a switch, but what was it?

People with walk-in souls are different people after the exchange is made. Others comment on the personality change. And the person knows they've got new memories and feelings.

Alison's mind was foggy with sleep. She carefully marked the page and placed the book back on the nightstand. She was too tired to consider the possibilities. Rob or her parents could come back into her life as different people. As wonderful as that seemed, it scared her.

Chapter 36

Alison

The day of the funeral came fast, yet slow. Alison was ready, but she couldn't say her last goodbyes with the lump in her throat, rendering her speechless. The funeral director—effective, kind, and calm—walked her through everything she needed to do without the emotion and hysteria she felt. His job was to help loved ones make sound and practical choices and soothe those left behind.

And now she was sitting in church, waiting. She was sure her mother's spirit had taken flight right after her death. But how was she to know? What did it matter? Mother was gone. Period. As much as she wanted her mother's soul to find another body, she didn't think the scenario was right for that to happen.

How many times had she heard "Amazing Grace" at funerals? She couldn't remember not hearing that hymn. And now she was listening to it again as her family left her one after another. She was the last of the family, with a few cousins scattered to the wind.

She hadn't handled her father's death well, certainly not with grace or anything close to it. Rob held her tightly during the service, his suit jacket wet from her tears. He handed her tissues, an endless supply from his pocket.

And then there was Rob's death. There, she clung to her mother's hand for support and rested her palm on her stomach, hoping this baby would see her through and be the link she needed with Rob's absence. But several weeks later, she miscarried. Then it was just Alison and her mother. And now, Alison sat alone, still and quiet. Although she heard people behind her, she felt alone. No one else had loved her the way Mother and her father had—the way Rob had.

She kept her eyes glued to the cross lit from the back and seemed to be hovering near the wall, not attached to anything. The way she, too, felt—not connected to any person or thing.

The box that held her mother's remains was placed on a small table covered with a white cloth trimmed in lace. Her mother had been reduced to a container of ashes.

She heard the attendees—shuffles on the carpet, whispers, someone blowing their nose. She turned to see who had entered the church—Cindy, several other teachers from the school, and Steve. She smiled a small smile, indicating she was glad they were there. And then she noticed HB in the back. Their eyes locked. She gave him a slight nod, and he returned the gesture. He remained standing even though there were a few seats left. Reluctantly, Alison looked away as a neighbor touched her hand and told her how lovely her mother had always been.

"Thank you," Alison whispered.

The woman took a seat, and again, Alison locked eyes with HB. His lean body hugged the door frame, not in or out, just in between.

Mark, Marilyn, and Emerson slid onto the bench

behind her. Alison reached over, squeezed their hands, and thanked them before turning around as the minister took the pulpit. He didn't begin immediately, shuffling his notes as the church slowly filled with mourners.

Alison imagined death was the void she felt now. She had no thought except to get through the service, go home, have a cup of tea, and fade away into the sofa cushions, never to be seen again. She'd put on an old black and white movie and watch the images flicker by—the sound turned off. Is that what being dead was like?

Mark put his hand on her shoulder, and she reached up and touched his fingers. They were as cold as touching a piece of granite. She realized he was trying to comfort her, but the emptiness she felt continued.

She turned back as the organist began "Abide With Me"—thankful for many friends, colleagues, and neighbors who had come to pay their respects to Mother.

The minister began by thanking them for coming to honor the memory of Irene Steele. She was a kind-hearted woman who loved her daughter and family and friends and had always looked out for others before herself. A woman who had served bowls of homemade chicken noodle, broccoli cheddar, and vegetable beef soup to Alison and her friends. Alison thought she heard a snort from Steve. Mother had been known for her soup. The Steele kitchen was a warm and cozy place for the after-school crowd who could warm up with soup and finish their homework. The world had been a better place because Irene lived in Clearwater.

She sniffled and felt Mark brush her shoulder with a tissue. She took it, nodded, but didn't turn around. She could thank him later for being there with Marilyn and others from school.

Mercifully, the minister's message was short, but how could that be? Her mother's merits should have taken the rest of the day to recite with the many good deeds she had performed for the community. Thirty minutes and it was all said and done. Sixty-nine years on earth, and it was summed up neatly and concisely in the time it took for a sitcom to run. Sixty-nine years equaled thirty minutes.

Chapter 37

Alison

The service ended with the minister inviting everyone to the gathering room for refreshments before stepping down and stopping at Alison's pew and offering his hand. She grasped it, grateful she didn't need to walk down the aisle alone.

He patted her hand and whispered, "How was the service? Was it what Irene would have liked?"

She gave him a watery smile. "Oh yes, Mother would have loved all the attention—I know she would have approved."

Behind them, people began leaving their seats and following them to the gathering area. Round tables had been set up, and there was a long table with dessert, coffee, tea, and fruit punch.

She took a cup of coffee with a trembling hand, spilling some before adding milk and sugar.

She felt someone at her elbow.

Mark said, "Are you sure you need all that sugar in your coffee?"

She whirled around, spilling even more coffee. "Yes, I need the sugar today." She leveled him with her best-no-nonsense-steely gaze. "I deserve something sweet today."

Marilyn sidled up and put her arm around her. "Of

course, you deserve something sweet."

Mark stammered, "I just meant…"

"Now's not the time," Marilyn told him and guided Alison away from the table.

"Thank you," Alison whispered. "I better thank everyone for coming today."

"Do you want me to go with you?" Marilyn asked, squeezing her hand.

"No, I think I'll be okay." But she felt the tears prick at the back of her eyes. She gripped the coffee cup tightly and made her way around the room to thank those who had stayed.

Alison saved the tables with her friends and students for last. She sat down with them for a moment. "Thank you for coming."

"Class isn't the same without you," Wayne said.

"I'll be back soon." She sipped at her coffee, now lukewarm. "I miss all of you!"

HB was staring at the table but looked up, and their eyes locked for the third time today. It was like an electrical cord between them, and she felt a buzzing tingling up her arms.

She turned from her students to the table with Steve, Marilyn, Emerson, Mark, and several others. "How are you holding up, kiddo?" Steve asked.

"Okay," Alison said. She leaned her thighs against the table as they talked.

"Is there anything you need?" Mark asked.

She needed her mother back, but that couldn't happen, could it?

Alison shook her head. "You were so very helpful the night Mother died, and I can never thank you enough." She saw Mark straighten and puff out his chest a bit. "I think I just need time," she said, her voice lowering.

"Take all the time you need." Steve patted her shoulder.

She was sure she wouldn't need more than another few days to sort out her thoughts and fill out the paperwork of her mother's death.

She backed away after telling them how much she appreciated their support.

As the cookies dwindled, so did the people—some slipping away without saying goodbye. Goodbyes were hard at a time like this.

Next, she went into the kitchen to thank the volunteers for the desserts and coffee, and then she slipped out the side door for some fresh air. A soft breeze swirled the leaves, and she leaned against the side of the church, lifted her head to the sky, and closed her eyes. At that moment, she felt her mother's comforting kiss on her forehead, telling her it had been a lovely service.

Moments later, HB joined her. "Alison? I was waiting for you to come out of the kitchen but figured you needed a moment to yourself."

"Yes, yes, I did. Thanks," she said, turning to face HB and patting his cheek. He didn't flinch or pull away. Instead, he seemed to lean marginally closer.

He cleared his throat. "You wanna know something weird?"

"What?"

"I feel like I've known you for a long time."

Alison studied him, looking into the eyes of a person who had lived more years than just twenty. Maybe that's what happened after a life-altering accident. Did it rob you of your carefree spirit?

"I've got to go to practice," HB said, shuffling his feet.

"Practice?"

He hung his head and shrugged. "I volunteered to help with baseball conditioning."

Alison raised her brows. "That's wonderful." She grabbed his hand and squeezed it. "I'll see you soon."

She drove home, selected a bottle of wine, and poured the first glass, which dulled her thoughts until they were bearable.

Alison awoke with the sun streaming through the window—unusual for this morning. She looked at the clock on the table. Oh, gosh! It was 12:26 p.m. She had never slept this late, but then again, she had never buried her mother before.

An empty wine bottle sat on its side. Ugh. Had she drunk a whole bottle?

Cautiously she sat up and put her hands on the side of her face, feeling as though her head would fall off if she didn't. The wine seemed a good way at the time to dull her thought process, so the memories weren't as sharp and painful. Now, she had a different kind of pain.

Like a disabled old lady, she stood, straightened, and rubbed her lower back. Everything hurt this morning. She pulled on an old sweatshirt and jeans lying in a heap on the chair and went to find coffee.

While she waited for the coffee to finish, she surveyed the scene of destruction in the living room. Family photos littered the coffee table, the couch, and the floor. Alison remembered looking through them—the images blurry through her tears. Pictures of her parents as newlyweds, Alison as a baby, photos of Rob and their wedding. She had dumped out the box, drinking, hiccupping, and laughing through tears at the contents.

When her coffee finished perking, she took two aspirins, grabbed a cookie from the tray Marilyn had left, went into the living room, and began pushing the pictures on the table into a pile, clearing off the couch and floor. She sat, cupping her mug and slowly sipping. Was she supposed to do anything today? Nothing. She was on bereavement leave from school and didn't have anywhere to be. She didn't even have to go to the store—she had plenty of food. The refrigerator was filled with casseroles and bread to last a lifetime from well-meaning friends and colleagues. Nope, she had no place to go and nothing to do. She supposed she could start on the funeral home list. Call social security to stop Mom's benefits, put the utilities in her name, and have the attorney help with other paperwork, but she just didn't have the energy. She'd think about all that stuff tomorrow.

She picked up her phone and stared at the blank screen. Figures. She stuck her tongue out—the battery was dead. She plugged it in, and while she waited for it to charge, she stretched out on the couch and wondered how many people were trying to reach her. She'd let the aspirin do its work.

She awoke to the sound of pounding. Not in her head, but the front door and the doorbell chimed repeatedly. She sat up, pushed her hair away from her face, and stood. Who could be knocking on the front door? It sounded like they were using a jackhammer. Bam. Bam. Bam.

She heard a faint, "Alison?"

Mark.

She walked toward the door and looked at her

distorted face in the mirror. She was a total and complete wreck.

"Coming," she said and slowly opened the door for him as she smoothed back her hair and tucked it behind her ears.

He looked at her appearance and gave her a forced smile. "Did I wake you?"

"I-I…" She hung her head.

"I've been calling, and I got worried." Mark had a bouquet of pink tulips tucked under one arm and a bag of Chinese takeout cartons.

Ugh, not more food, but she smiled at him.

"I didn't sleep well, and my phone's charging."

"Would you like me to go?"

"Oh, no." She welcomed the distraction and used her hand to gesture to the living room.

"These are for you." He handed her the tulips.

"Thank you. My favorite flowers."

"I remembered. But they're hard to find." He rustled the takeout bag. "Hungry?"

Her stomach flipped, her mouth felt sticky, and she realized she hadn't eaten since yesterday. "Yes. Yes, I am."

"I'll put these in the kitchen," he shook the tulips.

"I'm going to freshen up a bit. There's coffee. Help yourself."

"A vase?"

"Above the fridge."

In the bathroom, she brushed her teeth, splashed water on her face, and combed her hair. Better. She looked down at her torn and ratty sweatshirt, brushed a stray crumb from her chest, and rolled her eyes at her vision in the mirror. This was as good as it would be for today.

She entered the kitchen, but Mark was standing in the hallway studying the pictures on the walls.

"You have a nice-looking family," he finally said.

She waved a hand over the pictures. "Most of the people in these pictures are dead. It's hard to be the last person standing."

"No brothers or sisters?"

"I'm an only." She tossed her hands up.

"Aunts or uncles?" Again she shook her head. "Cousins?"

"A few," she said, "scattered around."

"No relatives in Clearwater?" Mark put his arm around her, and she again shook her head. He fished in his pocket for a tissue and handed it to her. She blew loudly and dabbed at her eyes.

He led her to the couch, and they sat together, his arm still around her. "I'm so sorry, Alison. And going through this alone. I want you to know I'm here for you." As he said those words, he squeezed her shoulders softly.

She nodded but didn't feel particularly relieved. Mark had said all the right words, but the spark wasn't there.

"I hope I'll be more to you than just the new Biology teacher. Have all the time you need to mourn your mother." He kissed her forehead. "Let me rustle us up some grub."

Long after Mark had left, she was still sitting on the couch in a trance. The evening shadows had shrouded the house in fog. Tiredly, she reached over and turned on the lamp, and heard a rustle outside by the window. She pushed herself up and peered out into the night. The snowball bush obscured part of the window, but it moved as if pushed by the wind, but the night was still. Had it been an animal rustling in the bushes or something or someone else?

The hair on the back of her neck prickled, and she felt tight in her stomach like something wasn't right. She closed the curtains and went into her bedroom to look out that window. She stood to the side so she couldn't be seen. The moon highlighted the shape of a person, making her step back with a gasp. Someone had been peeking in the windows.

She turned and hurried to the phone, dialed 911, and asked for someone to check out the prowler in her backyard. While she waited, she continued looking out the bedroom window. The shape was still there, moving as if to keep warm—dark on dark, but a bulky person— a man. From the front of the house, she heard gravel crunch in the drive. The figure froze. He had heard it too.

She opened the door for the uniformed officer. "There's someone in the backyard by the snowball bush. I've been watching him," she whispered, motioning to the left.

The officer nodded, switched on his flashlight, and rounded the corner. Alison hurried back to the bedroom to see the figure run away with the officer in pursuit. The figure had a head start and was lost among the neighborhood houses' trees.

Maybe the prowler was scared away by the police. She hoped so. It gave her the willies to think someone was watching her, assessing the break-in potential of an unarmed, single woman. Maybe she should take Mark up on his offer to stay and sleep on the couch. As soon as she thought that, she nixed it. She didn't want Mark to get the wrong idea.

The officer said he would file a report and advised her to keep the shades drawn and contact them if the prowler returned.

One by one, Alison turned on the outside lights, the house showed brightly, and she was sure the neighbors wondered why all the lights were on. She'd call them tomorrow, tell them what had transpired, and be on the lookout for a man hiding in the shadows.

Chapter 38

HB

"Aren't you going to school?" HB's mother asked, frowning at his morning stubble and wide yawn.

He scratched his head. "Yeah, I'll get around to it."

His mother raised her brows. "Is everything okay?"

"We have a sub, and it's not the same without Ali."

"Ali's a student or the teacher?" she asked.

"Teacher." He turned away and went into the bathroom for a shower.

HB didn't feel like attending adult ed with the substitute, but he went for Cindy.

Once there and settled, HB raised his hand.

"Yes?" the sub asked, nodding and smiling her encouragement. HB had already forgotten her name.

"Any word on Alison?" He paused. "Like, when she'll be back?"

"Sorry," the sub said. "I don't know. They didn't tell me how long I'd be here, just that Ms. Larkin was on bereavement leave."

"Thanks," he mumbled before turning to Cindy. "Should we send flowers or something?" They hadn't done anything before the funeral, but the church was filled with flowers. Alison might like something now from the adult education crew.

That would give HB an excuse to visit Alison to

deliver the card and flowers.

Later in the day, Cindy took up a collection, ordered flowers, and passed around the card for everyone to sign.

HB picked up the flowers, pocketed the card, and drove to Alison's house. Her car was in the drive. He got out and balanced the gifts and knocked on the door.

Alison opened the door, smiled, frowned, and looked behind him. Was she expecting someone else?

"Did I come at a bad time?" HB asked, looking around.

"No."

Her face must have revealed her surprise because he asked, "Do you want me to leave?"

"Of course not!" She pulled him inside. "Please come in."

"I'll only stay a short time," he promised though he wanted to stay forever.

"Are those for me?" She pointed to the flowers in his hand, a multi-colored bouquet of yellows, blues, and reds.

"From the class." He shoved them in front of her. He had wished they were pink tulips.

"How thoughtful!" She held them to her nose. "Beautiful!" she exclaimed.

"We wish we could do more for you as you have for us," he said.

She put the flowers on the coffee table and moved her hand toward the sofa. He sat, and she did too. "Didn't you have something you wanted to talk to me about?"

Momentarily, he couldn't remember what it was.

"Did you forget?" She gave him an encouraging smile. "So much has happened. It seems like ages ago."

Then it came rushing back to him—Dr. Sims—the

things he remembered and the yearbook pictures. He sat with his hands clasped and his head down, thinking. Was now the time to tell her? He jerked his head up. "I'm not sure this is a good time to tell you what I know."

She frowned. "That sounds serious."

"It is and a bit weird too."

She leaned forward and clasped her hands together. "Why don't you tell me, and I'll decide how serious it is."

HB shifted on the couch, trying to find a comfortable position. Finding none, he straightened and looked at her. "You know I felt like a different person when I came out of my coma?"

Alison nodded but remained quiet.

"And I wrote about the rescue at Cedar Springs?"

She remained stock still.

"I started adding one plus one, and I came up with something bizarre out there."

Clearing her throat, Alison finally said, "You're scaring me."

He noisily let out his breath. "I've been seeing a counselor, and he told me about one of his patients, Ashton." HB paused and rearranged his thoughts. "I talked to Ashton, who told me he had tried to kill himself but failed."

"Oh, no!" Alison cried. "Please don't tell me you want to kill yourself!" She leaned forward and tried to grasp his hand.

"No, I want to live again!" He let her touch his fingers before pulling back. Although contemplating suicide might be easier than telling Alison he was her dead husband—Robert.

"Anyway," HB swallowed, "Ashton told me about

185

soul walk-ins."

"What did you say?" Alison asked, alarm creasing her brow. "Wait!" She jumped up and hurried down the hallway while he waited. He moved his forefinger over his thumb, wondering what would make her leave like that.

She returned with a small book, sat, and clutched it to her chest as if protecting it. Then, slowly, she eased the book onto her lap and opened it.

He murmured the title. "*Communicating with the Dead*...So you believe in that?"

"I don't know what I believe. But this book mentions walk-in souls and—"

"I think I have Robert's soul in my body," he exclaimed before he could change his mind.

HB didn't mean to interrupt her, but it just happened. He couldn't help it. He watched as Alison's eyes rolled back, and she slumped over.

"Alison?" he patted her hand and then her cheeks until her eyes fluttered open.

"How..." She looked confused. "Why? What?" She fell back on the couch. "I don't believe it," she said with a shake of her head, and her features turned stony. "I think you should leave."

"What?" HB cried. "No! No. I'm sorry!" Tears immediately filled his eyes. "I knew it was a bad time."

"What a cruel and mean joke to play on me after what I've gone through!" Her eyes flashed with anger, something he couldn't pinpoint.

"I'll let myself out." He jumped up. He'd blown it with Alison, and she didn't want to believe him. And he might not have a chance to convince her.

Alison didn't return the next day or the next. Had his

revelation pushed her over the edge? After all, she had fainted at his news. While he waited and wondered, he studied with Cindy, helped with baseball conditioning, and worked.

A week later, when HB pulled into the parking lot by adult ed, Alison's Subaru was already parked, and light showed through the windows. He let his breath out, wondering how he'd be received.

He entered cautiously and stepped inside. Alison looked pale, drawn, and tired. When she looked up, he came forward. "Hi?"

"Hi, yourself." She gave him a forced smile, and he came to the front of the room and perched on the edge of one of the tables.

"I want to apologize for last week, the day I brought the flowers. I was wrong to tell you about Robert after losing your mother. I'm sorry."

"It was a shock. I reacted badly. I'm sorry, too." Her eyes slowly lifted to meet his. The pain was etched in the tiny lines around her eyes.

"We'll drop it," HB said, studying her features.

"No." She touched his arm. "There may be some truth, but it scares me."

He nodded and took note of the dark circles under her eyes. "Are you sleeping?"

"I haven't been sleeping. Someone was peeping in my windows."

HB's heartbeat jacked up a notch. "Really?"

Blood roared in his ears, his mind imagining someone hitting or hurting Alison.

"Someone was looking in your windows?" HB leaned forward, concerned for her safety.

"I filed a police report and have kept the curtains

closed."

That was no way to live. Anger burned in his gut and he clenched his fists. Maybe if he kept watch, he could observe who was doing the peeping?

His thoughts were interrupted by the rest of the students, who seemed to have arrived together, and with big grins, they crowded around Alison's desk. She said, "Thank you all for the card and flowers. Your thoughtfulness meant so much to me."

A murmur traveled around the circle, and feet scuffed the floor.

Later, as Alison moved around the classroom, checking with each student about their work, HB's gaze followed her as she spoke in a low voice. Cindy noticed his preoccupation and poked him.

"What was that for?" he whispered.

"You."

"Me?"

"I think you have a crush on Alison," Cindy said with a mischievous grin.

Was it that obvious?

"I don't know how you came to that conclusion. It's just good to have her back."

"It is," Cindy agreed.

When Alison finally stopped at their table, she said, "Get me up to speed on what you two have been doing while I've been gone."

Cindy volunteered, "We finished Section Fourteen and started Fifteen."

"You two are such fast workers!" she said, a smile on her face, the pain still etched between her eyes, but her once cloudy eyes were clearer now.

Cindy nudged HB. "He's been pulling me along."

Suddenly a flush started at his neck and blazed toward his cheeks. HB didn't want to look at Alison. Instead, he focused on a scratch on the table.

"I'm so happy you joined this class," Alison said to him. He glanced up to see a natural glow on her face, and his heart warmed.

"Me too," Cindy said. Alison's hand snaked out to squeeze his, and then she did the same with Cindy.

HB finally looked up and was bothered by the sadness in her eyes. Was her sadness one big ball of emotions after losing her mother, his revelation about Robert's soul, and now a peeping Tom?

"It was his idea to send the card and flowers," Cindy added.

It wasn't his idea. He just wanted an excuse to see her, and he blew it.

"So very thoughtful," Alison said before easing away from the table. "Thank you. The flowers were a bright spot on the dining room table, and I thought of you every day."

He hoped she meant him, but she probably meant everyone in the class, him included.

****

Getting back to work had been therapeutic and kept her mind off the last picture she held in her mind of her mother's slumped over body. She replaced that image with the excited expressions on her students' faces—joy, concern, and caring. Caring for her as a friend, a person, and a teacher, caring for them to better themselves.

When everyone had left for the day, she fixed a cup of coffee, tapping her spoon on the rim, before sitting at her desk, determined to review student work. But thoughts of her mother crowded everything else, and the tears began anew.

****

When HB got home, he realized he had left his sweatshirt at school. Would Alison still be there? Since it was only a ten-minute drive, he got in his truck and drove to the school. He let out a sigh when he saw her Subaru.

He knocked and then opened the door. Alison sat at her desk, head bowed. She looked up when the door opened, her face red and tear-streaked.

"Is everything okay?" He cautiously entered.

"Yes, sorry, yes." She wiped her eyes and motioned him in. "I'm so sorry you had to see me like this," she said, hiccupping and furiously wiping at her face with her palms. She fumbled with the tissue box.

HB rushed forward, pushing the box closer to her.

Alison blew her nose and whispered, "Thank you."

He picked up a chair and sat next to her, not saying anything as she calmed down. "I'm sorry you lost your mother," he said after the hiccups subsided and her body was still. "That must have been terrible."

"She was my everything."

He couldn't imagine losing his mother.

"Do you still have your parents, HB?" she asked, suddenly sitting straighter and assuming her role as a teacher.

"My mother." He shrugged, trying to be nonchalant. "My father? Who knows?" HB rarely thought of his father. It was painful to know his father wasn't part of his life.

"I'm sorry."

Could a person miss something they didn't know? He moved his chair closer so they were shoulder to shoulder, and tentatively put his arm around her. She didn't move away or protest, so he kept it there while trying to calm his racing heart. His fingers lightly stroked the silk of her blouse and he leaned closer to smell her perfume. Gradually, her shoulders relaxed as the tension drained away.

"Can I do anything?" he asked.

She shook her head. "No, just being here is nice." She was quiet for a long while. "My job and students are important to me."

At that moment, he wanted to be Robert for her and not a student, but he remained quiet, tightening his grip on her slightly, and still she stayed close, not resisting his touch. He leaned over to kiss her cheek, but she turned suddenly, and their lips touched, keeping their lips together until she moved away and dabbed at her eyes again. "That was an accident," she said.

"I'm glad it was an accident," he whispered. "I won't tell anyone."

"Thank you," she whispered back.

Reluctantly, he stood, smoothed down his jeans, and took his sweatshirt off the back of the chair.

"Will…will I see you tomorrow?" she asked in a small voice, almost childlike.

And the next day and the next. He nodded.

She smiled. "I'm glad."

HB curbed the desire to return and kiss her again, but he waved before opening the door and leaving. Once in his car, he put his forehead on the steering wheel, resting against his scar. He could still feel the soft pressure of her lips on his. He had never desired a woman like Alison—Ali—before.

He stopped by the batting cage and, not seeing

anyone there, parked and went over to where there were balls and extra well-worn bats. He needed to get his mind off Alison. He'd hit a few balls.

"Hey man, you're good," a voice behind him said.

HB turned and studied a boy of about sixteen. "I'm kind of rusty."

"Will you pitch to me?" the boy asked.

"Sure. What's your name?"

"Alexander. People call me Alex."

HB pocketed several balls before jogging away from the batting cage and turned back to face Alex.

HB watched as Alex took a stance next to home plate.

HB moved his shoulders around, then snapped his arm back and let the ball fly toward Alex.

The ball sailed by Alex.

"Hey! Can you slow it down for me?" Alex called.

HB did, and Alex managed to get a piece of the ball.

Coach Miller walked across the grass toward HB. "I've only seen that pitch from one other player in all my years at Clearwater."

HB raised his brows.

"Only Rob pitched like that," Coach Miller said.

HB felt the color leave his face. "Rob Larkin?"

"Yup."

HB handed the coach the ball and jogged away, calling over his shoulder, "I've got to go!"

****

With renewed resolve, Alison blew her nose and squared her shoulders, determined to get caught up on her paperwork. She began with Cindy's Section Fifteen post-test. Cindy earned ninety-five percent, her new normal since she and HB had been working together.

She stopped and licked her lips, remembering the accidental kiss she and HB had shared when there was a knock on the door. Had HB returned? Her heart skipped a beat.

The door opened. Her heart sank—it was Mark. He had been supportive during her leave, but she often just wanted to be alone.

She forced a smile on her lips.

"Hi," he said. "Getting caught up?"

She waved her hand over the towering pile of papers on her desk.

"Can I tempt you to join me at Happy Hour?"

She snorted. "That won't help me correct these papers." But she was in no mood to correct papers.

"True." He smirked. "But I'm better company than an empty classroom."

She snorted and thought to herself, *Are you sure*?

She could always take the papers home to do later. One drink wouldn't hurt, would it?

"Just one drink?"

"One drink unless you change your mind and have two." He gave her a beguiling smile and shrugged with outstretched hands. "Or if you're bad, want to add dinner?"

She laughed. "I can imagine what these papers will look like after two glasses of wine."

"Your students might like the results." Mark winked.

"Or not," she said over her shoulder as his face fell.

She packed the papers into her briefcase, followed him to the door, and locked it behind her. There was only one place to drink in Clearwater, and she followed Mark to the Moonglow Inn.

When Alison entered the restaurant, she scanned the room for HB, but she didn't see his smile, longish hair, or lean frame. Disappointed, she followed Mark to a table where they ordered drinks and an appetizer.

Over food, she had two glasses of wine and felt the tension flow from her body. Mark pressed her again about making their relationship exclusive. The pinched feeling in her neck and shoulders returned.

"I'm flattered, Mark, but I need to get my mother's affairs straightened out." She reached a hand up to rub her left shoulder.

"A guy has to try," he said with a small smile that made it clear he wasn't sorry for his suggestion. "Here." He got up and used his fingers to massage her shoulders. "Better?"

"Much," she lied. His touch made it worse, and she swallowed a wince of pain.

****

Later, Alison dreamed of a baseball game. The state championship when she and Rob were in high school. She sat in the bleachers and watched Rob, Steve, and the rest of the team take the field. The funny thing was Rob resembled HB.

She awoke with her heart pounding. Was Rob HB? The thought terrified her. Being involved romantically with students was frowned upon. Yet, their accidental kiss made her lips tingle. So was what HB had told her true?

Chapter 39

HB

HB couldn't get Alison out of his thoughts, especially since someone was spying on her. So telling his mother he needed to work, HB donned all-black, slipped out of the house, and drove to Alison's neighborhood. He drove slowly by the house, noting her car was gone, parked a few houses away behind a tree in an empty lot, cut the lights and motor, and waited for her to return. His watch told him it was 7:30 p.m. He took a sip of his energy drink and waited.

He didn't have to wait long before her Subaru went past. He waited ten minutes for her to park and go inside before he took off on foot to walk the property's perimeter, looking for the prowler.

Then, a familiar SUV drove by. It was hard to tell in the darkness whether it was black, brown, or navy, but the SUV was a dark color. HB was pretty sure it was that Hutchins guy. He had seen that kind of SUV parked by adult education several times.

The hair on the back of HB's neck bristled at the thought of that brute touching Alison. HB waited some more. By eight thirty, the skies had darkened entirely, and the street lights cast faint yellow circles on the pavement. HB kept to the shadows as he walked to Alison's house, passing the SUV. The bumper had a sticker for staff parking at Clearwater High School. Bingo. It was the Biology teacher's vehicle. Why was he parked this far away if he was visiting Alison? Or was he doing the same thing as HB? HB knew he didn't like the guy. Who said only women had intuition?

His sneakers crept across the grass. The front porch light was on, and HB saw the light from the back of the house. He pressed himself against the siding and listened for anything that would indicate someone else was watching.

Presently, he heard the faint scratch of branches moving apart and twigs breaking. Could Alison hear that from inside the house? He doubted it. The sound was coming from the backyard. Maybe it was a raccoon? With his heart pounding in his ears, he was confident it was no four-legged creature.

He heard it more clearly as he edged closer to the backyard. He ducked as he passed a window with shades drawn tightly, only a sliver of light showing where the two halves met. His eyes adjusted to the darkness, and he could make out his surroundings: a neatly coiled hose, a garbage can, and a broom leaned against the house.

In the distance, an owl hooted, and leaves scurried across the sidewalk. The owl's eerie "whoo whoo" asked the same question HB had. Who was Alison's prowler? He was almost sure it was the Biology teacher. But why, he wondered.

At the juncture of the side and back wall, HB peered around to see a bush moving, and inside was the partial shape of a person—a man—straining to peek into the window. Should he announce himself or watch and see what the man did?

From where HB stood, the prowler appeared to be a

big man. That Hutchins guy was a buff, military-type with close-cropped hair and a rigid stance.

Behind HB, he heard a crunch in the driveway. The prowler took notice, too, and stood still. Time stopped while they waited to see if Alison had called the police or if a friend was paying a visit.

The prowler eased out of the bush and crept around the right corner. HB saw a dark shadow hide behind a tree and then hurry across the street. HB followed and watched the man get into Hutchins' SUV. Mark. He was Alison's prowler.

HB eased back toward the front of the house as car lights swung around, and the vehicle backed away and continued down the street. Followed a short time later by a small navy or black Ford. A coincidence? Or was someone watching Mark too?

How was he to tell Alison what he saw without sounding like a creeper himself?

Chapter 40

HB

HB dawdled as long as he could, waiting for Alison to finish with some late-arriving students. He worked on English while willing the stragglers to finish and leave so he could talk to her alone.

"You're certainly working late tonight," Alison commented when she passed HB's table and glanced over his shoulder. "English?"

"Spending all my time with Cindy on math," he explained. One credit more, and he would be finished with English.

Alison folded her arms. "She's made remarkable progress because of your tutoring. You should think about going into a career that utilizes your math skills. Engineering. Or medicine."

"Medicine," he said without thinking about his answer. He would be a doctor.

"Oh! My husband was a doc—" She stopped midsentence as if she said something she shouldn't, and her eyes widened.

"I know that. I'm going to be one, too," he said. He was predestined to be a physician.

"That's very ambitious and takes a lot of education." Alison cocked her head to the side, sensing he wanted to talk further. "Do you have a question?"

"I want to talk with you."

Alison's face blanched as she looked at the clock on the wall and at Samuel and Wayne bent over their workbooks. "Class is over in ten," she whispered, "and then we can chat."

The door banged open, partly from the wind and partly from the force of Mark's arm. He grabbed for the door that crashed against the side of the trailer.

"Some wind today," he remarked as he came to where Alison leaned against the table by HB.

Damn. HB wouldn't be able to talk to her with that S.O.B. around—the stalker, window peeper, and total ass. He was sure Hutchins was the stalker and not a concerned party.

HB scowled and shrugged, implying their little chat would have to wait, and stood.

"Didn't you have something to tell me?" Alison asked.

"Tomorrow." He offered a small smile.

"Okay."

HB went home, changed for work, and when he got to the Moonglow, he donned his apron and started folding napkins and bussing dishes.

A few minutes later, Alison and Mark came in, chatting, and Alison was laughing at something Mark had said. Did she look happy with him? HB couldn't tell from this distance. Alison's laugh looked forced from his vantage point.

Alison spotted him and waved, and Mark shot dagger eyes at HB. *Right back at you, buddy!*

****

The waiter showed them to a table by the front window where Alison ordered wine and Mark a dirty martini. "And make sure it's dirty this time." Mark scratched at his chin.

"Yes, sir!" the waiter said.

"I've got something important to ask you," Mark said, reaching across the table to clasp her hands.

Alison stiffened. Mark had a peculiar look on his face causing her to frown. It was almost as if he was going to pop the question, but that was outrageous with the short time they had known each other. She didn't withdraw her hands but cringed at his touch and leaned marginally away from him.

"I'm going to take my ex-wife to court to gain custody of my children."

Alison relaxed slightly. This was about Mark's kids. Maybe he needed a letter of reference for court?

"Doesn't the mother automatically get custody?"

Mark moved his shoulders. "Usually, but if I can show the judge I've got a stable relationship, they may find me suitable to have custody." He chewed his lip as if he wasn't sure and scratched at the pimples on his chin.

A stable relationship? Surely, he wasn't implying...

He continued speaking, "I threatened her a couple of times." He frowned. "I should have married her sister instead," he said under his breath.

Alison's brows rose. "You threatened her?"

"She was following me," he said with a whine. "I guess I got carried away. I told her I'd kill her."

"That sounds serious."

He grimaced. "Just a figure of speech."

"True, but it could be taken out of context."

"That's why I need your help."

"How can I help?"

"Would you move in with me?" Mark asked.

"What?" She abruptly set down her glass and leaned away from him. "No, Mark." She shook her head. "I can't." She gave Mark a grim smile. "I'm sorry. No."

He tried to retake her hands, but she pulled them back. "But, this would mean a lot to me," he begged.

"I can't," Alison repeated, this time quietly but firmly.

His voice rose, and his cheeks took on a crimson color. "You're ruining my life, you know!" He slammed his palms on the table, making the silverware bang together and the glasses wobble.

Alison heard a couple of the other guests gasp.

"I have nothing to do with that." Alison's eyes widened.

"You do," he hissed, an unreadable expression of fury and disbelief on his face.

Several diners turned in their direction. "Calm down!" she said, motioning for him to lower his voice.

He grabbed her arm and jerked.

"Stop it. You're hurting me!" She struggled out of the chair, but it tipped over with a crash. Mark dug his fingers into her flesh, and she gave a little shriek. "That hurts!"

In the struggle, Mark's elbow hit a waiter who dropped a tray on the floor with a clatter and bang of dishes.

"Hey buddy," the cook said, coming out of the kitchen, wiping his hands on his apron. "What's going on here?"

"Shove off!" Mark growled. "This is a private matter."

"Not in here, it's not. This is my restaurant!"

HB came out of the kitchen and rushed to Alison's

side. Alison could tell by how HB moved his feet and the restless thumb rubbing that he was unsure of the situation and Mark.

Mark shook his finger at HB. "You again!"

"I work here." HB shrugged.

"Get out of my way!" Mark shoved HB into the table. Their drinks teetered and spilled, one of the glasses rolling over the edge and crashing to the floor. Alison watched it all unfold in slow motion. Mark's martini olives lay like eyeballs looking up at them.

HB managed to stay on his feet and muttered under his breath, "I'd like to kill that S.O.B."

Alison and several diners overheard HB's threat. She looked at HB and frowned. Surely he didn't mean that.

"The martinis suck here!" Mark yelled as he banged out the door.

Alison covered her mouth as a giggle tried to escape and turned to the cook and said, "Let me pay for the damage."

"No need. He's not welcome here again."

"Then let me pay for the drinks," Alison said.

The hostess nodded, and Alison located her wallet and pulled out a card. "Here. Put it on this."

Once in the house, she dialed Steve's number and told him what had happened. "Mark frightens me, Steve. He's out of control!"

Chapter 41

Alison

The following day, Alison's classroom phone rang as she unlocked the door.

"Hello?"

"It's me," Marilyn said. "There's a huge fight going on in the office. Mark threatened Steve!"

Alison digested the information and imagined Steve had confronted Mark about what happened at the Moonglow last night.

"Oh, gosh!"

"Watch your back," Marilyn said. "He's angry with you, too."

"I know."

She was on high alert for every crunch of gravel or footsteps coming up the steps. Each time a student arrived, she stiffened and relaxed when she saw who it was.

Cindy frowned at the jerky way Alison moved when the door opened.

"What's going on?" Cindy asked as Wayne came in and sat down.

"Someone's mad."

"At you?" Cindy frowned.

"Yes. I'm worried he'll interrupt class."

"The teacher from the high school?" Cindy asked.

Alison nodded but continued peering out the windows as she walked the room, helping students.

Mark roared through the front door moments later, yelling, "You've been leading me on! Now, you're jeopardizing my job! You're a real piece of work!"

There was a collective gasp from the students, and their work was forgotten as they turned toward Mark, barreling up the aisle toward Alison.

She held out her hand. "Stop!" But he kept on coming. Why had she thought he would?

Someone shoved a chair in his path. HB? But Mark pushed the chair out of the way.

"I've done no such thing!" She rubbed at the bruise he had left on her arm the night before. "Look what you did to my arm!"

Alison's students watched, wide-eyed at the drama, and then began to push back their chairs. Wayne stood as if he was going to tackle Mark, but Alison waved her hand, meaning she didn't want him to get hurt from Mark's tantrum.

Alison had her hand on the phone. "Get out of here, Mark! Go back to your classes."

"Steve told me to take a few days off to get my act together!" Mark's face got redder and redder. "My act together!"

Alison remained quiet but stepped around the table to put some space between her and Mark.

HB stood, and so did the other students. When Mark grabbed her, they piled on top of him.

"Call the principal!" Alison yelled. Mark wiggled out from under the students and ran through the door.

With Mark gone, the students had just managed to go back to their seats when Steve came in, asking,

"What's going on here?"

The students all began talking at once.

"Hold it!" Steve said. "One at a time."

"That guy came in and tried to attack Alison."

Steve's gaze shifted to Alison. "Was it Mark?" And she nodded. "I'm not sure what his problem is," Steve said.

Alison blew out her breath. "I think he's on steroids."

"Hmm," Steve said. "I guess that would explain his aggression."

"He's also going back to court against his ex-wife," Alison said, her voice breathless from the adrenaline pumping through her veins.

"We can't have that sort of thing going on, disrupting the educational process." Steve moved his shoulders as if they hurt him. "I'll call the sheriff and see if they can round him up."

When Steve left, the adult education classroom sat in stunned silence. No work today.

One by one, the students began gathering their things. Several patted her shoulder as they started leaving. Only HB remained.

"I'll follow you home," HB said.

"No, I hate for you to do that."

"I want to."

He paused. Now was the time to tell Alison what he had observed the other night. "He's your prowler and window peeper." He motioned his chin toward the door.

"Mark? Oh, God! I can't go home."

HB nodded as he picked up the phone, dialed 911, and explained the situation. "They're on the way to take your statement."

"Our statements," Alison said emphatically.

HB nodded as he talked. "We'll ask them to keep an eye on your house."

"I don't want to be alone." She shivered and rubbed her arms.

"I'll stay with you," HB said.

"Would you?" She grasped at his arm. "Thank you."

Soon they saw flashing rotating lights and footsteps outside. The police were here to take their statements.

Chapter 42

HB

When the police finished taking their statements about the window peeper—AKA Mark—the fight at the Moonglow—Mark again—and the altercation caused by—you guessed it—Mark at school, they finished by saying, "We'll patrol in your neighborhood looking for a brown SUV."

HB followed Alison home. There was no sign of Mark Hutchins, but the guy was clever and sneaky so he could be anywhere.

Once inside, HB looked out the front window before closing the drapes and said, "I want you to lie down. You're pale and clammy." He lifted her eyelid. "Shock." He was also acutely aware that they were alone. He had deep feelings for her, but he needed to keep those emotions in check at the moment.

"How do you know about shock?"

He placed a hand on her forehead, and she held his gaze. "I just do." He shrugged, but he did. His walk-in soul, Rob, had been a doctor in another life.

He saw her swallow and look stricken at the obvious. Was she reconciling that he was Rob?

HB shifted his feet uneasily before taking her arm and helping her stand. She leaned against him, and they stopped at the picture of Alison and Rob's wedding.

"That was a happy day, wasn't it?" HB asked.

She studied him before nodding. They continued to the bedroom, where she sat on the edge of the bed, took off her shoes, and unbuttoned her blouse. HB turned away, but she put a hand on his arm before slipping off her pants. She sat watching him. He nodded before easing her down and pulling the quilt over her.

"Please," she urged. "Stay with me." She patted the bed next to her. He paused before settling on the quilt and cuddling her in his arms. Their bodies turned toward each other, her head tucked under his chin.

She sighed and fell asleep. The best sleep she'd had in a long time, cradled in HB's arms.

She was prodded from her sleep by the rustling of the bushes outside her bedroom window.

HB jumped off the bed and looked out the window to see Mark's broad back leaving the yard. "Damn, that Hutchins guy again!"

HB ran to the front door and went outside. A few minutes later, he came back to her side. "Interesting."

"What?" She had donned a robe and clutched it to her chest like she was cold.

"There's someone following Hutchins. And I wonder who and why."

Alison thought for a moment. "If I had to guess, I would think it's his ex-wife."

HB thought out loud. "It could be a woman. I didn't get a close look at them."

"We should probably contact the police again and tell them he's returned."

"You can do that in the morning," HB said.

In the morning, Alison called the sergeant they had talked to yesterday and told him Mark was still bothering her.

"We tried his condo, but his car is gone, and the neighbors say he hasn't been home."

She reached up and massaged her forehead.

The officer said, "I'll send a patrol car tonight."

I thought that was the plan for last night.

Mark was still sneaking around, spying on Alison. But had he seen HB on her bed?

****

Maybe a threatening note might deter Hutchins, HB thought. On a gas receipt, HB wrote: LEAVE ALISON ALONE OR ELSE! "Or else" covered a multitude of threats. HB wasn't sure physically threatening Mark was possible. The man was pumped up from the gym and had a dangerous temper. It was probably better to have the police do the threatening. HB left the note under the windshield wiper of Hutchins' SUV.

After leaving the note on the SUV's windshield, HB drove slowly by trying nonchalantly to see who was behind the wheel of the Ford. The person had a Tiger's cap pulled low over their eyes and wore dark glasses. HB couldn't tell if it was a man or a woman. He got the impression whoever it was had a slender build and longish nose.

Chapter 43

Alison

When Alison was satisfied no one was lurking outside, she sank onto the sofa, tilted her head back, and massaged her nose. Sitting in the living room, insulated from the rest of the house where all the lights blazed, made her feel cocooned and safe. The soft glow of one lamp lighted the room. The drapes were tightly closed, and she seriously doubted her peeper would stand at the front window and look in. The neighbors were able to see someone standing on the front porch. So she felt reasonably safe sitting here. She thought back to the strange start to her twelfth year of teaching—she lost her mother and met HB and the brutish Mark. HB thought he might be Rob. Did it change things even if that possibility was genuine?

Next, her gaze wandered around the room, taking in the pictures on the wall—her graduation portraits from high school and college and their wedding picture.

She remembered the conversation when HB told her he might have Rob's soul. She was angry when he had told her, and unbelieving, but so many things about HB reminded her of Rob that it might be true. But what if HB was wrong?

She didn't know for sure. She had growing feelings for the likable twenty-year-old. Would it be worse not having Rob at all or having Rob in the form of HB?

Steve called later, rousing her from the awkward way she was sleeping on the sofa. "I'm checking to see how you're doing."

"He scares me, Steve. What if he attacks me again?"

"I'm going to the school board about his conduct. And I understand he's been hassling another female teacher. Can you lock your classroom door?"

"How will my students get in and out?"

"They may have to knock to come in."

That sounded like a prison, but she'd do it to keep everyone safe, including herself.

"They're pretty shaken up with what happened."

"I can imagine." He paused. "Do you have anyone who can stay with you?"

"A student stayed last night."

"A student?"

"Yes, HB Comstock."

There was a long pause before Steve continued, "Do you think it's wise to rely on a student?"

"He's a nice guy."

"So you've said. I can't help remembering what HB was like before his accident."

"He's changed."

"The board frowns on relationships between teachers and students."

"He's twenty, Steve."

"Still…be careful."

Chapter 44

HB

When HB got up the following day, he searched for his mother and found her at the kitchen table, having her coffee before she left for work.

He sat and stared into her eyes, not saying anything. Outwardly he imagined he was calm, but inside, his stomach sloshed around like the waves at the beach.

"You're scaring me, Henry." She lowered her coffee cup.

"I don't mean to." He thought briefly about how to phrase his request "I've got to ask you a question, and I want an honest answer."

She dipped her chin for him to go on.

"What was I like before my accident?"

He picked up a saltshaker and turned it over in his fingers while waiting for her answer.

"You were different," she said after a pause, her jaw opening and closing like she was considering her words and looking away from him as if she was embarrassed.

He took her hands, and she looked at him again. "I was a real jerk, wasn't I?"

"Well…"

"Come on! Truth," HB said.

"Yes, you were a…" She stopped talking and looked to the ceiling before continuing, "A jerk. I guess I didn't

212

like you at times."

"Fair enough," he said. He suspected as much by the subtle clues he had discovered in the once-black bedroom and his graffiti-covered backpack. He had tossed the drug paraphernalia he had found—everything pointed to a very different person than he was now.

"I thought you were headed in the wrong direction like your father."

"Am I anything like the old me?"

"Looks." She motioned toward his head. "The scar." She stopped and stared at the floor. "Your eyes though…Your eyes are clearer and not red all the time."

Undoubtedly the drugs had caused that.

"And you never let on how smart you were," she said.

"So, you'd agree—I'm a new personality?"

"Yes, but why do you ask?"

"Just wondering how such a thing is possible."

"The doctor…" his mother began.

"That's bullshit…"

"Now, that sounds like the old Henry."

And the new HB.

He stroked his chin. "I'm trying to figure things out."

His mother raised her brows.

"Do you love the new me?" he asked, finger tracing the swirling lines on the granite tabletop.

"I loved you before," she said, "I just didn't always like you."

"And now you do?" he asked.

"Yes, I do, very much. You've made me very proud."

He nodded and smiled at her.

"And adult ed!" his mother exclaimed. "That's made a world of difference."

"It's the teacher," HB said. "She's the reason."

"I'm glad."

And too, he was falling in love with Alison.

He stood. "I've got to go."

She didn't ask where and he didn't tell her.

As he drove, he thought about what his mother had said. She had confirmed he was a different person. He went to the Lake Michigan public beach—now closed for the cold weather and watched the white-capped waves and the tumbling clouds. On a chilly fall morning, the beach was empty except for a man throwing a stick for a black lab to chase.

HB remained in his truck and thought about what he remembered from the dream. Dreams were weird and often psychedelic and confusing. But his past life was becoming more apparent, and he remembered more and more—it was amazing he had at one time been a loser but now had the soul of a doctor and husband in him. Yes, amazing.

His mother hadn't raised him to be a churchgoer or believer, but there was something that ruled over this giant planet and the universe. It probably could happen the way it did—the walk-in soul.

Just looking at the endless beach was enough for a person to believe in things one couldn't see. He backed out of the parking spot and went to class.

Chapter 45

Alison and HB

Alison got up, showered, and readied herself for work. She opened the curtains and saw the clouds that tumbled like cotton balls in the air and hoped the school day wouldn't be turbulent or crazy.

She paused in the kitchen, expecting to see her mother drinking coffee and reading the morning newspaper at the table. The kitchen was the same but seemed to have aged since her mother's death. The flooring was scuffed and worn, the countertops were dull, and the overhead light was missing a bulb. If tables could think, the table was wondering where Irene was and why she wasn't there.

With a sigh, she got into her car and, as she drove, searched for the brown SUV, but also HB's red truck.

She was in luck when she pulled into the parking lot. HB was waiting for her. She walked up the steps where he leaned against the door, watching her climb toward him. He had a peculiar look on his face. They didn't speak. They just looked at each other as if using telepathy to communicate. Had they always had that? Or was this something new?

****

HB cleared his throat as she unlocked the door, flipped on the lights, and they stepped inside.

"Remember what I told you before?" When he told her what he had learned with Dr. Sims, she yelled at him, and he thought he'd have to drop out of her class. And like a dummy, he was bringing it up again.

Her expression froze—a deer in the headlights.

HB was quiet and rubbed his forefinger over his thumb—channeling…what? He didn't know.

"You're not saying anything," she said.

"I don't want to upset you again," he said quietly.

She nodded. "I didn't believe you."

"You showed me that book?"

"I guess anyone can write anything they want in books," she said, moving gingerly toward her desk and then dropping her coat and briefcase onto the chair.

"True."

"What is it you want, HB?"

"I'm just trying to get at the truth. The truth about me and who I am."

She hung her coat over the back of the chair, moved her briefcase under the desk, and sat.

"What if it's true?" he asked, leaning against a table and folding his arms. "What if it means another chance?"

"I guess it means another chance." She cocked her head at him. "You mean Robert and me?"

****

She blew out a ragged breath. "If only it were true." She'd have a chance to love him again, but could she do that with this lanky boy who looked nothing like Rob? He didn't have Rob's lopsided smile or dark hair. HB was fair and lean and sported a scar on his forehead.

"I'm scared." She rubbed at her arms like she was cold.

"Me too."

216

He stepped toward her as if to hug her but stopped.

They heard footsteps walk toward the door. "Let's talk about this later," Alison said.

Several days passed. Alison and HB were once again alone in the classroom.

"I remembered the Christmas dance in 2004," HB said.

Both he and Alison had stayed late. She was correcting papers, and he was finishing an English assignment.

"What did you say?" Her head jerked up, and the pen she was using stopped mid-air.

"The Christmas dance." He swallowed. "You wore a red dress with sparkles down the side, and I gave you a corsage of red and white roses. I couldn't find any tulips."

She watched him with her mouth open slightly.

"The gym was decorated with red and silver balloons, and we went to the Moonglow for dinner with Steve and his date."

Alison looked like she was miles away.

"There's more. I was the pitcher for the baseball team. I made the team when I was a freshman."

"How do you know that stuff?" she asked.

"I remember. And I say things like 'in a jiffy.' "

"That doesn't prove anything," Alison said quietly.

"Not even the Cedar Springs essay?"

Again, she shook her head vigorously.

He picked up her hand, rubbed her forefinger, and then took two fingers and did the same. "Do you remember I used to do this to you?"

She appeared to be frozen or paralyzed. "Why are you doing this? I don't know what I think or believe."

217

"I want to move forward. I can't do that without you."

"Why?"

"Because you're the reason I came back. Why I found you again."

"You're scaring me," she whispered, her eyes wide and terrified.

He took both hands and continued massaging her fingers as he talked, first one, then two, until he had her entire hand in his and slid up and down her hand sensuously, making electric charges run up and down his arms.

"I remember you were always doing that to my fingers," she said quietly. "It was a turn-on."

"I'd like to kiss you."

They leaned toward each other until their lips met and stayed that way until the wind shook the trailer, pulling them apart.

"How was that?" he whispered.

She remained quiet but leaned marginally closer as if wanting another kiss.

He kissed her again, and when they pulled apart, he searched her eyes for signs of recognition or confirmation. He didn't know which.

She licked her lips as he watched. She was making this difficult for him to concentrate. He wanted to take her home and make love to her. Instead, he said, "I remember sneaking into your bedroom window when we were seventeen. Do you remember?"

She smiled and appeared more open to his words. "I do."

"You were pregnant when I left." HB put a finger to her lip.

"I miscarried," she said softly, studying her lap as she spoke.

"You're only thirty-four…we could…try again."

"No!"

Now it was his turn to be silent and let her process their conversation.

Several days later, they picked up on their conversation as if days hadn't passed.

"How does something like this happen?" Alison said as though no time had passed since they had talked about what had happened to HB and Rob. It was the only thing HB could think about, and apparently, Alison. The elephant in the room.

"As I understand it, if someone wants to die, which I did before the accident, there is an opening for another soul to take over." He leaned against one of the tables and ran his sneaker over a worn part of the carpet. She started to speak, but he held up his hand for her to stop and then reached out to hold her hand. "Two souls need to be involved. One is departing, and one is seeking a new home. After my accident, it was a perfect scenario, I believe. I think it's a decision both souls need to make."

She gasped softly. "I read that."

"Seems like something out of a King novel."

She chuckled.

****

"But Rob died two years ago." She couldn't imagine the logistics of such a thing. She reasoned a person's gestures and voice inflection would be hard to copy.

"I spent a long time in the hospital and rehab," HB said.

She put her hands to the side of her head as if trying to consolidate the colliding thoughts.

If she stared deeply into HB's eyes, she remembered the first time she looked into Rob's eyes. She knew, even at sixteen, he was the one. They would come together for life's ups and downs, but she hoped for more ups.

Yes, he was in there. Alison could see—a feeling more than vision—and it was comforting.

HB stepped closer, put his arms around her, and nuzzled her ear. "This is our chance."

Rob had said something similar when he proposed. 'Will you marry me? Now is our chance to be together forever and ever. Will you do me the honor?'

She wanted to laugh at the absurdity of the situation now. She was thirty-four, and HB was twenty. "I'm so much older…"

"Does age matter? Our time to be together forever and ever—always," he whispered in her ear.

She gasped—Rob's words verbatim.

He had read her thoughts.

"I wish it were that simple," she said, her head spinning from the possible outcomes. Most weren't good. She could lose her job for loving HB—a student.

They pulled apart at the sound of footsteps on the landing leading into the trailer. Alison felt as if her cheeks were ablaze.

HB smoothed out his jeans, pulled his sweatshirt down, and adjusted his shoulders.

Cindy entered. "You two look guilty as sin!" She laughed.

Alison must have shocked her by the look because she said, "Just kidding."

"You're early today," Alison said, turning toward her desk and patting her hair.

"Chapter Seventeen post-test today!" Cindy sang,

obviously in a good mood.

"Seventeen already?" Alison asked, shuffling a few papers on her desk before turning toward HB and Cindy. HB remained quiet, but the conflict he felt was etched on his face and mirrored his eyes.

They weren't finished with that conversation in any way, shape, or form.

Chapter 46

Alison

As much as Alison wanted to disbelieve Rob's soul was in HB, she hoped it was true. And if true, how would they manage? Would people even believe their story? Or think she preyed on younger men? The very thought made her chuckle. There were jokes about such women, and she never thought she might be the brunt of such things.

Now Alison sat on the couch with her head tipped back, studying the ceiling and considering the ramifications of having a relationship with HB until she heard tires crunching on the gravel in the drive.

She stood and parted the curtains. It was dark outside, and she couldn't see the vehicle clearly, but she thought it might be HB. She opened the door as HB came up the walkway.

They stood at the door entrance, each watching the other—neither saying anything, before HB stepped closer, put his hands on her shoulders, and kissed her. She let him do it. Their lips fit together, and it felt like they had been kissing like this forever. She heard another car and looked out at the street for Mark's SUV. The only car visible was small and blended with the night.

"You better come inside." She tugged on his sleeve. She didn't want her neighbors watching and turned to see if any shades or blinds moved, but all was silent and still.

They stood facing each other. HB's face was unreadable as they stood in the door's shadow until HB stepped forward and kissed her again. She responded to him as before, and the acknowledgment made her gasp.

She led him to the couch. "What do we do now?" she whispered.

They sat side by side on the couch, and he slipped his arm around her shoulders, and she felt herself sinking into him.

"I don't know, but I think we need to be together."

She felt the same way and gave a slight nod, worrying about her reputation as a teacher. Did it matter? Life was short, and she wanted to have all the happiness offered.

"We may have to figure out the next steps as we go along," she said, thinking about her school colleagues and students. What would they feel about Alison with HB and an age difference of fourteen years?

"We may have to keep it on the down-low at school." He chuckled.

Alison turned to him to see why he was laughing.

"Cindy already thinks I'm the teacher's pet because of the credits I keep earning."

She moved her head. "No way. You earned them." She gave him a slight nudge in the ribs. And now she knew why he had flown through the pre-and post-tests, racking up credits.

"I had an advantage," he said.

"Been there, done that?" She suppressed a giggle.

"Sort of." He gave her a sideways look. They were quiet. The house seemed to expand and constrict around them.

"Ask me some questions," he said.

"Like what?" She frowned. "Math?"

"Something only I would know."

Alison looked toward the ceiling as she thought about what to ask him.

"Where did we go on our honeymoon?"

"That's easy. Paris," he said with a chuckle.

"Okay, where did we go on our first date?"

"A school dance," he said.

Alison figured many people started their high school dating lives by attending dances.

"What color was my dress?"

"Blue. Sky blue. I thought it matched your eyes perfectly." He leaned forward as he answered the questions without a thought. "And you have a mole by your belly button."

She gasped. "How...did..."

He kissed her palm. "Anything else?"

She chewed her lower lip. She had a million questions, but she needed to process this before asking more. Alison shook her head.

He stood and took her hand and kissed it. "I need to go now, Ali."

She felt her brows rise at the nickname.

"I called you, Ali," HB said. "I'm sorry if it upsets you, but you don't have to be upset...Ali."

"I think you called me that on the first day of classes this year." She was disappointed he couldn't stay longer. "Will I see you tomorrow?"

"Yup. And the day after and after and after. Forever." He walked to the front door, turned, and blew her a kiss before leaving and closing the door behind him.

This second chance was unchartered ground, and she felt lost but also excited—now they needed to move forward.

Chapter 47

Alison

The following day when Alison awoke, she felt like a different person—one with a secret. A secret only she and HB/Rob shared. Yes, she had begun to put their names together.

She usually thought about her day as a teacher when she first got up and had her coffee—smiling to herself at the milestones her students would reach during the day. This morning, her thoughts and the smile she saw in the mirror went immediately to HB/Rob. It was almost as if she was a student again herself.

When she got to her classroom, the phone rang, and she ran to answer it. Steve needed to see her immediately, chasing away all thoughts of last night's rendezvous. She drove the short distance to the high school, wondering what he could need this morning. Her mind immediately went to the kiss on the front porch with HB. Who in her neighborhood would tattle on her? Or was Mark still spying on her?

Once in the office, she ran into Marilyn, looking through her mail while getting coffee from the workroom. Marilyn looked up and said, "Hey, stranger, what are you doing here?"

"Seeing Steve." She rolled her eyes and moved her lips downward.

Marilyn frowned and whispered, "Mark's been put on leave and barred from going to your classroom."

Her brows rose, but she heard Steve calling her before she could respond.

"Alison." Steve had spotted her. "Come in!"

Alison shook her head as she followed Steve to his office, and he motioned for her to close the door behind her.

"This feels serious," Alison said as she sat down.

"I've been worried about you since your mother died." Steve raised his eyebrows. "You're different." His gaze bore into hers as if trying to see into her head. She didn't want him to read her thoughts and made her face neutral and calm.

She *was* different and nodded. She was utterly alone without her mother, husband, or baby. At times it felt as though she had been slogging through icy slush.

He blew out a breath. "The board president received an anonymous call about you and Henry Comstock."

Alison sucked in her breath. She had been right. Someone was watching them, and the realization made her spine tingle.

"This is hard for me, Alison. I've known you for a long time. Rob was my best friend, and I hate to see you throw away yourself and possibly your career with a punk kid like Henry."

She leaned forward and felt the flush flooding her cheeks and neck. "I'm not throwing myself away!"

"It seems that way to me, and I know Rob wouldn't approve."

"How would you know?" she demanded. "You'll never understand this situation, Steve."

"Maybe not, but I'm going to have to put you on

leave until I can sort this out."

"On leave?" The words shot from her mouth.

"How am I supposed to respond to reports you were sleeping with Henry Comstock?" Steve looked upset. His face mirrored the way she felt inside.

"No! That's not true, we're…"

He cut her off. "I've had three calls from school board members asking for your termination! Just this morning!"

She swallowed.

"I told them I'd put you on leave until we sorted out the details. This is serious, Alison." He put his palms decisively on his desk and leaned toward her. "I've never had this at Clearwater before. This stuff happens in big towns, not here." He ran his fingers through his hair and shook his head.

"I'm sorry," she whispered.

"Do you have a logical explanation for what's going on?"

"He's twenty, and we're friends."

"Only friends?"

She sat mutely. Her hands held tightly between her knees to keep from shivering. That darn Mark was still spying on them! "Yes."

"The school board is having a special meeting to discuss your conduct. I never thought you'd be the root of the problem with a staff member and a student."

She started to speak, but he held up his hand and continued, "The board wants to take care of this before the newspaper gets hold of it. You know how they like this kind of smut and garbage."

"I'm sorry," she said again. "Nothing happened, Steve." But her mind immediately went to last night.

"Folks don't like that sort of thing in a small town. Teachers with students."

"I-I've been tutoring him." Her voice lacked conviction. She was a bad liar. He wouldn't believe the explanation anyway.

"I'm not sure the board will buy that."

"What will happen to my students if I'm on leave?" she asked, clasping and unclasping her hands.

"I imagine they'll survive with a substitute for a while like they did when you were on bereavement leave."

Alison stood and placed her hands on Steve's desk. "That's not fair! He's twenty!"

"A student is a student no matter their age." Steve picked up a pen and shuffled some papers on his desk to avoid looking at her. "Leave some directions for the substitute and then go home. I'll handle it from here." He pushed his chair out and stood, indicating this conversation was over.

Alison nodded, tears threatening to explode as she rushed from his office.

"Alison, is everything all right?" Marilyn stood by the copy machine.

"No," she mumbled as she hurried to her car and the short drive to adult education.

Cindy was waiting by the door. She lifted her arm to wave but lowered it, frowning. "Oh, my gosh, Alison?"

"Something's happened." She unlocked the doors and went to her desk. Her class was all individualized. Students worked at their own pace. There was nothing for a substitute to do except administer some pre-and post-tests.

"Alison," Cindy persisted. "Can I help?"

She blew out her breath noisily. "There's going to be a substitute for a bit. Can you show them where I keep the testing material?"

"Are you sick?"

"No, it's something else."

Cindy faced Alison, biting her lower lip. "I-I don't understand."

"The principal wants me to take a leave of absence for improper conduct."

"We're all adults here!"

Did Cindy have a clue what was going on between her and HB?

Alison didn't respond to her comment. "I would imagine the substitute will be here shortly. Good luck," she said briskly before more tears could erupt. She drove home quickly, then locked herself in, drew the shades, and drank a whole bottle of wine until her thoughts were cloudy, hazy, and dull around the edges.

Chapter 48

Alison and HB/Rob

There was a substitute teacher for the second time since he'd been going to adult education. HB frowned when he stepped into the classroom and hesitated. He only wanted to turn and leave and go to Alison.

But instead, he slid into the chair next to Cindy. "What's up?" Was she sick, or had something happened? The feeling of apprehension made his skin buzz and tingle.

"Alison had to take a leave of absence," Cindy said. She crossed her arms over her chest.

HB frowned. "Why?"

"I heard rumors about that Biology teacher."

"The guy that attacked her?" HB whispered, but he knew.

"That one."

"I don't understand." HB had a sneaking suspicion *he* was the reason Alison wasn't here. His mind went automatically to last night's kisses. It was hard to believe something so wonderful could be so devastating. Alison could lose her job because of him. But he knew he had to be with her. And besides, if his plan for his GED and M-CAT worked, they'd be out of Clearwater by next year.

Several others overheard their conversation. "Is

Alison coming back?"

"What happened?"

"I think it has something to do with that Biology teacher," Cindy whispered furiously.

"Hmm," HB said.

"It's not fair to penalize her." Cindy folded her arms more tightly.

"We should start a petition and go to the school board," Wayne suggested.

"Whoa! A petition for what?" HB asked.

"So she can come back and teach."

Samuel got a sheet of paper, began writing, and then passed it to the others in the class.

"There's only twelve of us today." HB frowned at the short list of names on the petition.

"We could boycott class," Cindy suggested.

"I don't think that's the answer," HB said. "Alison would be one hundred percent against it."

"We need to do something," Cindy insisted. "We could go to the school board and ask that Alison come back to teach."

HB eased out of his chair and stood. He wanted to go to Alison. He was sure she needed him.

"Are you coming back?" Cindy asked, grasping his sleeve.

"Don't know." His mind was going in a million different directions.

"Tell Alison we're mobilizing to go to the board. Tell her we miss her," Cindy urged.

HB dipped his head in agreement and slipped out the door. Not even stopping to wonder how Cindy knew he was going to Alison.

****

At his knock, Alison opened the door, her hair a messy tangle, like she had run her hands through it or slept on it. She swayed slightly on her feet. She was drunk.

"What are you doing here?" She hiccupped.

"Checking on you." He put his hands on her shoulders and looked into her red-rimmed eyes.

She hiccupped again.

"Let me make some coffee."

She leaned against the wall until he led her to the couch. "Sit." He gave her a small but firm push. "I'll make coffee and get you something to eat," HB said.

In the kitchen, HB measured coffee into the machine and searched the cupboards for bread, peanut butter, and some strawberry jam from the refrigerator.

He made sandwiches while he waited for the coffee to brew. He saw the empty wine bottle and peeked around the corner at Alison slumped over on the couch, her head on a pillow, snoring softly. He brought in the food and coffee and shook her shoulder. "Ali, I've got coffee and a sandwich for you."

She yawned and struggled to sit.

"How much did you drink?" He held up the empty bottle.

"Not much."

"The whole bottle?"

"I guess." She swiped the bottle from his hands and peered inside. "I lost track." She hung her head, seemed fascinated by her bare feet, and wiggled her toes, discarding the bottle on the floor.

"You've never been a good drinker," HB said as he handed her the coffee and sandwich. "Drink," he demanded. "Eat."

She sipped and nibbled at the sandwich. "How did you know I was here?"

"Cindy said you had left, and there was a sub."

She hiccupped. "But how did you know I'd be here?"

"This is where you live."

"I'm in big trouble, aren't I?" She set down the sandwich and cupped her hands around the mug.

"I don't know," he said. "The class is going to the board to protest your leave."

"Can they do that?" she said after another hiccup.

He shrugged. "Cindy is pretty bent out of shape."

Ali had a smear of jam on her lip, and HB reached over, wiped it away, and kissed the spot. He remembered doing something similar many years ago.

"Was it about me? Us?" The question, the elephant in the room.

"Yes, I'm sure Mark went to the board."

She slowly sipped her coffee, and the pinched frown lines softened between her brows. She reached up and patted her hair. "I must be a fright!"

"You look beautiful," he said, setting down his cup and sliding closer.

She looked so innocent with her wide eyes and pursed mouth. "Do you want to kiss me?" she asked.

"I do." And so he did.

****

HB drove to adult education the following day with an uneasy feeling in his gut. There was one unfamiliar car parked by the door—the substitute, he reasoned. True to their word, students had boycotted the class. There was a fluttering piece of paper taped to the door. HB ran up the steps to see Cindy's handwriting. EVERYONE

MEET AT THE SCHOOL BOARD MEETING TONIGHT AT 7. He backed away from the door, returned to his car, and drove home.

He was scheduled to work the lunch shift at the Moonglow and would be done in plenty of time. He was happy to have work to keep his mind occupied.

When he finished his shift, he went to the school board meeting held in the multi-purpose room of the high school. Before going in, he noticed Hutchins' and Alison's cars parked by the front entrance. He hated that son of a bitch. He wanted to punch his lights out, but he was no match for the man. But he could fantasize, right? He could dream about putting the guy in his place.

HB went to the multi-purpose room, arranged with tables at the front and several rows of chairs for spectators. He slid in next to Cindy and the others. She whispered, "I asked if we could speak on behalf of Alison during the public input portion."

"Are you going to speak?" he asked.

"Yes, me and Wayne."

"That's good." He didn't want to say anything because several people looked at him and thought he was the same old HB—troublemaker and drug dealer. He didn't want to bring unwanted attention to himself, to them.

Alison and Hutchins were seated on opposite sides. Steve sat by Alison, and Hutchins sat by himself.

The chair was unyielding and uncomfortable, and all HB could do was watch the back of Alison's head as she waited to be summoned into a closed session with the board. He wanted to sit next to her, hold her hand, and give her husbandly support.

He hung his head and studied the floor and his

235

sneakers during most of the boring meeting. His mind shuffled through memories. Their hopes and dreams for the future. Favorite places to go. The memories made his eyes tear up. He shook away those thoughts and stifled a yawn. He'd never attended one of these meetings before. Budgets, paving projects, vandalism at the middle school. Blah! Blah! Blah!

It seemed like eons before the board asked Cindy and Wayne if they wanted to address the board. HB sat straighter as they walked to the podium and microphone.

"Hello, I'm Cindy, and this is Wayne. We're students in Alison Larkin's adult education class." She stopped, turned slightly, and smiled at Alison.

The president nodded for them to continue.

Wayne cleared his throat, "As you can tell, I'm older than most students." There was a twitter from several observers. "Because of Alison, I'm finishing my GED. She cares for her students and wants the best for us."

"Thank you for your comments," the president said. "Anything else?"

Cindy raised her hand for permission to continue. "As Wayne said, most of us aren't your typical students. We didn't do well at regular school. I'm sure there's nothing"—she air quoted—"inappropriate going on with her and that other teacher. There has to be a misunderstanding." Cindy stopped. "She gives her all for her students."

"We appreciate you coming to share your thoughts with us, but as with all personnel issues, we can't comment on anything in a public meeting. We'll take your messages under advisement. Thank you."

HB watched as the board members began to gather their papers.

"We'll now go into closed session," the president said. "The audience is welcome to wait, but it may be a while."

Cindy, Wayne, HB, and the others stood as the audience began to file out. Alison turned and gave them a half wave before they left for the "closed personnel" session. Hutchins, striding like a peacock, turned and glared at HB. The ass.

Chapter 49

Alison

Alison waited to be summoned into the closed session board meeting after Mark. She shifted on the hard seat, the metal back pressed into her spine, and she massaged her neck.

The door opened, and Mark stepped out and glared at her. As he was leaving, he punched the wall next to the door making her jump. Steve yelled, "Hey! Stop that!" to Mark's retreating back.

Mark laughed and slammed the door behind him.

Alison sucked in her breath at the dent in the wall before following Steve into the closed-door session.

The board members sat behind two long tables. There was a chair for the person being interrogated—maybe that wasn't the right word, but it sure felt like it. She sat down, smoothed her skirt, crossed her legs, and waited. She had never been summoned before the board. Mark's dramatic exit already jangled her nerves, and she slowly blew out her breath and waited. The board was in disarray—several whispered to each other, one had dropped some paper on the floor and was bending over to retrieve it, and the board president scratched his head and read something in front of him on the table.

Alison knew most of the members, the pharmacist, the 7-11 owner, a daycare director, and the assistant manager at the grocery store.

The president began, "We have several matters involving you, Mrs. Larkin." He looked down at his notes and shuffled several papers around before picking up his pen. "The first thing is the matter with Mark Hutchins. I understand there was a fight of some sort?"

"That's correct," she said. "He barged in and disrupted my class and—"

"That very reason is why it is frowned upon for teachers to date other teachers. It's hard to hide animosity at work." He folded his arms and looked pointedly at her.

She shrugged and hoped she looked unconcerned.

"He's been advised to leave you alone," the daycare director said, tapping her pen on her paperwork.

Alison wondered if that would deter him, but it was his problem, not hers. "He's been stalking me and peeking in my windows at night."

"That's a matter for the police, I believe," the board president said with a perplexed look. "He's not to go to your classroom at school."

Had they put Mark on leave too?

"Is he still working?" she asked.

"Yes, until we can find a replacement."

Interesting. Mark's teaching career was more valuable to the school than hers.

The board president cleared his throat. "Now to a more serious issue. Your relationship with student Henry Comstock."

"We're just friends—I've been tutoring him," Alison added quickly. Her heart began to beat faster.

"We have information to the contrary," the president said.

"Your information comes from Mark Hutchins, I assume?" Alison felt the hair on her neck rise in indignation. "He's hardly a reliable source."

The board president looked at the other members and pursed his lips as if trying to think of something to say.

"Mark has been stalking me." Alison continued, "I don't think talking to you will make him stop."

"That may be the case in part, but the Michigan Revised Statutes specifically forbid relationships of a romantic nature between teachers and students."

"As I said before, I've been tutoring him. He was in a bad car accident and is behind in his credits."

The 7-11 manager raised her hand. "There has been a complaint filed with the sheriff's department to delve into this matter."

"What does that mean?" Alison asked. What did the complaint allege? She wondered if they would explain it.

"We're going to have to keep you on leave until we can sort this out," the president said, grimacing.

Alison frowned. "I want to work."

The president shook his head. "Until the complaint is looked into," he said, removing his glasses, "you're on indefinite leave, and I would suggest you get yourself an attorney."

"An attorney for tutoring a student?" Had she heard him right? An attorney? She closed her gaping mouth with a snap and willed the twisting in her stomach to settle. .

"If there are any more inappropriate actions on your part with Henry Comstock, we will press for your dismissal from your job with the Clearwater School District. You may be prosecuted for inappropriate relations with a minor. Do you understand?"

"A minor," she gasped. "He's twenty."

The board members looked at each other with puzzled expressions, and the pharmacist scratched his head.

"We were told he was seventeen. This information sheds a different light on the situation."

"I'm sure it does," Alison said, folding her arms.

"Do you have anything more to say?" the board president asked.

She had a lot to say, but none of it would make sense to them. HB had the soul of her dead husband, but she could never tell anyone. She and HB/Rob would share a secret even if they left Clearwater and started over in another place.

"I have nothing to say except that I've been tutoring him, that's all." she slapped her palms on her thighs.

"Thank you, Ms. Larkin. You're free to go, and we'll be in contact."

"My attorney will be contacting *you*." She stood, nodded, whirled around, and stalked from the room, brushing by Steve in her hurry to leave the meeting. She'd call Gloria first thing in the morning.

****

HB/Rob parked behind a strand of trees in a vacant lot and watched for Alison's car to return from the meeting. Then he saw her. She was driving fast. That translated into the meeting hadn't gone well. He gave her ten minutes to park and go inside before walking in the shadows to her house.

She met him by the back door, and even in the dim night light, he could tell she had been crying.

"What happened?" he whispered as if the walls had

ears and put his arms around her and drew her close. He thought he could feel the hammering of her heart against his.

"Not much. They thought you were a minor, but I set them straight."

He gathered her closer, her head nestled on his chest, his chin resting on her head, keeping her safe.

"They warned me to leave you alone," she said, her words muffled against his chest.

He squeezed her. "Can they do that to two consenting adults?"

"I don't think so. I'll have to check the Michigan Revised Statutes concerning this and hire a lawyer." She pulled away and rubbed the back of her neck.

"A lawyer?" HB/Rob asked.

"Yup." She let out a long sigh. She couldn't believe it had come down to this.

Chapter 50

HB/Rob

The next night, when the night was velvety and thick, HB/Rob drove to Alison's, where he saw Hutchins' SUV parked down the street and the blue Ford Focus camouflaged by some large bushes. There was no movement from either vehicle, but he saw the outlines of people in the driver's seats. If the situation weren't so tension-filled, HB/Rob would have thought it was humorous that Hutchins was watching Alison and someone else was watching Hutchins. So much for the school board telling Hutchins to leave Alison alone.

HB/Rob snuck around the back of Alison's house and knocked once. Alison kept the lights off, took his hand, and guided him into the house.

"What's wrong?" she gasped.

HB/Rob moved his chin toward the road. "Hutchins is parked outside."

Alison went to the curtains, parted them, and squinted in the darkness at the SUV by the road. She blew out her breath. "Why can't he just leave me alone?"

"But you know what's even stranger?" HB/Rob asked.

"What?"

"Someone else is following him in a blue Ford with a Missouri or Mississippi license plate."

"I wonder who would be following him?" Alison closed and locked the door.

"I have no idea."

"I know he's in a custody battle with his ex-wife." She chewed on her lip. "I wonder if she's following him or hired someone to spy on him?"

HB/Rob shrugged. "I don't want to think about him right now." He stepped toward her and gathered her close. "We'll think about him after..." His sentence trailed away before he whispered, "Can I kiss you now?"

****

Alison remembered high-school-aged HB/Rob asking the same thing. They had parked by the beach, where he asked permission to kiss her.

"You asked me that before. Remember?" she asked.

He considered her question. It was dark in the hall, but his grin was unmistakable. "We were at the beach."

Bingo.

"Tell me what else you remember?" she asked. Reminiscing distracted her from the school board meeting.

"Besides loving you?" HB/Rob asked as he led her to the couch, where a single candle blazed on the coffee table, making shadows dance on the walls—sensuous, smoky undulations.

"Yes."

"My father wasn't around much. He worked long hours," HB/Rob said.

Alison remembered his absent father. She liked Rob's mother tremendously and enjoyed having tea with her and looking at pictures of Rob as a baby, toddler, and then in primary school. She felt grown up at seventeen, having tea and talking woman to woman.

"My mother adored you. The daughter she never had."

Sadly, Rob's mother died soon after Alison miscarried.

"She was excited to be a grandmother," he added.

Alison remained silent as she listened.

His hand covered hers. "You know, we could still have a baby."

"I'm thirty-four." But her eyes darted around as if considering it.

"Not too old," HB/Rob said, turning her head away from his shoulder and kissing her mouth. "Remember, I went to medical school."

"What if I have another miscarriage?"

"What if you don't?" He placed his hand on her stomach. "I'll take good care of you."

Alison had no doubt he would be attentive and caring.

"Would you be willing to try?" he asked softly.

She gave him a wide-eyed stare, but he saw acceptance, surprise, and excitement in her eyes.

"Then we should get a move on it, don't you think?" HB/Rob asked, already reaching for the buttons on her blouse.

One by one, he unfastened them before pushing her shirt aside, his fingers soft against her flesh, circling her chest and unfastening her bra. "Beautiful," he murmured, pulling her onto his lap and putting his nose on her breastbone. He pushed Alison back onto the couch and kneeled by her side, kissing her and running his fingers up and down her flesh. Her skin responded with tingles that raced around her body.

Alison's breath stuck in her throat like she had eaten

a cracker and was now in need of water. She didn't dare breathe, fearing she'd break the spell. She wanted him. Yes, she needed him as a woman desires a man. It had been so long—two years. She had memories to sustain her, but it wasn't the same. The flesh remembered his touch and the pressure of his fingertips. They had another chance at love. "Sha-shall we go into my bedroom?" she asked.

He made a noise deep in his throat and continued kissing her on the way to her bedroom.

"I've missed you so much!" Once settled on the bed, he continued the exploration of her body.

He slipped out of his clothes, kicking them to the side. She pushed his hands away as her fingers moved over his chest and lightly outlined the scars on his body from his accident. His forehead wasn't the only visible reminder. He had others, and she touched each one tenderly—the flesh raised slightly, feeling softer and different from the rest—a constant indication of all he'd been through to return to her.

Alison responded to his touch, her skin jumping with tiny electric shocks. She arched her back, and they were joined. Two years had left her pent up and wanting to swallow him whole.

"Slow down," he whispered. "Let's take it easy."

"I can't," she breathed. "I need you now!" She thrust her hips at him, and he responded in kind.

Their bodies remembered the way they had made love before. Alison felt her heart match HB/Rob's, beating together—the music and tempo of their lovemaking—slow, slow, fast, and faster! Their scents mingled—hers fruity and floral and his musky—their unique co-mingled fragrance. Her breathing quickened, and he inhaled her, taking a part of her as his own and she, his. They climaxed together, Alison quivering and HB/Rob shuddering as he collapsed on top of her. And then, there was a loud sound coming from outside the house. A gunshot?

"What was that?" Alison put her head back, gasping before settling her chest against his and going limp in his arms.

"Do you want me to take a look?" he asked.

She didn't want him to leave. "Could it have been a car backfiring?"

"Umm," HB/Rob said, easing off her body and sliding on his jeans.

"Don't go!"

"Then I'll stay here."

They lay together, Ali stroking HB/Rob's arm as he caressed her cheek. She shivered and snuggled farther into his arms.

When HB/Rob reluctantly left in the wee, inky hours of late night, she walked him to the door and peered out the window. Mark's SUV was still parked on the street. Did she care he would see HB/Rob leaving at 3:00 a.m.? She realized she didn't care and went back to bed.

How many couples got a do-over?

She drifted off to sleep until the phone woke her.

Her arm flayed around, finally finding the phone. "H-Hello?"

"Are you awake?" Marilyn asked.

She was now, her heart hammering with roaring waves.

"Someone shot Mark." Marilyn breathed the news into the phone and Alison's ear.

"What?" Her mind was slow to respond as she

247

pushed the fog of sleep away.

"Someone shot Mark in front of your house."

Alison was wide awake now. "Oh my gosh!" She sat upright. The sound. The gunshot!

"Did you see or hear anything?" Marilyn asked.

"Uh." Her mind was a scramble of thoughts. "Yeah, I heard a sound but thought it was a backfiring car."

Surely they didn't think she had killed Mark?

"I wonder if it was the person who was following him? In a blue Ford?" Speaking her thoughts.

"A blue Ford?" Marilyn asked.

"Yes, someone has been following Mark in a blue Ford."

"Do you know anyone that drives a blue car?" Marilyn asked.

Tons.

Cindy drove a blue Ford. But why would Cindy shoot Mark?

"Do you have an alibi for tonight?" Marilyn asked, sounding more and more like Emerson.

She did, and she didn't. HB/Rob was her alibi, and she wasn't supposed to see him. "I-I was home alone."

"Oh, gosh," Marilyn said.

Oh, gosh, indeed. Alison was in trouble with or without an alibi. She was doomed either way.

Chapter 51

Alison

When Alison hung up from speaking with Marilyn, she struggled out of bed, put on a robe and slippers, went into the living room, and peeked out the curtains. The street was lit up with police, ambulance, and fire trucks. If she hadn't looked at the clock and seen that it was 4:00 a.m., she would have thought it was daytime. She unlocked the front door, hugging her robe against the autumn chill. She stepped along the walkway toward the beehive of activity.

She spotted Emerson, Marilyn's husband, and waved. "Marilyn just called me."

"Alison," Emerson said, motioning for her to stay behind the yellow crime scene tape. "Did you see or hear anything unusual tonight?" He went from being a friend to a cop instantly.

"No, I had the television on," she lied. "What happened?"

"It looks like someone shot Mark Hutchins."

"That's terrible." As much as she disliked Mark, she didn't want him dead. "Do you have any suspects?"

He leveled his gaze at her, indicating she was the prime suspect. "I understand there were problems between you two." He cleared his throat.

She folded her arms. "Nothing I would kill over. We

just didn't hit it off, that's all."

He held up a baggie with a crumpled gas receipt with writing on the back. "Is this your writing?"

She squinted at the writing and froze. The handwriting looked to be HB's. "No, that's not my writing."

"Hmmm."

"Any idea who might write something like that?"

"N-no. Did you talk to the person in the blue Ford?"

"What blue Ford?" he asked.

"It seemed to have been following Mark. I noticed it parked behind him." HB/Rob had reported the blue car to her.

He rubbed his chin. "Did you get a license number?"

"No." But maybe HB/Rob had, she hoped. He was good with remembering sequences of numbers. "I'm not sure it was a Michigan plate."

"There are some tire tracks. We'll check it out," he said off-handedly. It was apparent he had a lot on his mind.

Someone came up and spoke to Emerson. He turned back to her. "I've got to run. Let me know if you think of anything that might help."

"Do...do you think I should call my neighbors?"

"No, we'll be knocking on doors," he said. "See if someone noticed anything unusual."

HB/Rob must have written the note to scare Mark away. It didn't work. Should she tell Emerson HB/Rob was with her last night? Her stomach flipped, and she turned and sprinted back into the house.

Chapter 52

Alison

Alison sat on the couch, watching the activity that began dwindling as the morning sun was full in the front of the house. She saw neighbors exit their doors and venture forth, some talking to the police, others craning their necks looking for the dead body. She only wondered who had shot Mark, knowing it wasn't HB/Rob, even with the incriminating note. Would they pin the blame on HB/Rob? Ruin their future together? A cruel twist of circumstances. Was fate going to always be against them?

She looked at the mantel clock and dialed Marilyn when it was six o'clock, with trembling fingers and an ache in her stomach. She knew Marilyn would be up and have news from Emerson.

"Any news?"

Marilyn sighed. "The fingerprints are Henry Comstock's."

Alison had recognized the handwriting immediately. The scrawl of a future doctor.

"Why would he kill Mark?" Alison asked, although she knew how Marilyn felt about HB (not knowing HB was Rob).

"Several people overheard Henry say he was going to kill Mark."

Just a trite phrase. There were many in the English language. The rest escaped her. "That doesn't sound like HB."

"From what I remember, that's exactly what he would do." Marilyn's words were definite.

"He's changed since his accident."

"A leopard doesn't change his spots," Marilyn said.

He did if he had a new soul in his body.

"I think they're on their way to arrest him."

"Oh, gosh! I've got to go."

"I'm sure they'll want your statement," Marilyn said.

"Thank you!" Alison hung up. She paused for a moment and looked out the curtains as, one by one, the lights dimmed as vehicles left the scene and Mark's SUV was towed away.

She needed to call HB/Rob and warn him. She dialed his number, but it went straight to voice mail.

"Hi, it's me. Someone shot Mark last night. The police have the message you wrote and your prints. I think they'll be coming to talk to you. You need to tell them you were with me."

****

HB/Rob listened to Alison's message moments before he heard pounding on the front door. Too late, they were here. He struggled out of bed and slipped on jeans and a sweatshirt as he listened to his mother's excited voice asking them what was wrong.

"Henry," she called. "The police want to talk to you."

He texted Alison:

—*They're here.*—

"Coming," he said.

"This is Detective Palmer and Detective Sanchez. We'd like to ask you a few questions."

HB/Rob and his mother sat on the couch, facing the officers. HB/Rob absently rubbed his thumb with his forefinger while waiting for the questioning to begin.

"What's going on?" HB's mother asked. "Why are you questioning my son?"

"A teacher at the high school was murdered this evening, and we think Henry might be involved."

"Why would you think that?" His mother took his hand. "Henry?"

One of the officers held up the baggie containing the note. "This was found in the victim's car. Henry, is this your writing?"

His mother gasped, her eyes widening as she read the threatening words.

"It is." He swallowed painfully, a peach pit lodged at the base of his throat.

"Why would you write such a thing?" his mother asked.

"He wouldn't leave Alison alone."

As HB/Rob and his mother talked, the detectives watched intently, writing on their tablets.

"Did you threaten that man?" she asked.

"No." But he had. "Well, kinda." He sighed. "Okay, yes."

"Stand up and put your hands behind your back. We're arresting you for the murder of Mark Hutchins. If you need an attorney, one will be provided."

"Henry!" His mother shrieked. "Surely, you don't think he did that?" She turned to the officers.

"We'll sort that all out at the station." They turned to go, but there was a knock on the door.

253

His mother frowned and went to open it. "Who are you?"

Alison stood in the foyer. She looked like she had just thrown on her clothes and hadn't had time to do her hair.

HB/Rob gasped, "Alison!"

"This is Alison, your teacher?" HB/Rob's mother turned first to her son and then back to Alison.

"I need to clear him."

His mother led Alison into the room.

Alison stopped and faced HB/Rob, and the officers. "He was with me last night. He didn't kill anyone. We heard a shot but thought it was a car backfiring."

"I see. Would you be willing to make a statement to that effect?"

"I would."

"Ali…" HB/Rob began.

She held up her hand. "You didn't do anything wrong. Can he go now?"

"No, we're taking him in for his statement. Someone overheard Henry threatening to kill Mark Hutchins."

"You have it wrong," Alison said, tears streaming down her face. "I was the one who did wrong. He was in bed with me."

"Can you prove that?" the officer said, tapping a finger on his nightstick as he talked.

How does one prove they were in bed with another? The stains on the sheets? "I-I guess I can't."

"Arrest her! She's the guilty party!" HB's mother gasped and sagged onto the couch. "Oh, Lord!"

"No!" HB/Rob said, turning to the officers and moving his arms. "Don't arrest her. She didn't do anything wrong. Neither of us did!"

"Henry!" his mother scolded. "She's guilty of seducing you!"

"No, she didn't, Mother."

His mother folded her arms, her face dark with anger, and she glared at Alison.

"We'll sort this out." The officer fastened the cuffs on HB/Rob. "I'd like you ladies to follow us to the station. We need your statements too."

Chapter 53

Alison

In silent horror, Alison and HB's mother watched as HB/Rob was put into the squad car, neither speaking nor looking at the other.

HB/Rob's mother broke the tension-filled silence. "I'm in no state to drive," she wailed. "They have my baby."

"I'll drive," Alison said even though his mother looked at her as if she was a poisonous snake.

They followed the squad car to the station while HB/Rob's mother stared straight ahead and didn't speak to Alison until Alison whispered, "I'm sorry."

"How could you do this to my son?" she said with a snarl, suddenly turning toward Alison, mouth bared in a grimace.

"It just happened," Alison said quietly. Life would have been easier if it hadn't happened, but then again, life would never be the same—good or bad. A second chance only they, she and HB/Rob, knew about.

"You should be ashamed of taking advantage of an innocent boy."

Alison hardly thought HB/Rob was innocent as far as sex was concerned.

"What's the matter with you? Can't you get a guy your age?"

Alison remained quiet. HB's mother built up to a shouting match.

"I'm sorry," Alison said quietly. "It just happened."

"I bet!" She glared at Alison.

Alison gripped the wheel and slowed for brake lights in front of her. She needed to keep her attention on the road.

HB/Rob's mother paused, gathering more steam. "I want something different for my son. Like college. Or a career!"

"I'll make sure he goes to college." To medical school. Alison nodded.

"I hope they lock you up!" she told Alison as they parked at the station. HB/Rob's mother flung open the door and marched toward the entrance, leaving Alison to lock the car and follow.

Once inside, past screening, HB/Rob's mother pointed at Alison and said, "This is the person who should be handcuffed! Not my son!"

Emerson walked by with a cup of coffee and frowned at Alison. "What's going on?"

"I'll tell you," HB's mother said. "She admitted she was sleeping with my son. He's not a murderer, but she's guilty of seducing him. Aren't there laws against that sort of thing?"

Emerson stopped and studied Alison's face. "Is that true?"

"I'm afraid it is."

Emerson rolled his eyes. "How old is your son?" He turned to HB/Rob's mother.

"Well, he's twenty, but still…"

"I'm sorry," he said to HB/Rob's mother. "This isn't a police matter."

Sue C. Dugan

"Well, it should be!" HB/Rob's mother retorted.

Emerson moved around his coffee cup. "Why don't you come with me?" he said to Alison. He turned to HB/Rob's mother and motioned for her to sit.

Alison followed Emerson to his tiny office, where she sat, wringing her hands. Hopefully, HB/Rob would be released. She didn't care if they kept her or not.

"I lied to you earlier."

He rubbed his neck as if it pained him.

"When you asked if I heard a shot. I said I didn't, but I did."

"I see. Did you go investigate?"

"No, I was in bed with R—Henry Comstock."

Emerson's brows raised, but he remained quiet. He had probably heard this all before.

She nodded. "Will Henry be released soon?"

Emerson punched in something on his desk computer. "I don't know. Suspicion of murder. Maybe not."

"He didn't murder Mark. He was with me," Alison gulped. "We were having sex at the time. We heard the gunshot but thought it was a car backfiring." She chewed on her lip. "Please, don't tell Marilyn."

Emerson shook his head slowly, "This is all confidential." He paused and cleared his throat. "I hope you know what you're doing, Alison."

He studied her as he leaned across the desk.

Alison hung her head and studied her folded hands.

"Here!" He slid a piece of paper and pen toward her. "Write out your statement on what happened."

Alison did and gave it to Emerson, who quickly scanned the page.

"Good luck." Emerson gave her a sympathetic

258

smile. "You better call your attorney. This might turn into a circus."

Gloria was the attorney who helped Alison settle her mom's and Rob's estates. She'd call Gloria. She'd know what to do or who to call.

Chapter 54

HB/Rob

HB/Rob sat facing two officers in another part of the station. "We've got a problem," one of the officers said to HB/Rob.

It's never a good sign when they start with "we've got a problem."

"How so?" HB/Rob asked, shuffling his feet. But he knew. His animosity toward Hutchins was palpable.

"Some fellow workers overheard you saying you were going to kill Mark Hutchins."

HB/Rob thought back to that night. Hutchins pushed Alison against the table at the Moonglow. He was mad, sure, but murder? "An expression only. He was bothering Alison."

The officer nodded as if he understood, but did he? Would anyone realize what had happened on that day at that particular moment except the people involved? "Probably not a good phrase to say during the heat of the moment." HB/Rob shrugged.

The officer continued looking at him.

"I wasn't thinking." HB/Rob shoved his hands deep into his front pockets.

"So you did say it?"

"I guess." He shrugged. "Just a figure of speech."

"Do you own a handgun?"

"No."

"But you admit to writing the note found in Mark's vehicle."

"Yes."

"Anything else?"

"Find the person in the blue Ford. They've been following Hutchins around."

The officer wrote something down. "Did you look at the person or persons in the blue Ford?"

"It was dark, and they wore black clothing. I only saw one person. I remember the car had an out-of-state license plate that started with a C E. From Missouri or Mississippi."

Not Michigan, but it started with an M.

"We made impressions of the tracks and'll look at your tires to see if they match."

They wouldn't. HB/Rob was sure of that.

HB/Rob sat quietly while the officer squinted at his notes and gave him a direct look. "Do you know who shot Mark Hutchins?"

"No, but I would imagine a man with that temper would have plenty of enemies."

Another officer brought in some papers, set them on the desk, and shot a look at HB/Rob before leaving.

"What's that?" HB/Rob asked.

"Alison's statement." HB/Rob watched as the man's eyes moved over the words. "She says you were with her."

"I was."

The same officer came back with another piece of paper.

"Your mother wants to press charges against Alison Larkin, stating she raped you."

HB/Rob laughed. "That's not the way it was. I love Alison."

"How old are you, Henry?"

"Twenty."

"Did she coerce you?"

He laughed. "No, it was mutual." He smiled inwardly, remembering her body's warm feel against his.

"I'll need to talk to your mother."

HB/Rob shrugged before his mother was brought in and sat down. "How are you, dear?" She patted his hand.

"I'm fine, Mother. I want you to drop the charges against Alison."

"But she seduced you!"

"No, she didn't. It was consensual."

Her facial expression was shock, confusion, and disbelief, all in one. "Where on earth have you learned those big words?" she asked.

He chuckled. "I'm pretty smart, Mother. Alison made me see my potential, and I plan to attend medical school."

The listening officer asked HB/Rob, "Are you willing to waive the charges?"

"Yes."

His mother, still holding her purse, said, "I still think it's wrong for you to be with her."

"We didn't do anything wrong!" HB/Rob retorted.

"I'll release you on your recognizance. Don't leave town," the officer said.

"I won't." He turned to his mother. "Did you drive?"

"No, that woman did."

"Alison," he corrected her.

"We can have an officer drive you home."

HB/Rob and his mother stood. "Thank you."

When HB/Rob and his mother returned home, the house was a mess—drawers and cupboards opened, and the beds ripped apart. The frames of the doors and windows were black with dust. No doubt they were taking prints. His computer and truck were gone.

"Why on earth did they have to make such a mess?" HB/Rob's mother said, frowning and clicking her tongue in disgust.

"Looking for evidence. The gun."

"We don't own a gun!" she retorted.

"They don't know that."

"You were released!" She made clicking noises with her tongue as she continued the tour of the mess.

"They were probably searching while we were at the station."

His mother was busy the rest of the day putting stuff away and cleaning off the dust. She wore yellow rubber gloves and carried a spray bottle of cleaner, spritzing and wiping away the police destruction.

The police kept HB/Rob's cell phone. He'd need to get a throwaway phone to call work and vice versa.

While he put his bedroom back in order, he stewed about Alison, wondering if she had made it home okay. If she hadn't told them he was with her, he'd be in jail on murder charges.

Chapter 55

Alison

Alison called her attorney, Gloria, and made an appointment to talk to her the next day.

When Alison arrived, Gloria beckoned her into her office. "I was quite surprised by your call," Gloria said as she put a pad of paper and pen on her desk. "So tell me, what's happening? You were a bit garbled on the phone."

"There was a murder in front of my house two nights ago, and they think my student did it."

Gloria cocked her head, waiting for the rest.

"The boy in question was with me."

"How old is this boy?" Gloria took off her glasses, peered into the lenses, and wiped them with a tissue.

"He's twenty."

"I don't see the problem." Satisfied with her glasses, Gloria returned them to her face.

"The school board has a rule against teacher and student relationships outside of class. They want to fire me. And have put me on leave."

"Many districts still have those clauses," Gloria said, shrugging. "They're easy to get around unless the student is under sixteen, the age of consent."

"The principal says it's against district rules. Teachers and students."

"State laws take precedence over school district rules, Alison. It won't get far in the court system, but it may snarl up your life a bit." Gloria tapped on her notepad. "I'd like to talk to this boy, man."

"Henry Comstock," Alison said. "HB." Rob.

"I think we can get around the board and get you working again."

Alison exhaled some of the tension.

"Let me talk to Henry."

Alison wrote down Henry's address, and telephone number, slid the paper to Gloria, and let out her breath. "I will."

Chapter 56

HB/Rob

HB/Rob went outside to get the morning newspaper his mother still insisted on subscribing to, but he wished he hadn't seen the headline. Hutchins' murder was front and center. He opened the paper, smoothed it out, and began reading:

LOVE TRIANGLE MURDER

Teacher Alison Larkin, and Henry Comstock, her teenage lover, allegedly plotted and then killed Mark Hutchins, a popular Biology teacher at Clearwater High School. Mark Hutchins, the spurned lover, turned in Alison and Henry to school officials after seeing them in a compromising position. People reportedly overheard Henry vowing he was going to kill Mark Hutchins. It appears the student and teacher plotted to kill the Biology teacher. Henry is out on bail. This is a developing story, and we will report on the latest updates.

HB/Rob grimaced. The newspaper had the details all wrong as usual. Where had they gotten this information? Popular Biology teacher? Was Mark Ali's spurned lover who saw them in a compromising position? Had he comforted her? Was compassion a compromising position? Come on. Alison's mother had died a month earlier! He was glad Hutchins was out of the picture, but he didn't wish him dead.

And then he thought about the Moonglow. And did he still have a job there? They had taken his phone for evidence, so there was no way of contacting him. He wanted to keep his job, but the Moonglow either would or wouldn't want him after what had happened.

In the distance, HB/Rob heard his mother answer the house phone.

"Henry? There's someone who wants to speak to you."

He left the bedroom and took the phone from her hand.

"Hello?"

It was Alison's lawyer, Gloria, trying to help Alison get back to work.

HB/Rob sensed his mother hovering just around the doorway, listening.

"Yes, I've given the police my statement."

She continued asking questions.

"It was consensual." There was a pause as Gloria wrapped up the telephone interview.

"Thank you. I hope she gets back to work soon."

Later a police officer came to the door and knocked. It seemed everyone wanted to talk to him.

HB/Rob heard his mother invite the woman in. "We're still cleaning up the mess your people left!"

HB/Rob smiled.

"Henry! Someone else to see you!"

The officer handed him a summons for a lie detector test on Monday morning.

"I thought Alison Larkin's statement cleared me." He frowned at the summons.

"It's standard procedure," Officer Garcia said.

HB/Rob hadn't considered they'd make him take a lie test. What kind of questions would they ask, and would he know what to say?

HB/Rob wasn't sure how accurate the test would be. Did he answer the questions as HB or Rob? The line was blurred between his two soul personalities. He wasn't sure why he was doing this. Lie detector tests were faulty on many levels. A lie detector test wouldn't prove guilt or innocence. And he knew lie detector tests were rarely used in court.

They arrived at the Clearwater police station. His mother drove him because his truck was impounded. As they parked, HB/Rob scanned the building. The four-story white complex with small windows looked modern and stark, contrasting with some of the historical houses they had passed.

HB/Rob gave his name as Henry and followed a detective for his polygraph test. "We're going to start with some baseline questions. Name, date of birth, address."

When they finished those, the officer asked, "Have you ever been involved in illegal activity?"

Here was the sticky part. Had HB been involved in illegal stuff?

"I don't know," he answered truthfully. "I was in a bad accident, and my memory has holes."

"Have you been involved with drugs?"

Again, HB/Rob shrugged and repeated his answer about his faulty memory and the accident.

"Do you take drugs?"

"Prescriptions or otherwise?" he asked for clarification.

"Either."

"Yes."

"Did you take part in the murder of Mark Hutchins?"

"No way!" he answered. "Sorry." He sat straight up. "No!"

"Do you know who murdered Mark Hutchins?"

"No."

They finished, and he was led into another room to wait. A detective slipped through the door and sat down. The look on the officer's face told HB/Rob he had failed the test as he had expected.

"I failed, didn't I?"

"That's only one aspect of determining if you're guilty or not."

"I'm not guilty. I was with Alison." HB/Rob leaned forward. "What's happening with the blue Ford?"

"Looks like it was a rental."

"Then that's your murderer!" he insisted.

"The car was rented under a fictitious name," the officer said.

They had ways of determining who it was, he was sure.

"Prints?" HB/Rob asked.

The officer cleared his throat. "Yes, we're running them now."

"Is there anything else you need from me?" HB/Rob asked.

"We'd like you to surrender your passport."

HB/Rob snorted. "Passport? I don't have a passport!"

"Don't leave the area," the officer continued.

He wasn't planning to go anyplace.

"We have more questions." The officer shuffled his

papers. "Do you have a lawyer?"

HB/Rob looked at his hands. He seriously doubted the $2,500 in his savings account would get much of a lawyer.

The officer said, "One will be assigned to you if you don't have one."

"Can…can I go now?" HB/Rob asked.

The officer studied HB/Rob. HB/Rob pushed back his hair and revealed his scar. It usually elicited sympathy from most who saw it.

"Yes, we'll be in contact." The officer set down his pen and folded his hands.

"And the lawyer?" HB/Rob asked.

"That too."

He got into their car, where his mother turned to him with a frown. "Well, what happened? Was it like on TV?"

"A bit."

"Can I use your phone to call the Moonglow?" His mother handed him hers, an outdated phone with scratches on the face. "Hi. HB. I just wanted to check the schedule."

The hostess sounded flustered. "Just a minute. Let me get the boss." HB/Rob frowned as his mother drove.

"HB, so sorry to keep you waiting, but we can't have you working at the Moonglow with the murder charge hanging over your head. Not good for business."

Damn, he said to himself. "So I don't have a job?"

"Afraid not."

The money would be especially tight. It didn't matter that HB didn't do it. He was already labeled as "tried and convicted."

He looked over at his mother, whose fists tightened

on the wheel in a white-knuckle grip. "You heard?"

"Yeah," she said. "You don't have a job anymore."

Chapter 57

Alison

Alison sat on the couch with her telephone close by in case HB/Rob called. If his mother had allowed it, Alison would have gone to their house. HB/Rob's mother's words were still fresh in her mind from the ride to the police station.

Instead, it was Marilyn that called.

"So…" Marilyn dragged out the word.

Alison heard Marilyn exhale noisily and could tell she had something secret to say to her. Alison hoped it was about the murder.

"I'm not supposed to share this, but they found the blue rental abandoned by the airport and have processed it for prints."

"Do they know who rented it?" Alison gasped, leaning forward in anticipation. HB/Rob could be cleared!

Marilyn paused dramatically. "They are still searching for information. I do know it was a woman! They found long strands of blonde hair."

"Really?" Alison's mind immediately went to Mark's ex. "His ex-wife, do you suppose?"

"I'm not sure. Could be. Do you know anything about her?"

"Nothing except she lives in Houghton with her new

husband and daughters."

"They found incriminating information on Mark's computer, and the Houghton police are searching the house."

What sort of incriminating information? "Anything you can share?"

"No, Emerson didn't tell me what they found."

Alison tilted her head back and ran her free hand through her hair. What kind of stuff had they found on Mark's computer? She knew he was mad at his ex-wife and had a volatile temper.

What kind of woman was Mark's ex-wife? If she had stood up for herself, as Alison had done, she was sure there would be fireworks.

"Marilyn, I need to tell you something." She blew her breath. "Can you come over? This isn't something I should tell you over the phone."

"Now, you're scaring me! I'll be right over."

Marilyn arrived thirty minutes later.

Alison motioned for her to sit on the couch. Alison sat opposite her in a chair, clasping and unclasping her hands. "This will sound way out there," Alison began and stopped. "You know that I bought that book about spirit communication?"

Marilyn lowered her chin in a nod.

"I think HB has Rob's spirit in him."

Marilyn's mouth hung open. "What did you say?"

"You heard me."

"How did you come to that conclusion?"

"Lots of things. It started on the first day of classes when he called me Ali."

"That doesn't mean anything." Marilyn folded her arms defensively.

273

"Then he wrote an essay about something that happened eighteen years ago."

Marilyn frowned.

"He knew other stuff," Alison said, dropping her head and studying her clasped hands. "We're involved."

Marilyn studied her. "Involved?" She sat up, straightened, and lengthened her neck as if to see better. "Oh, my gosh. You and HB Comstock?"

"Yes."

After a long pause, Marilyn continued, "You're jeopardizing your career."

Alison considered teaching on the one hand and HB/Rob on the other. HB/Rob won over teaching. Maybe it was time to write that best-selling novel. Perhaps it was time to tell their story. Would that be classified as science fiction?

"I don't know what to say," Marilyn finally said after another long pause.

Alison watched Marilyn's jaw muscles move like she was having trouble with the words.

"I hope you know what you're getting yourself into." Marilyn stood and picked up her purse, her face stony and unbelieving.

"If you hear anything else about the murder case, will you call me?" Alison asked.

"Of course." Marilyn stopped with her hand on the doorknob. "I'm worried about you, Alison."

"It'll be fine," she said softly.

With that, Marilyn left.

In a way, it was good to tell someone, get it off her chest. If Marilyn reacted the way she did, Alison could imagine Steve and others would have far different responses. Had it been a mistake to tell Marilyn?

****

Alison had called HB/Rob repeatedly and got voice mail each time. Where was he? Surely they didn't put him in jail with his airtight alibi.

Someone knocked on the door, and out of habit, she looked out the curtains for Mark's SUV but saw an unfamiliar car. She peeked out the door, and when she saw it was HB/Rob, she flung it open and fell into his arms. "I've been calling," she said, tears flowing as she nuzzled his neck.

"They have my phone."

"I've got so much to tell you," she said and pulled him in.

"Good news?" He rubbed at his neck and made his way over to the couch.

"I spoke to Marilyn earlier, and they've recovered the rental car, and now they're searching Mark's ex-wife's house in Houghton." She clasped his hands in hers. "You should be cleared soon!"

"I didn't pass my lie detector test," he said, shoulders slumping.

She frowned. "Why not?" Alison sat up straight and cocked her head at him.

"Half the questions I couldn't answer." He threw up his hands in frustration. "Do I answer as HB or as Rob?"

"I didn't think of that." She sat next to him and automatically reached for his hand.

"When I'm HB, I can't remember much of anything."

"Then I guess you're stuck with Rob."

He absently rubbed her fingers as they talked.

"I hope they clear you soon." She gave him a tight smile before biting her lip in worry.

"Me too." He moved his shoulders around.

He looked tense to Alison, and she reached over and began to massage his shoulders. Knots relaxed, and he gave a low moan.

They both looked at each other—the shock of the last few days on their faces. HB/Rob had a crease between his brows and red-rimmed eyes, and when Alison looked in the mirror, she noticed her mouth was dipped at one corner with worry.

"I told Marilyn about us."

He raised his brows. "How did she react?"

"I should have expected her to think I was insane or off my rocker!"

"As much as I hate to leave Clearwater. I think we'll have to," he said.

"There's not much keeping me here," she confessed. "I might not have a job if the district pushes the teacher/student thing. Gloria didn't think they had a leg to stand on, but it could be a messy court trial."

"I'm going to take the GED test as soon as possible," he said, reaching up to take her hands that still massaged his shoulders.

"I can coach you?"

"Do you think I need tutoring?"

She thought for a moment. "No, you'll do great!"

"Then I'll take the SATs and see if I can't go into college in the fall."

"It sounds like you have it all figured out," she said.

"Nope, there's one more thing."

She put her hands in her lap and tilted her head at him.

"I want to get married."

Married—the thought hadn't even crossed her mind

with this murder thing hanging over their heads. "Married," she said breathlessly.

"I want you as my wife."

"What will people say? I'm so much older."

"As I recall, marriage is between two people, and they are the only ones that matter." He got down on one knee.

Was he going to ask her now? She clasped her hands together and felt tears pushing against her eyelids.

"Will you?" he asked, untangling her hands and taking them in his.

He touched the engagement ring she wore on her right hand, slid it off, and moved it to the left. "My grandmother's ring," he said.

"Of course!" she said breathlessly, almost as tingly as the first time.

"I was hoping you'd say yes again." He touched the antique ring with an old-fashioned setting with swirls of diamonds surrounding the center stone.

Alison felt the tears begin. "I know. I love that ring."

"But can you love me again?"

"I already do." She paused. "What will we do?" Her mind was going at warp speed—thoughts colliding with each other.

He held up her left hand. "There! It's official." He kissed her goodbye. "I better go and return Mom's car."

Chapter 58

Alison

The only sound was the television. Alison watched half-heartedly, hoping for a resolution to her leave and the murder charge hanging over HB/Rob. And, too, the house was lonely without her mother, with only memories and pictures to sustain her. She didn't even have schoolwork to distract her.

Finally, the phone rang. Alison muted the television and grabbed it, hoping it was HB/Rob. It was Marilyn. Did she have any news?

"Was it Mark's ex-wife, the one following him?" Alison asked. Her mind raced at warp speed, and she blurted out what was foremost in her mind.

"No, the prints don't match. The DNA is close but not exact. Maybe a relative?"

Alison chewed her lip as she listened. She vaguely remembered Mark telling her Barb went to Clearwater High School. Alison kind of remembered Barb had been Homecoming Queen, and everyone knew her.

"We went to high school together," she said. "But she was three years older."

"What was she like?" Marilyn asked.

"Popular!"

Then a memory popped into Alison's head. Barb had a sister—Belinda. Had they been twins? They were so different from each other that Alison had assumed they were cousins. Belinda worked as an aide in the library, was studious, and was a chess club member. Although the two looked similar, Barb wore makeup and the latest clothes, whereas Belinda never dressed up or wore makeup, a pale, uninteresting version of Barb. At least, that's what Alison thought at the time. Belinda seemed to blend into her surroundings, whereas Barb didn't. It was easy to overlook Belinda and focus on Barb.

Alison vaguely remembered they both went into the military after high school. Barb wanted to travel the world, and Belinda enrolled for a college education.

"Have they checked Barb's sister? Or maybe she was a cousin? But I think Mark said twin sister once."

There was silence at the end. "Emerson didn't say anything about a twin sister."

"Check it out. Her name is Belinda, but I don't know if she's married or not."

"Thanks!" Marilyn said. "I'll pass on that information."

Anything to help HB/Rob get out of this mess.

"And Marilyn…"

"I won't say anything to Steve about what you told me."

"Would he even believe it?" Alison asked.

"I don't believe it, and I'm into that sort of thing," Marilyn said, trying to make light of the HB/Rob thing, but ended by saying, "I've gotta go. Talk to you soon."

****

When HB/Rob came over later, Alison squealed when she opened the door for him. "I've got the most amazing thing to tell you!"

He sank into the couch and rubbed his neck. Logan Jefferson was the man, the lawyer, working his magic on HB/Rob's murder charge.

"Have your attorney check out Belinda, Barb Hutchins' twin sister."

"A twin? Didn't the cops check all leads?" HB/Rob lowered his head and ran his fingers through his curls as if scrubbing away images in his brain.

"I vaguely remember Mark saying his wife had a sister. It slipped my mind after everything that's happened. Marilyn's husband is going to check it out. The DNA was close but not a match."

"I'm thinking about DNA sequencing from medical school." He glanced off into space, and she could tell he was processing how his lips moved, and his forefinger rubbed his thumb.

Didn't this kind of twist only happen in the movies? Or detective novels?

They each remained quiet, lost in their thoughts. How convenient to have a twin sister do the dirty work. Maybe, just maybe, there was hope after all.

"I've got to call my attorney with this info."

HB/Rob took out his phone and called. "Alison told me Barb Hutchins has a twin sister. The cops haven't checked out that lead. Maybe she was the person following Mark?"

HB/Rob put the phone on speaker. "What do you think about the twin sister bit?"

"Might just be what we need to get you cleared," Logan's deep bass voice resonated from the phone.

HB/Rob grinned when he hung up, and so did Alison. She gave him a thumbs-up.

Chapter 59

Alison

As they waited for HB/Rob's attorney information on Barb's twin sister, Steve called and asked Alison to come to the school for a meeting. His voice was neutral, and he said he couldn't comment more over the phone. Her stomach flipped, never a good sign.

Something was up, and she was apprehensive, of course. She had been off for almost a month, and although she still received her salary, she couldn't help fretting over what could happen to her teaching career. She and HB/Rob would be leaving Clearwater at the end of the summer. She didn't want a black mark on her teaching record.

Alison went to the high school the following day and passed by adult education and was pleased to see three cars in the parking lot. The students weren't boycotting classes with the sub.

She parked, went inside, and said hello to several staff members she had once worked with. Before going into Steve's office, she checked her mailbox—only announcements and flyers for conferences. She dumped them all in the garbage.

"Alison!" Steve's secretary said, waving her arm. "He's waiting for you. Go right in."

Steve gave her a small smile and asked if she'd like

coffee.

"No, thanks." Alison waved a hand.

The atmosphere was chilly and formal—nothing like the old days. Alison sat, crossed one leg over the other, and waited for him to begin.

"The board voted to reinstate you until this matter can be sorted out."

"I see." Her foot jiggled as he talked.

"It has come to our understanding that Henry is an adult. The board has a clear policy banning romantic relationships between underage students and teachers."

As Alison listened, she jiggled her foot faster.

Steve continued, "The board wasn't sure about legal-aged students and teachers. It could be viewed as favoritism, but adult education is murky, a gray area."

Alison nodded, wondering where Steve was going with this rambling explanation.

"We're going to reinstate you, but not as a teacher. We'll have you at the district level doing clerical work but at your same salary."

She frowned. Not the answer she was expecting. "But what about my students?"

"I'm sure they'll work for a substitute until we can get things straightened out."

"But I'm a teacher, not a secretary."

"I'm not sure what the board's ultimate decision will be. Our attorney is looking into the legal aspects of it."

"What do you think, Steve? You've known me for a long time. Is this because of Rob?"

She thought she saw the almost imperceptible shake of his head. "You're different this year, Alison, and I'm worried." He leaned over his desk. "I think your judgment has been affected by your mother's death."

She stared at him, mouth gaping open, unsure how to respond. "This has nothing to do with my mother."

Steve remained quiet, his hands one on top of the other on the desk blotter.

"Is it so wrong I found love again?"

"No, but he's almost half your age and your student."

"Not for long. He will take his GED test, so he won't be in the class much longer."

"I'll share that with the board and see if that makes a difference," Steve said. "In the meantime, report on Monday morning to the district office at 8:00 a.m."

"You'll be hearing from my attorney." Alison pushed herself to stand, gave Steve a glare, before whirling around and stalking to the door. She'd have Gloria get on this right away.

"Alison," Steve called after her.

She stopped and held her hand out, cutting him off. "I'm not working at the district office. I'm a teacher! And I want to teach."

Steve's face paled, and he cleared his throat. "I'm sorry you feel that way."

"That way, Steve?" She folded her arms and tapped her foot.

"We thought you'd like to be back to work and earning your salary."

"How can Mr. Burns, in the Chemistry Department, have a DUI and still keep his job? Was he put on clerical duty?"

Carl Burns was the head football coach, that's why. He spent a short time in jail but kept his job. He was a menace and a threat to society. She couldn't recall him being penalized in any way.

"I can't discuss personnel matters with you." Steve's eyebrows shot up.

"It sure looks like discrimination to me!" She grabbed her purse, slung it over her shoulder, and stalked away. The secretary seemed surprised when Alison marched by. So was Marilyn, who was using the copy machine again.

"Alison!" Marilyn called. "I've got something to tell you."

Alison waved her hand, signaling she wasn't stopping to talk, but Marilyn followed her out of the building into the parking lot.

"You look upset," Marilyn said, folding her arms against the chill.

"Steve put me on clerical duty!"

"Why?"

"Because I've been..." How to phrase her relationship with HB/Rob. She blew out her breath. "HB."

Marilyn frowned. "I didn't say a word."

"I know you didn't. Mark saw HB comforting me and told Steve, who told the board."

"I'm still worried about you."

"Steve said I've changed this year." Alison moved her shoulders. "Maybe I have, but HB's changed since his accident."

Marilyn's brows rose in surprise. "He must have changed a lot."

"He's Rob now. And...I've fallen in love with him."

Behind them, the bell for the start of classes sounded, and Marilyn reluctantly turned away. "I'm still your friend."

"Thank you," Alison said before going to her car.

Clerical! She snorted. She didn't want to do clerical work. She was a teacher! And her students deserved to have her back.

In the parking lot, she sat in her car, caught her breath, and drove to the adult education building.

They were excited to see her. "Are you back?"

Alison shook her head. "I just wanted to see you."

There was a chorus of questions.

"No"—Alison raised her hand—"I'm not sure when I'll be back."

"We've missed you!" Cindy said, and there was agreement from the class.

"Thank you for going to bat for me at the school board meeting. That meant a lot to me."

A chorus of "Mmms" rippled around the class.

Alison turned to the substitute, who was watching with an amused look on her face. "I'm sorry to have interrupted the class."

"That's okay."

Alison looked around. No HB/Rob?

Cindy must have guessed who she was searching for. "He's at the district office taking his GED test."

Thank goodness. She could come back sooner rather than later.

Alison drove home, her stomach in knots from her conversation with Steve. The sensation of having to vomit came on suddenly—nerves, no doubt.

When parked, she fumbled with her keys to unlock the door while feeling like she would vomit. Once inside, she ran to the bathroom and spewed into the toilet. She rinsed her mouth and studied her now blotchy face, bloodshot eyes, and the hammering of her heart.

She splashed some water on her face and filled a cup

with water. She sat on the toilet seat, sipped the water, and waited for the churning in her stomach to quiet.

She brushed her teeth before calling Gloria. "I need your help."

"What do you need?"

"My job."

"Oh, dear."

"They want me to work as a secretary in the district office." Alison chewed a fingernail. She paced around as she talked, kicking off her shoes at one point and padding around on bare feet.

"What about your teaching position?"

"That's what I asked."

"Let me check the state regulations about teachers and students and see what the statutes say."

"Thank you, Gloria."

"I hope being with this guy is deserving of all the trouble," she said with a laugh, not an unkind sound, though.

Having Rob back was worth all the hassle.

The day stretched out before her. First things first—coffee. Alison went to fix some coffee, but the smell made her stomach turn over. She closed the bag, put it back in the cupboard, and decided on tea with honey. Was it more than nerves? Or was she coming down with something?

Chapter 60

Alison

Later, Marilyn called. Marilyn had proved her friendship by sticking by her even when she learned the truth about her relationship with HB/Rob.

"Are you sitting down?"

She was. Alison was half lying/sitting on the couch, propped up against pillows with her legs stretched out before her, the book she was reading resting on her lap. On the table, within reach, was ginger ale and crackers. "I am. Why?" Her stomach still felt queasy.

"They located Belinda Collins."

Alison's breath stuck in her throat. "They did?" It came out as a croak.

"Yup!"

Alison could barely breathe. A lump threatened to render her speechless.

Marilyn continued, "Apparently, she and her sister hatched a plan to do away with Mark so Barb could keep the kids and not share custody."

Marilyn paused for a cough. "Belinda's prints were in the car, and a partial print on the murder weapon and the car tires match those found by Mark's SUV. There were incriminating messages in their texts. They're holding both of them, one for murder and the other as an accessory."

Alison's remembrances of Belinda and Barb were fuzzy from high school twenty years ago. "I don't remember her well from high school. She was studious and quiet."

"Now, she's a studious, quiet murderer." Marilyn chuckled, obviously amused with her humor.

And Barb was a social butterfly. At one time, Allison had envied her for her popularity, but she didn't now. Both would go to prison, it seemed.

What a twist to this story. Something from an Agatha Christie tale or her mother's favorite, Perry Mason. This was the stuff of fiction, not real life.

"So is R—I mean, HB off the hook?" Alison asked, her main concern.

"I think he'll be cleared."

Marilyn didn't sound very enthusiastic about HB/Rob's acquittal. She was undoubtedly still mulling over Alison's confession about HB having Rob's soul.

Alison could picture the headlines in the local newspaper. "Former Local Twins Plot Teacher's Murder. Henry Comstock Exonerated." It had a nice ring to it.

"That's great news, Marilyn!"

She couldn't wait to tell HB/Rob.

"I gotta go. The girls are home and want dinner. Talk to you soon."

Marilyn hung up as Alison whispered, "Thank you." And cast her eyes upward and thanked the heavens for the good news.

She set her phone down and picked up her book but had no desire to read. She couldn't wait to share the news when he was done taking the GED test. The results weren't always instantaneous, but…he'd have a pretty good idea if he had answered most questions correctly.

Alison went into her bedroom and rummaged around in the trunk in the back of the closet looking for her freshman yearbook and found the Collins twins' pictures side by side, looking nothing like each other. Only their blonde hair was similar. She wouldn't have guessed they were twins. They seemed so different from each other. She continued thumbing through the yearbook, reading what friends and teachers had written.

Rob: MY FOREVER VALENTINE.

Steve: YOUR FAVORITE SIDEKICK.

She grimaced at Steve's comments. He certainly wasn't her favorite sidekick anymore. Steve had changed, or maybe they both had? She couldn't reconcile him wanting her to work in the office. She closed the book, set it on the coffee table, and picked up the novel she had been reading, but her eyes closed, and she dozed until she heard the rap on the door and struggled off the couch.

When she opened the door, HB/Rob grinned down at her. "I passed!"

She struggled off the couch. "I knew you would!"

He frowned at the ginger ale and crackers. "What's up?" He took her by the shoulders.

"I'm excited, and my stomach is upset because of all that's been happening."

He felt her forehead. "You don't feel warm. Do you have a thermometer?"

She shook his hand away. "No. No. Marilyn called, and they have Mark's ex-wife and her twin sister in custody for Mark's murder."

"That's even better than passing the GED!" He sat next to her and put his arm around her shoulders.

He studied her face.

"What?" she asked.

"You look different." He frowned and looked pointedly at the crackers and soda on the table. "What else is bothering you?"

"Nothing. I'm excited, is all."

He continued studying her before picking up her hand and kissing the underside of her wrist. "Could you be pregnant?" he asked softly and touched her engagement ring.

Alison blinked rapidly to keep the trickle of tears at bay. "I don't know. Do you think so?"

"I hope," he said.

It had been two years since the last pregnancy, but she could clearly remember the feeling of buoyancy at the person growing inside her. Did she feel that way now?

"Let's go buy a drugstore pregnancy test." He continued grinning. "My Ali." And patted her stomach.

Chapter 61

Ali and HB/Rob

They took Alison's car to the drugstore, and as they rounded a sharp curve, they came upon a vehicle up against a tree and a woman waving frantically. HB/Rob jammed on the brakes before rolling down the windows.

"Help us, please! I think my husband's had a heart attack!" A distraught and frantic woman waved at them.

Alison surveyed the situation. The car's front fender was crumpled against a tree. The driver's side door was open, and a gray-haired, ashen-faced man lay on the ground.

"I'll call 911," Alison said and fished out her phone.

HB/Rob jumped out, ran toward the man, and felt his neck.

The woman frowned at HB/Rob. "You're nothing but a kid. Do you know what to do?"

"I've had training," he said.

While Alison talked to the dispatcher, she watched HB/Rob spring into action.

"Roll him on his side, so he doesn't aspirate on his vomit."

They did so. HB/Rob checked the man's pulse.

"How do you know this stuff?" the woman asked, wringing her hands in frustration.

What was a plausible lie? He certainly couldn't tell

291

her he was a doctor in another life.

He concentrated on his work and listened to the man's breathing and heartbeats before rolling him on his back and beginning CPR.

"Do you know what you're doing?" the woman asked, tugging on HB/Rob's sleeve.

"Yes, I've had EMT training," he gasped in between breaths and compressions.

Alison remembered HB/Rob going through training right out of high school. Alison took the woman's arm and guided her away as HB/Rob worked on her husband. "It's going to be okay. He knows what he's doing."

"Your son?"

No use telling the woman anything else. "Student."

They stopped talking when the man vomited and coughed.

Presently, the ambulance rolled to a stop near them, and three paramedics jumped out, rushed forward with medical equipment, and took over for HB/Rob.

"Your quick thinking possibly saved this man's life," the attendant said to HB/Rob.

HB/Rob joined Alison and the woman near the road. He put his arm around her as they waited and watched.

"Thank you," the woman said to HB/Rob, "I don't know what we would have done without you."

"Are you going to be all right?" Alison asked.

"Yes, thank you. Our son's coming." The woman clutched at Alison's arm. "How can I repay you?"

"Help your husband recover, that's all."

HB/Rob shook his head as he wiped the dirt and vomit from his jeans from kneeling by the man. "Just want to help."

"You should be a doctor, you know," the woman

said.

They knew.

"Let me go home and shower," HB/Rob said.

Alison patted his arm. "I'll pick one up in the morning or see my doctor."

The following day, there was a small blurb in the Clearwater newspaper about Henry Comstock's heroic efforts in saving a man's life after a car accident.

Marilyn called. "I read about HB in the paper this morning." She paused. "I could hardly believe he saved that man's life."

"He did. I told you he'd changed."

"You told me he was Rob."

"Yes, and that's something Rob would have done."

"Oh, gosh, Alison. It is true!"

Chapter 62

Alison

Alison bought the pregnancy test, followed the directions, and watched as a result appeared. She hugged herself. Wait until she told HB/Rob. She scheduled an appointment with her gynecologist just to be sure.

She guessed it could have been stress from not teaching and the horrible ordeal with Mark's murder. She had spent two weeks pushing paper around, answering telephones, and taking messages before Gloria convinced the district, with the help of a multi-million-dollar lawsuit, to reinstate Alison to her old job. It appeared as though HB/Rob would be cleared of murder charges and was scheduled to take the SATs next Saturday.

But Gloria's help had come at a cost. Alison had spent most of Rob's insurance money on legal fees and bail.

They were sitting at the kitchen table, and Alison was quizzing HB/Rob for Saturday's test. She wanted to tell him, but she didn't want him distracted. He kept glancing at her.

"Did you take the test?" he asked.

She realized she hadn't answered him because of the peculiar way he looked at her. His head tipped slightly to one side with brows raised.

"I did."

He raised his brows further before taking her hand.

"I don't want to distract you."

"And you think not knowing isn't distracting?"

"It was positive," she said, squeezing her eyes shut, but she felt him get out of his chair and put his arms around her. She burst into tears. A chance at parenthood again!

"Shh! What's the matter?"

"Mother isn't here to be a grandmother."

"I know, and I'm sorry." He put his hands on either side of her face and held his nose to hers.

Alison sniffed.

"I'll take good care of you!" He nuzzled her neck and ear before their lips melted together.

****

When Alison returned to school the next day, Cindy said, "You seem different."

Alison shrugged. "I've been through a lot." And she had a secret lurking in her body, making her feel self-contained and smug at her good fortune. How many people had a second chance at love?

"True," Cindy said, giving her a look of speculation, eyes penetrating and searching. "I imagine it was tough working in the office answering phones."

"It's not a place I ever want to go again." Alison folded her arms, leaned against her desk, and willed herself to stop touching her stomach. It was good to be back in the classroom and keep her mind focused on something else besides the baby and her life with HB/Rob.

"You just have a more confident air."

"I just appreciate having my job back." And she had

fought for it, or rather, Gloria had.

Cindy grimaced with a pout. "I wish HB hadn't taken and passed the GED test."

"Didn't he promise to come back and help?" Alison asked, picking up and studying some papers on her desk.

Cindy nodded. "He's taking his SAT on Saturday."

Alison shook her head. "Yup, he sure is! I've been tutoring him."

But he didn't need her help.

Cindy grinned. "Wish him luck for me and tell him I need his help in math."

"I'll pass that on."

Later as she and HB/Rob worked at her kitchen table on questions for the SAT, she relayed Cindy's good wishes.

"That was nice of her." He looked up from the manual. "How's everyone doing?"

"They miss you."

"I'll stop by next week and say 'hi.' " He turned his attention back to the test questions.

"They'd like that." Alison rubbed her neck and moved her shoulders around.

"Do you want to take a break?" HB/Rob asked, pushing away from the table and massaging his back before kneading her shoulders. "This is getting kind of monotonous."

Alison agreed as she stifled a yawn behind her hand. She reasoned it was close to bedtime, but when she looked at her watch, it was only seven o'clock.

"Maybe you need to go to bed?" HB/Rob asked, taking her hand.

He was going to make a good doctor and father.

He nuzzled her neck. "Why don't I tuck you in?"

"Why don't you spend the night with me?" She felt the heat move through her body at the thought of him in bed with her.

"I'll send my mother a message I won't be home tonight."

"That's sweet of you." She was already shedding her clothes and would sleep naked.

"I owe her that much," he said, shucking his clothes after sending the message to his mother.

She stroked his scars and kissed the mark on his forehead.

Even though she was tired, she awoke to his touch as his fingers stroked circles on her belly before leaving to explore more.

Chapter 63

HB/Rob

HB/Rob had been spending most of his time at Alison's. He didn't want to go home in the dead of night and wake up his mother, so now, she begrudgingly accepted the new living arrangements. But he worried about her. She seemed to drag herself to work and back and didn't watch her favorite television shows. He needed to be there for her until he and Ali left. His mother had done everything for him. He owed her the peace of mind that he was here for her.

He and Alison were finishing breakfast when his phone pinged. He ate with gusto, whereas she picked at hers, eating a small bite of toast and ignoring the eggs. She sipped a little orange juice, eating sparingly, and he worried about her health.

HB/Rob squinted at the unknown number but answered anyway. "Hello?"

"Hey! Henry, this is Logan."

Was his lawyer's call just a formality? Alison's source said the charges were dropped. He hoped there would be something in the newspaper heralding the news so he wouldn't have a cloud hanging over him.

"I talked to the judge, and the state has dropped all the charges."

"I heard it was the ex-wife's twin sister who did it,"

HB/Rob said and winked at Alison.

Ali watched intently as HB/Rob spoke to Logan, a quizzical look on her face, to which he mouthed "love you," and she grinned at him.

"Certainly an interesting twist, don't you think?"

"Saved me!" He winked again for Ali's benefit and saw her eyes light up.

"Yes, it did."

"Great! Thank you!"

Now it was a done deal and not just hearsay, the facts getting skewed, like the game of telephone they played as kids.

"Keep yourself out of trouble," Logan said with a laugh.

"You betcha!"

"You are officially cleared?" Alison asked when he put the phone back in his pocket.

"Yup!" He hoped she'd feel up to what he had in mind.

The telephone call cinched it, and he finished studying for the SAT.

"I'm not studying anymore," HB/Rob said. "Let's do something fun today! How about we go to Grand Rapids, visit Meijer Gardens, have lunch, and kick around?"

The Gardens, Frederic Meijer Gardens, had been a favorite of Alison and Rob's. Ali and Rob liked to walk hand in hand, staring in awe at flowers and plants and the impressive art installations.

They drove there, parked, went in, then strolled through the displays. "I can't believe I still feel so grounded and calm when I'm here," Alison said. The fresh aroma of the plants and flowers commingled into an enticing aroma and made Alison think of new life, budding bushes and trees, and the rebirth in her belly.

"I'm glad you suggested this," Alison said, marveling at the abundance of flowers on display held in climate-controlled rooms so they would thrive in their natural environment. She bent over to take in the aroma before standing and smiling at him.

"I knew we liked it here. The perfect place to celebrate the baby before taking my SATs and making college applications."

Alison's stomach grumbled. "Let's have some lunch."

They drove to a favorite Italian café that had once been "La Strada," but it was now called "Luciano's."

"How disappointing," Alison said. "I can't believe it closed!"

"Let's try this new place."

A cheery bell chimed, greeting them with a familiar interior. A wine bottle on each table held a candle, and the wax had dripped down the side. The atmosphere was the same as before, and the smells—tomatoes, red wine, and oregano beckoned, and they were seated.

They ordered iced tea as they looked at the menu. Alison had already decided on Chicken Piccata, her favorite. And she assumed HB/Rob would get the Chicken Parmigiana. A waiter wearing a red and white checked apron took their order.

"Let's talk about our future," HB/Rob said, taking her hand across the table.

She felt her heart beat faster.

"I was thinking we should get married soon."

"Soon?" She took a sip of her tea with one hand, holding his with the other.

"The sooner, the better." He squeezed her hand. "That calls for a celebration!" He held up his iced tea, Alison did the same, and they touched glasses.

"A new start!"

Alison's heart lurched. "No dying on me," she said firmly.

"I won't. I'll be on the lookout for new drivers and foggy nights."

"Good. I don't want to lose you again."

"Let's go home and tell my mother."

"Will she be happy for us?" Alison asked, unsure how HB/Rob's mother would take the news. Her twenty-year-old son and thirty-four-year-old teacher were expecting a baby. It did seem as if Alison had robbed the cradle.

"I'm sure she'll be upset, but I think she'll be excited to be a grandmother."

****

"We have something to tell you, Mother," HB/Rob said, taking Ali's hand and guiding her to the couch where they sat holding hands.

His mother had just returned from work and struggled out of her jacket before frowning at their entwined hands.

"Alison and I are getting married."

His mother slumped back into the chair. "But, Henry, this is all so sudden!" Then she leaned forward as if to get a better look at them. "What do you and she"— she pointed to Alison—"have in common?"

There was so much. They nurtured each other, loved the simple things in life, the butterflies in the spring, baseball, long walks, a good book, they lit a fire in the other (but wouldn't tell her that!)—they completed each other's sentences. What more could they ask for?

Simply, he said, "She completes me."

"I don't understand any of this, Henry." As she talked, her head moved side to side in denial and disbelief. "You haven't been the same since you came out of that coma."

Exactly.

"I'm not the same person. I've had time to examine what I want in life, and I want Alison by my side."

His mother frowned as if she hadn't heard them. But she remained quiet.

"And...we're going to have a baby," he said, squeezing Alison's hand ever so slightly.

"A baby?" his mother asked, her face skeptical, and then the look of understanding changed her features. "You don't have to get married to have a baby."

"I know. I asked her before we learned we were expecting."

"But you're only twenty and haven't finished your GED yet."

"I'm an adult and can get married if I want. And besides, I passed my GED test and am officially graduated from high school." He was sure he had mentioned passing the test to his mother.

His mother glared at Alison but softened as she said, "You passed?"

He looked over at Alison. Her face had paled slightly, and he saw her swallow and sink back into the cushions.

Alison said, "I love HB with all my heart."

"His name is Henry," she snapped.

"I love Henry." Rob. Whoever.

Maybe the first sonogram would sway her?

"I'm sorry, Mother. We thought you'd be pleased to be a grandmother," HB/Rob said.

"But she's almost my age!" his mother snorted.

"We'll monitor her pregnancy closely," he said. "She'll get the best care. I'm going to be a doting father."

His mother folded her arms. "And where did you learn to talk like that? You sound like a doctor or something. 'Monitor her pregnancy?' " She shook her head. "I don't understand the change in you!"

HB/Rob couldn't tell her the real reason for the personality change. "Remember I shared what the doctor told me about people coming out of comas speaking different languages?"

"Yes, but you're a whole different person."

"You said you liked the new Henry," he said.

"Yes, but the old Henry wouldn't be throwing away his life marrying a much older woman!"

The old Henry would be throwing away his life on drugs and probably go to prison for his actions. He rolled his eyes. Besides, they weren't throwing away their lives. They were making up for the lost time.

"You'll see. It's not a mistake. I love her." He held up Alison's hand and kissed her knuckles.

"Oh, God!" his mother wailed.

"I hope you'll accept our decision."

His mother bowed her head, sniffled, and began to cry. "I don't understand! Was I such a bad mother? Or is it because of your deadbeat father?"

HB/Rob got up and put his arms around his mother as she hiccupped and raged through her sobs. "It was nothing anyone did. Hush." He tightened his grip on her shoulders. "We fell in love and want to be together. Age doesn't make a difference."

She continued to wail, and Alison brought the box of tissues which she snatched from Alison's hand.

"I better go," Alison said, edging toward the door. "You and your mother need some time together."

HB/Rob nodded and kissed her on the cheek before returning to his mother's side.

Chapter 64

Alison

"Hey!" HB/Rob said, making smacking noises into the phone.

"Miss me?" Alison asked with a giggle, feeling almost as giddy as she had many years ago at the start of their high school relationship.

"Do I ever!"

"Any word yet?"

The SATs were last weekend.

"I keep checking my emails and the mailbox. So far, no word. Do you think that's bad?" he asked.

"No," she assured him. "I bet you did great!"

"I did have an advantage," he said.

"True. You took it seventeen years ago."

Later, HB/Rob arrived at the front door wearing a big grin and waving a piece of paper.

Alison gasped and clapped her hands together.

"I had an almost perfect score!" he said, kissing and twirling her around.

"That calls for a celebration," she said.

"What should we do?"

He shrugged. "Since I'm broke, it'll have to be cheap."

"How about a romantic dinner here tonight?" she suggested and moved her arm to encompass the kitchen and dining room.

"Sounds great!" he said.

****

Life was beginning to take on a more normal routine. Alison wasn't on pins and needles about the murder charge. She had shared with Marilyn about her relationship with HB/Rob. It felt good to get that off her chest and tell someone about their soul transfer.

The phone rang with good news, not updates on Mark's murder.

"Hello," Marilyn said. "Can you go shopping next Sunday and out to lunch?"

"Sure thing!" Alison exclaimed, still excited about HB/Rob's SAT score, impending motherhood, and marriage.

"What's happening with you?" Marilyn asked.

Alison took a deep breath before responding.

"Are you still there?" Marilyn asked.

"I'm pregnant."

Now it was Marilyn's turn to take in a breath. "Oh, no!"

"Oh, yes! I'm thrilled." If Marilyn had been with her, she would have seen the broad smile that made Alison feel giddy with anticipation.

"Is it HB's?"

"You know it is." Rob's baby with HB's DNA.

"That was the last thing I thought you'd tell me."

"I figured I should tell you before word got around." Had anyone seen her at the obstetrician recently?

"Have you told Steve?"

"No."

"He's not going to be happy."

"I don't care. I'm finally going to be a mother!"

"I'm happy for you," Marilyn said. Her sentiments were heartfelt, but her tone was neutral.

"I'll see you Sunday?" Alison asked.

"Yes! You can tell me more then."

Marilyn shared her opinion about the subject when she and Marilyn went shopping.

They were looking at crocheted baby bonnets at the antique store when Marilyn grimaced. "You're doing this, aren't you?"

"Yes, I love him."

"What will you do?"

"He passed his GED and had an almost perfect SAT score, so he can pretty much write his ticket."

Marilyn stepped back from her and put her fists on her hips. "How on earth had he managed that?"

Alison shrugged, put the bonnet back, and moved toward an old-fashioned cradle. Was something like this practical these days?

"He's brilliant."

"He sure didn't act like it in my class," Marilyn said, frowning at an old-fashioned potty chair from a bygone era.

"Come on!" Alison huffed. "He had a terrible accident and a second chance at life. He has Rob's intellect!"

"I'll say!" Marilyn moved to a child-sized cup and saucer with the Peter Rabbit picture on the side. "This is cute."

Alison smiled and nodded.

Marilyn gave Alison an unexpected hug. "I hope it all works out for you, Alison. I hate to see you throwing your life away when he reverts to his old self."

"He won't. He's committed and wants to go to

medical school."

Marilyn quirked a brow and carefully replaced the cup and saucer. "Like Rob?"

"Not 'like Rob.' He *is* Rob."

"It's almost as if we're talking about two different people," Marilyn said.

"Now, do you believe me?" Alison asked.

"I did before, but wished I didn't."

The enjoyable time she and Marilyn had spent shopping and out to lunch vanished when she got a terse message from Steve: SEE ME ASAP.

On Monday, Alison crept into the office at noon, hoping he'd be too busy to see her. She didn't want his negative attitude to impact her feeling of euphoria of a baby.

He glanced up from his desk and motioned her to come in as he pushed the papers on his desk aside as if they were impeding his thoughts and said, "Close the door!"

She bowed her head but jerked it up. She didn't need his approval, she realized, and glared at him.

"Did you think people would accept you and that kid being together?" he said. No pleasantries. He just launched into it, scowling as he did.

"I don't care at this point, Steve."

"How can you do that to Rob's memory? He'd be insulted you chose that boy!"

"He reminds me of Rob."

"There's no way in hell!" Steve's face turned red, and he seemed to have trouble breathing, coughing and sputtering.

Oh, how she wished she could tell Steve HB was Rob. But would he understand? It had taken her months to believe it herself fully. She didn't know precisely how Rob had become HB, even though she read several books with plausible explanations, but would Steve? What would she say? "Steve, HB is Rob. Rob's soul moved into HB's body." A soul could move from one body to another if needed.

She waited until he was calmer and said, "I don't think he'd be insulted. I know he'd be pleased I found another wonderful man to love me." She thrust her jaw forward.

"He's not a man. He's a boy! A delinquent boy!"

"You're wrong, Steve. The accident changed him." She gestured wildly with her arms. "He's different."

"Ha! People are judging me by the actions of my staff. People doubt my leadership abilities because of you!"

"This isn't a reflection on you, Steve." She gestured, hoping to emphasize her words.

He continued her gestures and all. "Oh, it isn't, huh? I'm getting messages from parents questioning my judgment and criticizing staff on the relationships with their children. It may all be lies, but it makes us look unprofessional and not fit to teach." He glared at her.

She remained quiet, waiting for his tantrum to end and his face to return to its normal color. She sat looking at her fingers laced together in her lap. "We'll be leaving this summer for a new place. You won't have to worry about it next fall."

His mouth dropped open. "You're going to quit after this year?"

"Don't you think it's for the best?"

"No!" He threw up his hands. "I want you to stop this nonsense. You're the reason adult education is so well attended. The students love you—" He stopped after saying love you. "I meant they respect your caring manner and how you help each of them."

"I'm not staying, Steve. HB is applying for colleges, and we're moving as soon as he decides which one offers him the best scholarship."

"He thinks he's going to get into college?" Steve looked dumbstruck.

"He had an almost perfect score on the SAT."

"Did he cheat?"

"No!" Her face reddened. "I tutored him, but he did it on his own."

"There has to be some mistake."

"No, there isn't."

"Well," he said, still shaking his head and glaring at her. "Don't say I didn't warn you. If you leave and want to come back, I'm sure the board will deny your application with all the flak we're getting about you and your teenage lover!"

"He's not a teenager! He's twenty!" she shouted.

With that, she stood, smoothed down her skirt, and went back to adult education, where they loved her.

Steve had forgotten his exchange with HB about the hunting trip and having to hike out of the woods. Would Steve connect the hunting trip and the new soul? Probably not.

It seemed like most people weren't keen on her and HB/Rob being together again.

Chapter 65

Ali and HB/Rob

A few weeks later, Ali and HB/Rob set out for South Bend and Notre Dame early on Saturday morning. They drove US 31 along the Lake Michigan shoreline past Holland, Saugatuck, and Benton Harbor, where they saw glimpses of Lake Michigan, white caps frothing in the wind.

HB/Rob reached over, took her hand, and squeezed. His intense gaze seemed to look past her eyes and intrude into her thoughts. "Ready for our new life?"

Alison smiled. That phrase meant several things to her. Was she ready? Was anyone prepared for parenthood? Or for a move to a different state? She wasn't ready, but she was excited. They would figure it out together like the last time they had made a move from Clearwater.

"Yes."

"Good. You're quiet. No change of heart?"

"No." She patted her stomach and settled back in her seat. "I'm ready for something new." She turned toward HB/Rob. "I never realized how opinionated and backward some people are in Clearwater." She was thinking of Steve—once a good friend and now...She didn't care if she saw him again.

"Let's not burn any bridges—we might want to

311

come back," HB/Rob said.

She looked sideways at him. He was going to leave his mother behind. And Alison? No relatives to speak of in the area.

They crossed the state line from Michigan into Indiana. Ali rolled the window down and smelled the green of this fertile area: newly mowed grass, budding trees, and the pungent scent of cow manure.

South Bend was similar to Clearwater in some ways, only differing in size and Notre Dame's long shadow over the city. Folks in the Midwest were friendly, open people, and when she and HB/Rob stopped for a bite to eat, the waitress engaged them in a lengthy conversation.

Her name badge read "Stella."

"What can I get you, folks?" Stella stood with her pen poised over her pad to take their order.

"What is the soup of the day?" Ali asked.

"Creamy mushroom—a favorite."

Alison raised her brows and, when she didn't get a grumble from her stomach, said, "I'll try that." None of the diner's onions, bacon, and beef smells bothered her.

HB/Rob had a burger made with local cheese.

"You folks just passing through?" Stella asked.

HB/Rob tipped his head toward the street. "Thinking about attending Notre Dame."

Thinking? Alison was pretty sure they'd stay here.

"We're looking for a place to live."

"Try Georgetown."

Alison pursed her mouth. "Georgetown?"

"Not that Georgetown," Stella said with a laugh. "We have our own Georgetown."

Ali and HB/Rob looked at each other with raised brows.

"I'll get your order in," Stella said, placing her pen behind her ear and hurrying toward the kitchen.

"Would you like to stay here?" HB/Rob asked.

She tilted her head. "It has a small town feel in a big place."

"I was thinking the same."

"If we find a place to live, I vote for South Bend," Alison opened the straw and took a sip of her water.

"We'd only be four hours away from my mother."

"Do…do you…think she'll visit?"

"Once she meets the baby, I don't think wild horses will keep her away."

Alison giggled nervously.

"What's so funny?"

"This whole situation."

He shrugged. "Give it time. People will eventually accept us."

And if they didn't, Alison decided, who cared?

When they had finished lunch, Stella placed the bill on the table. "I hope you and your son will be happy here."

So that was the way it would be. Everyone assumed HB/Rob was her son, but that was okay, she guessed.

"You're quiet," HB/Rob said.

"Does it bother you that people think I'm your mother and not your girlfriend? I've got a few strands of gray hair."

He was quiet, thinking, and said, "To paraphrase Randy, I don't care about your hair!"

They laughed and said, "Always," together.

They held hands and continued on their way, driving slowly through the town and past the university. University towns were similar in their composition the

313

closer to campus they got. There were more bars, microbreweries, fast food places, and specialty coffee shops.

"What do you think?" HB/Rob asked after their second pass-through before pulling into a parking lot.

"I'll be happy any place you are."

"I always wanted to attend Notre Dame."

"It's a good school."

"I know." He shrugged. "I'll only go if they give me a full ride." He shook his head. "I wish I could play baseball for them." He felt his arm. "I don't have the right build for baseball."

"But you have the right build for me."

He turned to her with love and took her hand in his. "True. I was desperate for any body to get back to you. I should have been more specific and asked for a jock body."

Chapter 66

Ali

After they returned from South Bend and HB/Rob had accepted a full-ride scholarship from Notre Dame, Alison turned to her students and said, "This is my last semester teaching at Clearwater. I'm leaving for Indiana."

It seemed the right time to tell them her plans not to return. Spring was around the corner and, with it, new beginnings—for many things, not just her and HB/Rob.

Moans and shocked expressions followed her announcement.

"I'm expecting a baby too." She patted her stomach.

Wayne laughed. "And I thought you were gaining weight from eating too many chocolates!"

Alison gave him a shy smile. "Motherhood is a dream come true."

Cindy shook her head and laughed. "That darn HB! I've only got two more credits, and I'm finished, and I wanted you to give me my adult ed diploma." But Cindy looked pleased for them.

Alison smiled at the class. "You'll all be fine with or without me. Look how resourceful you were when I was on leave. You'll need to pull each other along. I'm counting on it."

With downcast eyes, they returned half-heartedly to

their work.

****

May was over, and they would be moving in a few short months. Alison had been packing up the house bit by bit. What to take and what to store, and what to give away? To keep the house and rent it out or sell? At this point, she didn't have the heart to sell her childhood home, so they'd rent it out.

On the last day of classes, Alison arrived to find the classroom festooned with balloons and streamers and music seeping under the doorway. She smiled as they yelled, "Surprise!" No doubt Cindy had arranged the party. But how had they gotten in to decorate? Who was the likely culprit? Probably the janitor.

She had overheard some whispering during classes, and when she came nearer, the whispering stopped, and everyone looked guilty. She suspected something was up, but not this. A card and flowers maybe.

Marilyn told her Steve wasn't planning on a going-away party for her after twelve years of service, and that was just as well. Marilyn walked to the adult education trailer and handed her a card, and Alison smiled at her old friend.

"I'm going to miss you," Marilyn said, giving her a quick hug. "Who am I going to shop with?"

"One of your daughters?"

"No," Marilyn shook her head sadly, surveyed the room, and reached over and squeezed Alison's hand. "I'd look pretty silly with ripped jeans and a stretch-mark-covered stomach hanging out!"

"I'll miss you too. We've been through so much." They stood looking awkwardly at each other. Goodbyes were hard.

"Would you like something to eat?" Alison moved her hand over the table laden with snacks, a cake, and all sorts of food.

"Looks good." Marilyn helped herself to a handful of nuts and pretzels mixed with cereal.

"How about a slice of cake to eat later?" Alison offered.

"And let Steve see me with 'going away' cake?" Marilyn asked in mocked horror.

"I don't want you to get in trouble."

"I'll take some cake," she said and laughed.

Alison fixed Marilyn an extra big helping of cake and hugged her.

"You'll come to visit?" Marilyn asked.

"Of course. Ro—er, HB's mother's here, and we'll come with the baby."

"I'll look forward to holding your baby," Marilyn said simply with love and emotion, making her voice crack.

Chapter 67

HB/Rob

Summer blossomed in western Michigan, the trees flowering along with Ali's rounded belly. Everything was awakening, it seemed. Birds were busy with their newest offspring, quarreling and chasing after the marauding jays.

After the first sonogram, HB/Rob shared the picture with his mother. "See, here she is."

"It's a girl?" His mother had an incredulous look on her face as she peered closer at the picture. "A girl," she breathed.

"Yup, so it appears."

"A little girl," his mother whispered. "I always wanted a girl."

HB/Rob knew his mother had secretly harbored the desire to have a daughter and knew she was thinking of pink dresses and hair bows by the way her eyes darted around and clasped her hands together.

"Think of how much fun you'll have dressing her up." He knew he was baiting her and getting her to accept Alison and the baby as her own.

HB/Rob could tell his mother was dreaming of fairy princess dresses. He had hooked her and now to reel her in.

"You'll be the only grandparent," he said.

"What about your father?"

HB/Rob shrugged. "I've not heard from him. You?"

She shook her head. "Thought he had a new family."

Screw his father. "You'll get to spoil her." His mother looked away, her eyes misty and her mouth pursed. HB knew from experience she was imaging something wonderful—a grandchild all her own to love and spoil.

"Oh, yes." She nodded.

When it was time to schedule the second sonogram, HB/Rob asked his mother if she'd like to come.

"But does she want me there?"

"Call her Alison, not she," he said with a smirk, "and maybe she'll want you there."

"Okay. Alison. Does Alison want me there? I haven't been very excited about you two." His mother clasped her hands together and lowered her head in contrition.

HB/Rob untangled her hands, took her right one, and squeezed. "Of course, she hopes you'll be a big part of our baby's life."

His mother appeared to digest and turn this information over in her mind. HB was familiar with his mother's moods. She was considering what he said by the way she moved her mouth and clasped her hands together.

"Maybe I should have her over for dinner and get to know her better," his mother said while chewing on her bottom lip. HB/Rob pulled up the first sonogram on his phone and showed her again. His mother covered her mouth as if she didn't know what to say about the blurry picture of her granddaughter.

"I'm sure she'd love to get to know you better too."

"I'd like to come to the sonogram," she whispered, touching the screen of his phone and looking again at the baby shaped like a lima bean.

Bingo. His mother was on board with the baby. Would she agree to attend their wedding?

First things first, and dinner needed to be a success.

Several nights later, HB/Rob and Alison arrived for dinner, holding hands. HB/Rob sniffed the air—Chinese.

His mother greeted them and shyly nodded to Alison. "I'm sorry I didn't cook, but I couldn't get away from work. I hope you don't mind Chinese."

"Chinese is wonderful!" Alison said enthusiastically. She appeared to accept take-out for dinner without hesitation.

HB/Rob led Alison to the sofa and pulled over an ottoman for her to prop her feet. "I'll get you something to drink."

He returned with sparkling water, lemon, and a glass of wine for his mother.

His mother sat across from the sofa and leaned forward as if she had questions.

"I-I don't know much about you, Alison, but people at the bank say you're very nice."

"Thank you." She sipped on her water and looked over the glass at HB/Rob's mother.

"One of the tellers got her GED with you several years ago. Callie Baldwin."

"Oh, yes! I remember Callie. How's she doing?"

"Training for a management position and taking some college classes." HB/Rob's mother clasped and unclasped her hands. "Callie said we'd get along."

To her credit, Alison remained quiet but smiled at his mother and sipped her drink.

HB/Rob watched the expression on his mother's face. The way she moved her lips, he could tell she was thinking things over and trying to decide if she liked Alison or not.

What wasn't to like about Alison? She was beautiful and looked to be twenty-five, not thirty-four. She was intelligent and caring, and he loved her for all those things.

"What...what do you and Henry like to do?" she asked.

Alison leaned forward, cupping her glass with her hands. "We're crazy about Meijer Gardens."

"Me too!"

"Why don't we all go together before the exhibit leaves?" HB/Rob asked.

"That would be wonderful," his mother said, giving Alison a shy smile. "Maybe we could even go shopping for baby clothes in Grand Rapids?"

"Oh, yes!" Alison agreed.

And just like that, the two ladies had become friends.

The following week they visited the butterfly exhibit and went shopping for some pink baby sleepers. While at dinner, Alison slipped HB/Rob's mother a handwritten invitation to the wedding.

"Oh my!" his mother gasped.

"We'd like your blessing," HB/Rob said.

"When?"

"Right before we leave for South Bend."

In South Bend, HB/Rob would attend college classes, and after the baby was born, Alison was offered a position teaching English at a private Catholic high school. Alison could put the baby in the daycare run by the university when she returned to work.

His mother put her hand to her chest. "I guess you'll go through with it whether I'm there or not." She looked from Alison to HB/Rob. "I'll be there," she said after a long pause.

"We'd love that," Alison said, snaking her hand toward his mother. With a shaky smile, his mother touched the offered hand and squeezed, signaling an agreement.

Chapter 68

HB/Rob and Ali

As they sat at breakfast one morning about a week before their scheduled wedding, HB/Rob asked, "Is there anyone else we should invite?" He frowned. "Your friend from school? Marilyn?"

Ali shook her head. "No, just the three of us are perfect." She wiped her eyes.

"If you're sure?" He tipped her chin upward. "What's the matter?"

"I wish Mother was here."

He put his arms around her and squeezed. "She'll be with us in spirit, I'm sure."

On the morning of their appointment with the judge, Ali and HB/Rob walked hand in hand toward the courthouse, his mother trailing behind, holding a large bouquet of pink tulips for the bride. HB/Rob couldn't stop grinning and wanted to pump his fist in the air and shout to the world, "We're getting married again!" He felt his mouth would break in two from his happiness. Alison squeezed his fingers while leading the way with her ready-to-pop belly.

A little girl.

He couldn't believe his good fortune!

In the judge's office, they stood before a kindly man whose eyes twinkled as he studied her shifting belly.

"Due any time now?" he asked, pushing up the glasses slipping down his nose.

"Yes," Ali said as HB/Rob placed his hand on her abdomen. The baby girl responded with a kick.

"I think she knows her daddy!" HB/Rob said.

"She does," Ali mouthed.

"And who is your witness?"

So far, his mother had been quiet. "I am!" HB/Rob's mother said, handing Alison the tulips. "I'm going to be a grandmother."

"A wonderful experience," the judge said. "I've got three myself!"

HB/Rob gripped Ali's hand tighter.

"Let's get on with it, folks, and have you married before you become parents and…grandparents!"

Before the judge, they continued holding hands and smiling at each other before he pronounced them man and wife. They slipped on the bands and kissed.

This time, it was different from the first wedding when Alison wore a long white gown as her mother walked her down the aisle.

This time, his mother hugged them. "I wish I could go with you, but I've got to return to work."

"Thanks, Mom, for all your help!"

She kissed each of them before leaving. She turned to study the couple at the door. "I love you all! I'll be there for the baby!"

HB/Rob crooked his arm. "My wife. I've been waiting a long time to say that, and I won't be apart from you again."

"Have a good marriage," the judge called as they left.

"We will!" HB/Rob turned to Alison. "I can't wait

to see what the future holds for us." He tightened his grip on her hand and nodded toward her stomach. "And for her. I won't be apart from you anymore!"

The van was packed and parked outside city hall. HB/Rob helped her in before starting the van. "Can you fasten your seat belt?"

"I'll try." Ali tugged and just barely fit it under her stomach.

They had rented a two-bedroom apartment in South Bend, and Alison had a job when she finished her maternity leave. A promise from his mother to help when the baby was born—only a few weeks to go and the baby had shifted downward, making it uncomfortable to walk or sit or sleep.

HB/Rob maneuvered the van out of the parking lot. The road leading away from Clearwater took them past the high school and the adult education building with the "Walk-ins Welcome" sign.

"Are you going to miss it?" HB/Rob asked, squeezing her fingers over the center console.

"Yes and no. The only people I'll truly miss are Marilyn and my students."

"We're going to have a good life. I can feel it," HB/Rob said with more bravado than he suddenly felt. His stomach tightened suddenly. Why was he responding this way? He gripped the wheel, looked at the speedometer, and kept it right at 55. He didn't want anything to spoil their trip to a new life. But this was the same road he had been killed on before. Of course, he was apprehensive.

"This road makes me nervous," he admitted, a bead of sweat popping out on his forehead. The winding road with hairpin turns and blind spots had caused many accidents, including his.

"That was a foggy night," Ali reminded him.

Since his accident, he had driven this road many times, so why the feeling of apprehension? Was it because they were leaving? Was he worried about leaving Clearwater?

The logical part of his brain knew he was being silly. The road was void of cars, and the sky was blue and cloudless. A perfect day for a drive, so why the needling in his gut?

He mentally checked himself, berating himself for thinking thoughts of gloom and doom on their wedding day.

In the distance, he saw a car, not unusual, but the car seemed to be weaving over the center line. Maybe his eyes were playing tricks on him? The vehicle was a distance away.

"Do you see that?" Ali asked, gripping his arm.

"I do."

This couldn't be happening again, not after all the trouble he had gone through to get back to Ali. He should know what to do. The first time the car had blindsided him, he hadn't expected the collision. This time he could react and get out of the way.

He slowed, hugging the right side by the barrier, but a truck was on his bumper. HB/Rob put on the blinker, hoping the truck would go around them. The truck swerved around them on the blind curve when the oncoming car slammed into it, bouncing the truck in slow motion. HB/Rob only had time to catch his breath before the truck flipped into them, pushing the van down the embankment.

He leaned over as if to shield Ali from the flying

glass, the screeching sound the metal made as it hit the guardrail, rocks, and trees. Then the airbags deployed, smacking HB/Rob in the face. Alison shrieked. They were both pinned by the airbags. That was good, but why did he feel pain in his chest?

When the rolling stopped, he realized he didn't die this time. HB/Rob tried to push aside the airbag. "Ali! You okay?" he screamed.

She moaned.

He panicked. No! No. "Hold on. Let me see if I can reach my phone and call for help." He exhaled and willed himself to focus and stay positive. This accident was different from the last time. They were alive even though Ali hadn't spoken a word.

She moaned again and said, "Baby."

He finally was able to move his arm around to the pocket with his phone and told it to call 911.

"911, what's your emergency?"

"We've had a car accident. We're trapped, and my wife's pregnant."

"Can you give us your location?"

"We're past the Clearwater High School southbound. I think my wife might be in labor. Can you hurry?"

"Can you repeat that?" asked the operator.

"Just past the Clearwater High School by Beechwood Drive. Down in the embankment."

"Help is on the way."

"Hurry!"

"I'll stay on the line with you."

"Thank you." He felt for Ali's arm or hand and grasped it. "Ali! Can you hear me?" He squeezed her fingers.

A low moan. The van had tipped on the passenger side. "It hurts."

"Ali? Stay with me! Squeeze my fingers."

When she didn't respond, HB/Rob pushed aside the airbag and felt for her. She moaned again, as he touched her hand that was clenched around her stomach. He laid his palm on her spasming abdomen. "Help is on the way!"

The low whine in the distance signaled the paramedics were coming.

"Ali? I hear them."

Nothing. All was quiet outside the van. Even the birds stopped their calls. Everyone and everything waited silently.

He grabbed her arm and squeezed. "Hold on, baby!"

The crunch of tires signaled impending help and an army of footsteps hurried down the embankment toward them. "Help is here, Ali!"

"Everyone okay in there?" a voice called.

HB/Rob's vision was blocked by the airbag. "No, my wife's not responding!"

The driver-side door was pried open and three faces peered down at him. "What's your name, buddy?"

"Rob—I mean Henry. Henry Comstock, and that's my wife, Alison. We're expecting a baby soon."

"Alison, can you talk to us?"

No sound.

"Alison?"

A moan this time. A promising sign she was still responding.

They cut the belt from HB/Rob, helped him out, and placed him on the gurney. Then they began cutting away the front of the van to get to Alison. One of the paramedics started pushing HB/Rob toward the ambulance. "No! I don't want to leave her!"

"We've got to get you checked out. You might have internal injuries."

"I don't care about me. I know I'll be fine. I need to know she's okay!"

Mercifully, the man didn't push anymore. HB/Rob propped himself up and watched the jaws of life cut through the van getting closer to where Ali was trapped. He brushed away the hand with the blood pressure cuff.

"Alison, we're here to get you out. Can you talk to me?" an attendant asked.

HB/Rob strained to hear anything from her. Tears filled his eyes as he watched and waited.

The metal protested being cut and pried apart. The scraping sounds grated on his nerves, but he knew they were getting closer to rescuing Ali. Once done, they pushed a gurney over and carefully lifted Alison. She was covered in blood but clutching a pink tulip in her right hand.

"Ali! I love you!" HB/Rob shouted.

Thankfully he was rewarded by a low moan.

"We're going to airlift her to Grand Rapids."

"Can I go with her?" HB/Rob asked, swiping at the tears blurring and spilling down his cheeks.

"You can be with her. First, we need to get out of this ravine. The chopper won't be able to land here."

HB/Rob jumped off the stretcher, went to her side, and used the tail of his shirt to wipe the blood from her face. "I love you!" he told her.

She moaned and even managed a weak upturning of her lips. "Me, too," she whispered.

****

HB/Rob climbed up after the stretcher. It took four paramedics and firefighters to keep Alison level as they got to the mangled guard rail. At the top, he turned to look at the overturned van. One of the back panels had ripped open, spilling the contents. The baby's crib lay in pieces next to an overturned chair.

He turned back to Alison and took her hand. "You're going to be all right. Both of you!" The force of his words made her eyes flutter briefly. She heard him, he was sure.

The road had been blocked to traffic while they worked on Alison, the truck driver, and the person in the sedan. Moments later, the medical chopper, a huge white bird, throbbed overhead. The motion from the blades kicked up dirt and rocks. HB/Rob shielded Alison with his arms and whispered, "Hold on, baby. They'll get you fixed up in a jiffy."

The helicopter landed on the road.

****

Alison heard the voices and tried to speak, but she had a weight on her chest and spasms in her belly. Something metallic and sticky clung to her face and hair, and she smelled smoke. Dimly she thought the baby was coming. And where was HB/Rob?

As if being lifted by the wings of angels, she felt herself floating toward a giant white bird whose wings beat in the air with a *thump thump thump*.

"My baby," she whimpered.

"No worries, Alison. We'll take care of you and the baby."

The pressure descended toward her thighs. "She's coming!"

She was loaded into the bird when she heard, "The

330

head's crowning."

Finally, the pressure slid from her body. "A girl!" A voice exclaimed. Then she heard the baby's cry.

"Her name is Maxine for my mother," Alison whispered. "Irene Maxine. Maxi."

But they had heard. "Nice name," a faraway voice said.

"Maxi," Alison whispered again, her hand moving to her stomach.

They placed the baby on her chest, and she nuzzled her head. She couldn't see, but she knew the baby was beautiful. She remembered their stillborn baby and how beautiful she was too. "You came back," she tried to whisper.

In her mind, Alison heard Maxi respond. "Yes, he came for me. This is how it was supposed to be." HB/Rob had returned for their baby? Momentarily Alison felt disappointed, but this was what it was destined to be. HB/Rob and Maxi would be together.

Alison felt something taking over her body. It was peaceful, and prisms of light sparkled and danced right out of reach. Her mother touched her hand, and she felt her father's whisper kisses on her cheek.

"She's coding!"

Alison lifted from her body and watched as the dancing crystals surrounded Maxi.

And she was glad HB/Rob would have Maxi by his side.

And with that, her body went limp, and she floated away from the white bird, past HB/Rob and Maxi.

She saw the future, HB/Rob holding his daughter's hand and walking into the sunset.

Alison was guided forward by her parents.

Would she be able to return like HB/Rob had and be part of their lives? She hoped so.

Was there someone willing to let her walk into their body?

It wasn't about her and HB/Rob, but their child. The little girl wanted to come back and be a part of their lives, of HB/Rob's life. Maxi would learn about her mother by looking at pictures and hearing stories. But she knew the child would be loved and cherished by HB/Rob. He would be an excellent father to Maxi, and as soon as she could, she'd find a receptive soul and body and return to them. She could only hope she would soon be part of their lives again and not just watch from afar. But she would watch over them and send messages with feathers and pennies, signaling she was with them even if they couldn't see her.

Maxi would pick up one of the feathers and exclaim, "Look what I found, Daddy!"

And he would know it was from her.

****

"We're sorry, Mr. Comstock."

HB/Rob tipped his head back and screamed, "No!" This situation wasn't supposed to end like this! He had come back to her so they could be together. His anguished cries were heard over the helicopter's rotating blades. "No! No! Ali!" His heart was ripped from his chest, suffocating him, but still, he continued to scream.

One of the paramedics patted his shoulder, but he shrugged them away.

"We're sorry." He blinked at the medics, who were also looking shocked and sad.

"We did everything," they said.

HB/Rob hung his head as tears and snot flowed

down his face. He was nothing without Ali—no heart or soul—a shell of a man without her.

The baby cried, and he lifted his head. He had a baby and no wife.

Chapter 69

Ali

Alison began walking—no, gliding—as if her feet had wings. She moved effortlessly through a long dark tunnel toward the light. Usually, she would have felt claustrophobic in the constricted space, but now only the feeling of calmness and well-being cloaked her.

The light grew as she moved closer; contentment consumed her. Alison stopped and surveyed her surroundings—a bright place clouded with mist. A beautiful place, though shrouded, was comforting and familiar. She felt her mother touching her hand, guiding her, and even Aunt Penelope stroked her hair as she had done when Alison was small. And best of all, a feather kiss on her cheek from her father.

Alison touched her now-flat stomach. No evidence remained of just having Maxi or the injuries from the accident. They were gone too. She was whole and uninjured in this place.

A girl limped out of the mist and approached her. "Hello? Can you tell me what to do?" the girl asked.

Alison wasn't sure what the girl meant. "I'm new here."

"I'm deciding," the girl said and then shuddered.

"Are you sick?" Alison asked.

"I guess so." She shook again as if an earthquake

moved her body violently. "I was in an accident." She paused. "I caused an accident."

"I was in an accident, too," Alison said. "I'm not sure where I am." She looked around again as if the scenery had changed, which it hadn't.

"I think this is the in-between place," the girl said. "I have to decide to stay or leave."

The realization that this must be the annex to her heavenly place comforted Alison.

"Do you want to leave?" Alison asked.

"I caused the accident on purpose. I wanted to die. I hate my life since we moved."

"So you get to decide?" Alison asked, unsure of what the girl meant. "I didn't get to decide."

"I'm the girl in the car. I hit the truck that hit you," the girl said. "I'm Sabrina."

The girl's revelation didn't evoke any strong emotions, only more of the comforting void Alison felt. So this was the girl who ran into the truck which plowed into their moving van, veering them off the road, pinning Alison against the dashboard, causing internal injuries, and the birth of Maxi? Alison wasn't mad at her, instead felt overpowering acceptance. Mad wasn't even an emotion she possessed any more. She only felt love, caring, and acceptance.

"Would you like to trade places with me?" Sabrina asked.

"You mean now?"

Sabrina shuddered again. "Yes, they're trying to revive me, and I must decide."

Alison would have a chance to be with HB/Rob and Maxi if she switched places. HB/Rob had done it, so why not her?

"Yes, I'll switch with you." She felt herself elevating and saw Sabrina's limp body as the paramedics worked on her through the blinding white light and mist.

And with that, Sabrina's soul walked away, and Alison's soul took over.

From far away, down the dark tunnel, she heard, "We have a heartbeat!"

-4EAEA-

A word about the author…

Sue writes 5-star LitPick novels that keep readers of all ages turning pages long into the night. When she's not writing, she's reading, attending author events, or walking her dogs. Snack wise, Sue is a salty-type gal, but wouldn't say no to a chocolate kiss or two! She's not sure she's a reincarnated former novelist, but if she was, she'd want to be Jane Austen, Mary Shelley, or Emily Bronte.

www.scduganauthor.wixsite.com/mysite

CPSIA information can be obtained
at www.ICGtesting.com
Printed in the USA
BVHW051746150523
664203BV00006B/96